OPEN LINE

OpenLine

A NOVEL BY

ELLEN HAWLEY

COFFEE HOUSE PRESS
MINNEAPOLIS
2008

COFFEE HOUSE PRESS books are available to the trade through our primary distributor, Consortium Book Sales & Distribution, www.cbsd.com or (800) 283-3572. For personal orders, catalogs, or other information, write to: Coffee House Press, 27 North Fourth Street, Suite 400, Minneapolis, MN 55401.

Coffee House Press is a nonprofit literary publishing house. Support from private foundations, corporate giving programs, government programs, and generous individuals helps make the publication of our books possible. We gratefully acknowledge their support in detail in the back of this book.

To you and our many readers around the world, we send our thanks for your continuing support.

LIBRARY OF CONGRESS CIP INFORMATION

Library of Congress Cataloging-in-Publication Data
Hawley, Ellen.
Open line : a novel / by Ellen Hawley.
p. cm.
ISBN 978-1-56689-209-4 (alk. paper)
1. Radio personalities—Fiction. 2. Radio talk shows—Fiction.
3. Conspiracies—Fiction. 4. Fame—Fiction. 5. Political satire.
I. Title.
PS3558.A82335O64 2008
813'.54—DC22
2007046387

FIRST EDITION | FIRST PRINTING
1 3 5 7 9 8 6 4 2
PRINTED IN CANADA.

ACKNOWLEDGMENTS

I'm indebted to many people for advice, encouragement, critique, editing, and information. They include: Betsy Amster, Larry Bensky, Chris Fischbach, Ringo Hallinan, Barb Lakey, Stewart O'Nan, Deidre Pope, Marcie Rendon, Linda Rice, Ida Swearingen, Gregg and Catherine Swedberg, Gregg Swedberg, Lucy Vilankulu, and Jane Whitledge.

DISCLAIMER

This is a work of fiction. Any resemblance between the characters and real people—living, dead, or otherwise—is purely coincidental. Where the names of historical figures have been used, it is beyond unlikely that they did in reality anything even close to what they do in the following pages.

FOR IDA

CHAPTER 1

Annette didn't believe it herself at first. It was a slow night, and some caller had a bug up his ass about Vietnam. He said it marked the beginning of the end of American greatness, led directly to September 11th, to Saddam Hussein, not to mention to America's loss of pride, and how many kids these days even knew this great nation's history, and rah rah rah until it was getting up Annette's ass too and there was nothing to do about it but scratch.

"Brian," she said into the mic, but he kept talking—taxation, terrorists, and it all traced back to et cetera and so forth. God, he was boring. Annette was damn near asleep on her own show. She had a good voice for radio—low, sexy when she wanted it to be— and she pitched it at him hard, but he wasn't having any of it. He ran right over her, going on about individual responsibility, the decline of educational standards, stuff she didn't disagree with but that didn't mean she wanted to hear it from him.

"Brian, sweetheart, if you don't let me get a couple of words in here I'm going to have to cut you off."

"I'm just trying to make a point," Brian said, but he stopped talking after he said it, which was good because she only had one other caller standing between her and dead airtime. She lived in terror of dead airtime.

"Here's what I'm trying to tell you," she said, drawing it out now that she had space to work in. "And listen carefully, because this is important. This is what the government doesn't want you to know: there was no Vietnam War. It never happened."

Brian went ballistic, talking about weapons, graves, photographs, costs. The open phone lines lit up and the callers' names lined themselves up on her screen as fast as Nick could single-finger them on the keyboard. With the hand that wasn't typing, he gave her a thumbs-up sign through the window.

"Brian, sweetie," she said, cutting in. "I've read all that, I know what they say. What I'm telling you is it's a fake, a phony, the biggest scam a government ever put over on its citizens."

Brian splattered himself all over the phone lines. The dead, the injured, their families, and what kind of a person . . . Annette grinned at Nick, although he was still looking at the keyboard, searching for the space bar, or the enter key. This was too good not to share, even if she had to share it with nothing better than the top of Nick's head. The waiting callers glowed on her screen, as lovely to behold as money in the bank.

"On top of which," Brian said, "the photos . . ."

"Hey, pictures can be faked. Anything can be faked. You read the papers? We've had the Department of Agriculture, the Department of Defense, the Department of Warm Feelings about Your Government, all of them planting news stories that are really just P.R. pieces and the media gobbling them up as if they were the real thing. We've had reporters getting paid to say what the government wants them to say. We don't know what's real anymore. I see a tree these days, I have to kick it to make sure it's not metal. Brian, baby, a photo's nothing."

Brian said yes but . . .

"O.K., answer me this," she said. "If the Communists won the Vietnam War, how come the Soviet Union collapsed?"

She punched a button and cut Brian off, then gave his silence half a second to prove he couldn't answer.

"Can you answer me that?"

He couldn't and she took another caller—not the one who'd been on hold, who wanted to talk about the Islamic hordes piling up at the borders to attack America, or so she'd told Nick, who'd left the *s* out of Islamic. Annette would've been fine with that last night—she'd done a pretty fair riff on Islamic hordes and they were a thousand times better than having to talk about the fishing season—but the thing about them was that she didn't own the topic. The best she could do with it was come off like a pipsqueak echo of everybody famous who'd already defined how America thought about the issue. So screw the Islamic hordes. Vietnam was *hers*, and tonight Annette was rich. She could skip anything that didn't interest her and take the first of the callers she'd drawn out of the deep night silence.

"Diane, talk to me. Did you fall for it too?"

"What I think? I don't know. I know the last caller was rude to you and I don't think that's right, but I do know some people who went over there and one of them lost, you know, a part of his leg and all, so I don't know, when you think about it, how it could help but be true, you know?"

"So you're telling me you fell for it."

Annette uncapped her bottle of Evian while Diane explained how she wouldn't say she'd fallen for it exactly, but when you know someone, and she'd seen him in shorts and all, and there was no question about the leg . . .

Diane had an invertebrate's voice, a jellyfish voice. She was the kind of caller who'd talk all night without ever committing herself to an opinion but who'd never let herself be budged from what- ever it was she sort-of believed. Annette set her water bottle down without drinking from it.

"Diane, Diane. I'm not talking about a leg here. I believe the leg, but have you ever asked yourself if you really know how he *lost*

the leg? Have you ever wondered why more people came back
from this war with their heads messed up than from any other war
in history? It's because of the disjunction between what really
happened and what they believe happened."

Disjunction, her mind echoed. A great word, *disjunction*.

On the other side of the window, Nick shook his head and
grinned at her. The lines were full, and he had nothing better to do
than look moony. That was Nick's great gift: he looked at her as if
he'd never seen a better looking woman, and night after night
Annette rode on that. For the full length of the show, he let her
believe that she was more than just pretty enough not to embarrass
the truly beautiful, let her believe it so intently that her voice
became the voice of a blindingly gorgeous woman. The forgettable
brown hair and the thick knees dropped away. Hell, it was all a trick
anyway, this beauty business. First she had to believe it, and then
the men would. Or maybe the men had to believe it first, and then
she could. Whichever way it worked, it didn't matter. This was
radio. She was the best looking woman her listeners could imagine.

She let Diane dither: she didn't think people should be rude,
of course, even when they disagreed, but on the other hand . . .

It struck Annette that Diane was arguing with her seriously—
that a full bank of callers was waiting to argue with her seriously—and that could only mean one thing: Annette was really
good at this. It was ridiculous how good she was.

Half a long minute later, Annette lost any hope that Diane
would complete either a thought or a sentence, so she cut in.

"What I'm saying," Annette told her, "is it was a massive
experiment in mind control. Mind control and god only knows
what else. I don't think anyone knows yet what they were really
trying to hide, but I'll tell you this much: this isn't the first time
the government's tested weapons on its own soldiers. You know
about the A-bomb? The atomic veterans? They lined these guys

up, stood 'em at attention, set the bomb off, and then studied 'em like guinea pigs to see what happened."

Nick was still watching her with cow's eyes, but he was chewing on a slice of dried pineapple now. He grazed his way through the show every night—dried fruit, nuts, fried-looking things that came from health-food stores, compact slabs that looked like candy bars but promised energy, long life, infinite job security. They'd given him a cow's bulk—not fat but not muscular either. Just big.

Diane was going on about her friend's leg again. Annette took a sip of water.

"Gotta move on, Di, we've got half of the greater metropolitan mosquito control district on the line here, but I want to tell you this first: I'm not questioning your friend's honesty. I know he believes what he's telling you. What you have to ask yourself is how *he* came to believe it."

She punched the button for the next line.

"Michael, talk to me. What do you think?"

Michael was a vet. He'd been over there. He'd seen people die. She heard a break in his voice, tiny but unmistakable, and she clutched—couldn't force a single word out into the air, couldn't think anything more useful than *holy fuck*. Diane was one thing, but this guy was real.

This guy was also leaving a bald spot in the middle of the conversation: dead airtime, the one unforgivable sin on a talk show, but she couldn't—could not—force herself to step in and fill it.

"The thing is," Michael said, his voice under control again, "is the war, the reasons they gave us for the war, never made much sense to me anyway. We were fighting over there so we wouldn't have to fight here? Come *on*. The Vietnamese weren't about to invade us. We knew that. So now that you've asked the question . . . I mean, it sounds insane, right? But the whole war was insane. I mean, people think Iraq is nuts, and they're probably right and all, but I was *in* Vietnam. I saw some things . . ."

There was that break again, that pause, and it wasn't exactly like she clutched this time, it was more like something clutched her, dug its claws directly into her guts to keep her from saying a single syllable.

"I'm not the same person I was before, and that's the truth. So I'm not saying you're right, o.k.? I'm not saying you're right. All's I want to tell you is I did some things. And I've lived with the things I did. All my adult life. So if you're right, if I've been carrying that around for nothing. . . ."

His voice flew sharp-edged and painful through the wires to the control board, through the soft night air of the suburbs, into Minneapolis, into Saint Paul, out to farmland that would turn into suburb in the next two weeks; it materialized in people's cars, in their bedrooms, in their kitchens and prison cells, slipped down their ear canals and into the mysterious workings of their brains. The claws had let go of Annette's insides, but she didn't notice any mental shift as Michael's voice lodged in her brain. It was nothing she could have told anyone about, nothing she even remembered later, when people asked about it, although she remembered the caller clearly, because Michael was the turning point. He spoke and the joke erased itself, leaving no traces in her memory. She had in all seriousness raised a possibility, and Michael had confirmed it. That was all. The moments that came before Michael erased and reformed themselves so that the idea—the possibility—had now come to her the way rain came from the sky. She was an open channel, a set of wires, a control board with knobs and slides and stuff whose names she'd never bothered to ask about, carrying the idea into the world without knowing its source, or even thinking to ask.

It was a humbling experience.

★

She wrapped up the show with all the lines still lit and she and
Nick settled themselves on the steps outside to drink a beer from
the cooler in his car. They were wired, both of them, adrenaline
pumping through their veins, driving them to talk too fast, laugh
too loud, open a second beer apiece and pour alcohol into their
agitated bloodstreams. Moths stuttered through the parking-lot
floodlights, and behind a screen of trees the late-night traffic fled
the northern suburbs for the southern and the southern ones for
the northern, leaving nothing behind but a wisp of noise and a
gradual tendency toward warmer weather and extreme storm
activity worldwide.

"Where do you come up with this stuff anyway?" Nick asked
during the second beer. He was leaning against the locked door,
grinning at her like he was in on some huge joke.

"It came to me."

She said it seriously, almost angrily, taking as much fun out of
the joke as she could.

"You are something else."

She drank.

"Sure I am."

He set his beer down and dropped heavily to his knees at her feet.

"Sleep with me, Annette. It'll make you happy. And if it doesn't,
then at least it'll make me happy. Shouldn't one of us be happy?"

She laughed.

"Fuck off, Nick."

He reached for the last of his beer, chugged it, and heaved
himself upright.

"It's what you want, you know."

"What I want is a daytime show in a town where they don't
know which end of the cow eats hay, that's what I want. Christ,
Nick, don't you want to *be* someone?"

"I am someone. Everyone's someone."

Annette shook her head. Had he even grown up in America? Where was she supposed to start with this guy?

"Besides, I don't sleep with people at work. It's bad for the complexion."

They watched each other for a few seconds, measuring the shifts that had taken place in the distance between them. Or that hadn't taken place. They both felt something different in the air tonight. Neither of them could have named it yet, but it wasn't about sex. Or it wasn't primarily about sex. Nick asked her to sleep with him once a week, give or take a few days, and she always turned him down. She wasn't sure he'd even want to sleep with her if she said yes. Asking was what he thought he owed her, that was all. Or what he thought he owed himself. It was oddly restful, that absence of any real want between them. It let them stay friends. So nothing new there. Still, he seemed further away than usual, and the distance made her feel like she'd left a sweater somewhere during the day and had only now missed it.

"Nick, I'm going to make a confession here, o.k.? And don't let it go to your head. If I did ever sleep with someone from work, it'd be you."

He slammed a fist to his chest, right over the heart, as if he were saluting the flag or having a coronary, and he grinned so thoroughly that she forgave him for acting as if her show tonight had been a joke. How could she not? Sure, Nick dressed like he reached into the laundry basket blindfolded every morning, and sure, his life was going nowhere, but he was also the only person she'd ever known who she didn't have to read for hidden plans or meanings. And he was the only Minnesotan she'd met who liked her, who didn't think she was too pushy, too loud, too New York. Who didn't fault her for not having that Minnesota-nice surface. Maybe if she slept with people from work she really wouldn't sleep with him. He was the kind of guy who got hurt. He was the kind of guy who people like her had to protect. A gust of good feeling blew through her: for Nick because he was who he was; for herself because she could protect him; for the two of them together because they could drink beer and not do anything more than make jokes about sleeping together.

He reached a hand down to pull her to her feet.

"Ready to go to your lonely bed?"

"You go ahead, Nick. I want to sit here a minute and see if I can't slow down a little."

"You sure? You'll be all right?"

"Go on. You think the moths are going to attack me?"

He looked doubtfully at the trees that separated the station from the houses on either side, from the freeway in front, measuring the threats gathered in the darkness—the dangers only a man could assess or protect against, the risk he was taking in leaving her.

"Up to you, I guess."

He packed their empties into the cooler and left her to the uneven whoosh of the freeway and the surge and swoop of her tightly strung nerves, which hurled her from elation to the verge of tears. She'd been good tonight, damn it. She'd been brilliant. Limbaugh, Stern, none of them were any better than she'd just been. And who'd heard her? Nick and his fellow cows, that's who. No one who'd help her career. Christ, if anybody deserved a show in New York, she did. She wasn't asking for syndication. Yet. She just wanted her chance. Couldn't any American boy be president? Didn't any girl just maybe have a shot at it in this new century? And what was a president, after all, in this day and age? There were better things to be, and she was owed her chance at them.

In the meantime, she was lonelier than she would ever have believed possible, and all she really wanted was a chance to move back home.

Was that so much to ask?

CHAPTER 2

History's made by accident as much as it is by plan. If Stan Marlin hadn't come home from a Minnesota Liberty Constructive meeting mad enough to chew his way through the door of his Jeep, he would never have heard Annette on the radio that night, and regardless of what she believed or didn't believe about the Vietnam War, she wouldn't have talked about it for long. Something else would have come up. History would have flowed around her like one more rock in the river, and it would never have noticed her contribution.

But Stan did come home mad, and he slammed through his front door to find Steve Flambard—his friend, his more or less permanent houseguest, his fate in life—sliding his sock-feet off the coffee table and trying to act like they'd never been there.

"Good meeting?" Flambard asked.

"Don't even ask."

Flambard already had asked, but at least he didn't ask again. Instead he held up one of Del Reiss's books to show Stan that he'd been absorbing wisdom underneath the television's laugh track.

"You were right about this one," he said. "Listen to what he says here."

He flipped pages until he found a passage he'd marked.

"'Through the courts, and through its network of extralegal agencies, the government has no hesitation about telling the citizen how to conduct his family life.' That's deep, Stan. That's beautiful. And it's what you've been telling me, isn't it? The courts won't give me custody because they're stacked against the father."

Stan grunted. He didn't have the patience to listen to Flambard's woes tonight. Even if they were wrapped up in quotes from Del Reiss, who Stan respected greatly and whose books formed the philosophical root of the Liberty Constructives, they'd still come back to Steve's kid, Steve's ex, the judge, everybody's lawyers. Flambard picked through Del Reiss's books like a four-year-old picking through chow mein for the chicken bits, shoving everything else to one side of his plate. All that mattered was the wreckage of his marriage. Never mind what Reiss had to say about how the Constructives could return America to the purity of her roots. That was nothing but celery and sauce.

"I've got to get some sleep," Stan said.

"Sure, Stan. Didn't mean to hold you up. Wasn't thinking."

Stan lay in the dark and listened to the TV, which clawed its way down the hall and scratched at the closed bedroom door, and he tried not to think about tonight's meeting, which meant, of course, that he couldn't think about anything else.

The meeting hadn't actually been a Liberty Constructive meeting. It had been a caucus, a faction, a handful of members, most of them loyal enough to Stan to set one foot on the slippery ground of becoming a breakaway organization, although that wasn't what Stan wanted for them. What he wanted was to get the Minnesota Constructive out from under the spell of Cal Anderson, that fine-looking former soldier who'd engineered Stan's ouster as president six weeks before. Anderson had a gift, unhindered by the subtleties of intellect, for stringing together borrowed bits of theory and presenting them as if they'd sprung fully formed from Del Reiss's writings. He did it so well that a solid majority of the membership hadn't noticed that Anderson's real goal was to wave Del Reiss's writings through the air like

Chairman Mao's *Little Red Book* and scurry under the Republican Party's umbrella with them, where they'd stay nice and dry and pretty and unread.

It wasn't that Stan didn't welcome the Republicans' rightward surge—they weren't bad on taxes and might eventually work up the courage to axe Social Security, although they'd never say that outright—but the minute they'd gotten their hands on the machinery of government they'd made it bigger instead of smaller. They'd handed the deficit over to NASA to strap on a rocket and shoot into outer goddamn space, and they'd found new and hair-raising ways to intrude on individual liberties. If Anderson had understood Del Reiss's books at all, he'd know that. He'd see that the Republican umbrella had only moved close enough to the Constructive to drip rainwater down its organizational collar. If Stan couldn't take the Minnesota Constructive back within a year, it would be unrecognizable. Within two years it would cease to exist at all, and then who would remind the state's citizens that terrorists weren't the only threat to liberty, that there was also the U.N. and its domination of the federal government; the federal government and its domination of the American citizen; compulsory education, which had swamped the schools with the uneducable and undermined respect for learning; Social Security, welfare, unemployment insurance; government regulation of everything from the environment to the production of shoelaces while terrorists strolled in and out of the country illegally *and* legally; the whole network of regulations and guarantees tying American businesses in knots and keeping people from taking their lives in their own hands and making of themselves what they could. Not to mention the pandering to every immigrant group that wanted to turn America into a replica of whatever godforsaken country they'd left.

The problem, though, was that people—even Constructive members—liked simple explanations, and Anderson's explanations were simpler than Stan's. The Arabs were coming, the Arabs were coming, and Americans had to set aside their differences, their rights, and their independence in the name of patriotism. It wasn't what you'd call a program, but it was enough to rally people, and that was all Anderson wanted: followers, people who didn't think too deeply. Anderson must miss all those soldiers lining up to salute him. If life had carried him in another direction, he'd have started a religion.

Hell, if Anderson had a program Stan could respect, he'd still give Stan hives, and that was the truth.

Even at the best of times, Stan had trouble shifting from the public person to the private, and this wasn't the best of times. So instead of falling asleep, he was lying awake with a sour stomach and a headful of arguments he hadn't been quick enough to make at the meeting because who'd have thought he'd need to argue at what was supposed to be a friendly gathering. He'd gone out of his way, damn it, to make sure Ed and Penny Cole were invited, and they'd done nothing all evening but repeat Anderson sound bites and demoralize the group Stan had assembled so carefully. He told himself not to worry about them—they were only two people—and he answered himself back that they were two well-respected people, with a lot of energy and free time. With big mouths. With money they didn't mind contributing.

He sat up and sipped the glass of lukewarm water he'd set on the bedside table the night before. If he couldn't win the Constructive back, he couldn't imagine what he'd do with his life.

Half an hour later, when sleep still hadn't caught up with him, he turned on the light. Sleep was the refuge of mediocrities, of depressives, of people with nothing more on their minds than the alarm clock tomorrow morning, and Stan was none of those. He was a man with a mission: to help America reclaim its greatness. Did that sound arrogant? He'd tried to live the standard-issue life, and in some ways he'd done a better-than-average job of it. Here he was, fifty-six years old, and if he was reasonably careful with his money, he'd never have to work again. How many people could claim that? So he'd learned a lot of things, and one of them was that without a purpose, life isn't worth living. In Del Reiss's books, and in the Liberty Constructive, Stan had found his purpose, and it was with a great sense of relief that he'd given himself over to it and dropped the effort to live what someone else might have called a personal life.

He pulled on his robe and headed for the kitchen, crossing the living room between Flambard and the TV.

"Guess I'm too wound up to sleep," he said.

Flambard had just pulled his feet off the coffee table again and was adjusting the rest of his body to the disruption. Stan didn't mind if Flambard sat with his feet on the table. What he hated was the way he pulled them off, as if he had Stan confused with his ex-wife.

"Sorry I didn't get to the meeting," Flambard said.

"Wouldn't have changed anything."

"Worked till past seven. Supposed to get rain tomorrow, and they wanted to get the job finished."

Stan grunted.

"Time I ate, got cleaned up . . . Well, you know."

Stan grunted again.

Flambard worked off the books so his ex wouldn't take half his paycheck in child support. He did roofing, painting, a few handyman jobs—not a lot of them, but then he wasn't paying rent, so he got by.

When Flambard first moved in, Stan had assumed it would be for a few weeks, just until he got on his feet, but that had been months ago and neither of them had made a move to destabilize the arrangement. They were comfortable together, in an awkward way. It was nice, sometimes, to find another human being in the house.

"Might've been better if I'd gone anyway. The ex called and pitched me a fit. Says she won't let me see Cortney till she gets some money."

"Hell, I'm sorry, Steve."

"Yeah. I don't know. Sooner or later she'll want a free babysitter, don't you think? Want to get out for the evening, maybe do the grocery shopping on her own."

Stan agreed—sure, why not, what did he know about ex-wives. Flambard's eyes drifted back to the TV, and Stan turned on the radio in the kitchen, squirted soap into the sink, and ran the water.

Stan was a big man, a bit more than six feet tall and broad in the shoulder and waist, and he felt silly standing in front of a sink. His hands were too big to fussbudget around with cups and glasses, and so he prided himself on getting his dishes washed every few days. Standing barefoot on the linoleum with his arms deep in soapy water, he was an urban survivalist, practicing the most genuine form of self-reliance. Sometimes he wished he had married, but a wife and kids made a man vulnerable. All he had to do was glance into the living room to understand that. And a woman wanted more from marriage than a kitchen to keep clean. He understood that too. Respected it even. And if that meant that a couple of times a week he washed dishes, so be it. No job was unimportant if it maintained your independence.

The call-in show came to him in snatches, whenever he shut off the rinse water. He didn't listen to call-in shows as a rule. Del Reiss said call-in shows were a direct line to the nation's unconscious, and Del was a man of rare intelligence, but Stan didn't have much patience for them. Or for the unconscious. They struck him as shared ignorance, and even though he tuned in now and again to see if he could bring himself around to Del's way of thinking on this, he never came away wiser or better prepared to reach the American mind, sluggish as it was with televised entertainment and the pseudonews the liberal media passed off as information.

What caught his attention as he turned off the rinse water was a single phrase: *the biggest scam a government ever put over on its own citizens.*

Right, he thought. It'd have a shitload of competition for that honor, but he left the water off so he could hear what the scam was. He was inclined to like the woman who said it. She saw through the government's facade, even if she was exaggerating whatever this was. And she had a nice voice—confident without being pushy. Likeable. He ran the sponge silently over the dirty dishes and stacked them in the left-hand sink to rinse later. Whatever fragment of government betrayal this woman had latched on to, she was someone the Minnesota Constructive—his branch of the Minnesota Constructive—should get in touch with. Someone *he* should get in touch with. He had information about government betrayals that would make her measly scandal look like business as usual, which it probably was. His mind spun off into the network of media contacts that would follow from this one, and the intellectual framework he could provide for them, and how Cal Anderson didn't have the imagination to do that, or the independence, and he was so involved in it all that he almost missed what the woman on the radio was talking about and had to piece it together retroactively. The Vietnam War never happened? Disappointment landed inside him as heavily as if some little guy in black pajamas had dumped a fifty-pound sack of rice on the floor of his stomach and run off to join the Vietcong. His network of media contacts unwove itself in less time than it had taken to imagine, and he was once again just some guy who couldn't sleep, washing his dishes because he didn't know what else to do with himself. The woman on the radio, whatever her name was, was certifiable. He'd gain squat from being associated with her.

His hands held a coffee mug underwater as if it were the IRS he was drowning.

Still, it was a hell of a comment on the nation's unconscious that people were still dissecting the Vietnam War. If only the politicians had gotten out of the way and let the military do what it did best, the country would be a different place today.

He noticed the cup. He was damn near strangling the thing.

The Vietnam War. How could anyone claim it hadn't happened?

Well, it was true that the politicians had lied about it, but that's what politicians did best. And yes, he had to admit it, even the military had lied. Everything they touched had been a victory. Victory piled on top of victory until suddenly—oops, how'd that happen?—they were hustling the last technocrats onto helicopters and flying them out. And there was that business on the Tonkin Gulf. Everyone pretty much agreed at this point that it hadn't . . . He didn't like finishing the thought but intellectual honesty compelled him: it hadn't happened. No North Vietnamese gunboats. No enemy attack. Just a bunch of sailors out in bad weather, their equipment picking up ghosts and pings and echoes. And the government had known that. The whole picture had been available to them, and they'd buried it. So it made sense that people didn't believe anything or anyone.

Still, the claim was crazy.

Wasn't it crazy?

Slow down. Del Reiss would tell him not to be afraid if the institutions that out of patriotism he had held sacred turned out to be corrupt. Be angry, Reiss advised, but don't be afraid. Don't turn away. So O.K. He had to learn more about this before he dismissed it. He owed that to Del. He owed it to himself.

The Vietnam War, though. The very thought of it made him dizzy. In his deepest moments of fear, even of paranoia, he'd never dared imagine a betrayal on this scale. If this turned out to be true, then everything he'd been outraged by up to now was nothing. Sticks and stones. He felt the cracks and clicks of an intellectual chiropractor realigning the elements of everything he'd thought, until this moment, that he knew.

If, he reminded himself. He was still deep in the realm of If.

But the Vietnam War. Holy Jesus. If she was right, the Constructives were barely touching the furthest fringe of what had gone wrong in America. If she was right, taking the Constructive back was tiddlywinks compared to what he'd be able to do.

If she was right . . .

Shit, she had to be right. Too much rode on her being right to allow for other possibilities.

"Steve," he yelled into the other room, "turn off the TV and get in here."

He unclenched the mug and let it sink onto the reef of plates at the bottom of the sink, and he let himself sink onto a kitchen chair so he could give the radio his full attention.

CHAPTER 3

Afternoon was always Annette's low time. Once she'd eaten breakfast, once she'd read as much of the paper as she could stand to read, once she'd stared out her apartment window at the nearly empty parking lot, the fact was that she didn't have much to do with herself. Afternoon was when she came nose to nose with how out of place she was in Minnesota, with how few people she knew, with how many fewer of them she liked. Or liked her. The dark afternoon of the soul. It was when every rotten opinion she had of herself made itself known: she was no one; she was nothing; she knew shit about radio and even less about journalism, and everybody at the station could take one look at her and see that. She could go back to school and study both of them, but her mother would never give her the money, and Annette was up to her eyeballs in debt already. She hadn't made a mark on the world and never would.

Everybody thought she was a loser.

She thought she was a loser. If there was a wrong move to make, she'd be sure to make it.

Et cetera.

Afternoon was when she got depressed. There. She got depressed. Well, why wouldn't she? She was living in a town where nobody loved her and hardly anybody liked her. In New York people at least made sense to her, and even if her mother drove her nuts, Annette knew someone loved her. Living in Minnesota, though . . . It was like being the one girl in the high school who's dyslexic about clothes, the one who can't say the right thing even when she says exactly what everyone else is saying.

Why had she left New York, then? The usual reasons: to put some distance between herself and the dead zone that was her mother's apartment; to reinvent herself; so she could go back when she was so famous that not even her mother would upset her; because Minnesota was where she got a job offer.

Right. So there she was, the host of a show no one listened to and two-thirds of a step away from crying for Mommy to come get her.

Annette turned away from the window. Her building's parking lot was nearly empty. Everybody but her had someplace to go. They had real lives, real families, real friends, real business to take care of. She rinsed the dishrag, wrung it out, and gave the kitchen counter a wipe, but she'd wiped the counter just a little while ago and she hadn't gotten it dirty since then, so the gesture depressed her even more.

She sat back down at the table to read a little more of the paper than she could stand because she was supposed to be up to speed on all topics, and who knew what bit of obscurity some caller would want to talk about. Besides, reading the paper made her feel more professional than wiping the kitchen counter—or playing computer solitaire or watching the soaps, for that matter—and that gave her the illusion that something better was on the horizon and she was preparing herself to meet it.

When the phone rang, she was, in fact, not actually reading the paper but staring at the sports page and feeling dumb because sports made no sense to her and never had.

She dove for the phone. Never mind that it was an unidentified caller—it was human contact. She didn't care if it was someone selling lightbulbs or hustling donations for the Police

Benevolent Whatever It Was. She'd have opened the door to a Jehovah's Witness right then. But the caller hung up before she'd gotten the second syllable of "hello" out of her mouth. And called back. And hung up again.

On the third call, it came together: her show. Someone had gotten themselves bent royally out of shape and was trying to tell her about it. So who cared about the sports page?

The phone rang.

"Do we have a problem here, sweetie?" she said.

The caller hung up.

Annette was thrilled. Here she was, sitting barefoot at the kitchen table with her hair still not washed and the air conditioner blasting overcooled air on her shoulder, and she was still enough of a factor in somebody's life that they had to call her.

The phone rang. She set the answering machine to pick up on the first ring and turned down the volume.

The phone rang. The machine clicked on.

Fuck journalism. If she projected a powerful enough presence, she wouldn't need journalism.

All the way down to her fingernails, she felt alive.

Annette's boss studied her from behind the cleanest desk on either side of the Mississippi, a small man with a huge desk. Annette had never subscribed to the theories about small men and Napoleon complexes, but for Len Bitterman she could make an exception.

"What the hell were you thinking?" he said.

He left an empty space at the end of the words, but it wasn't really a question, it was a mallet pounding on the top of her head.

"Do you have any idea what I've been dealing with since I got in this morning?"

He opened a folder, ruffled some slips of paper.

"Veterans groups. VFW. American Legion. Groups I never heard of. Vietnam Veterans for a Fair—shit, I can't even read this. Looks like 'lemonizing.' You say anything last night about unfair lemonizing?"

Annette shook her head.

"Not to mention a couple dozen pissed-off individuals Kathi screened out before they got to me. Shit, you've got more complaints here than you've got listeners."

He held up maybe half a dozen pink message slips and stared at her, waiting not for her to talk but to give some visible sign that his words were sinking in: throw herself on the carpet and howl, maybe. Weep. Lemonize. She looked back at him, unblinking, with no access to the memory of ever having doubted herself. She felt nothing. She could have pierced her thumb with a roofing nail and not noticed.

"Every line lit up," she said finally. "As soon as one was empty, it lit up again."

He wasn't ready for that yet, though.

"We're a responsible station. We can't have you out there on the fringe telling people the earth's flat."

As she understood it, actually, she'd been hired to shake people up—to say the earth was flat or square or triangular if the mood took her, as long as people listened and the station didn't get sued. But this wasn't the time to debate that. Maybe some small print somewhere said that shaking people up was all right, but Len getting angry phone calls wasn't.

"I didn't say it was flat. I raised a question, nothing more. If there's nothing to hide, what are people upset about? Len, I had a vet call up almost in tears last night, asking himself if all the memories that've been haunting him maybe are false. Almost in tears, Len. Did you listen to the show?"

"Parts of it. Enough."

Parts of it. And whatever parts she brought up, they wouldn't be the ones he'd heard.

"You're going to tell me you believe this shit?"

"Len."

She leaned forward: regret, sincerity—hell, one of the emotions. Even in Len's presence, she remembered what emotions were. For a while when she was in high school she'd thought about being a performance artist, but she'd been put off by the way people made fun of them. She hadn't learned yet that opposition's as good as approval. Or she'd known it but hadn't been brave enough to do anything with the knowledge. It was just as well, as it turned out—there was no money in performance art. Shit, life itself was performance art, and she must have sensed that, even then.

Whatever name the emotion she was channeling carried, she let it flow into her and then outward toward Len.

"I might've raised the question more aggressively than I should've, but that's all I'm doing is asking a question, and if there's nothing there—no secret, no cover-up—that'll come out. And that's good, Len. That's as it should be, and we'll be a stronger society because of it."

Len sat back cautiously in his chair, not quite trusting it to hold him but relaxing in spite of himself. He liked this kind of talk—democracy, a stronger society. She made herself relax into her own chair and wait while he stared at her. It was harder now that she'd felt something. She had to lock her hands together to keep the shakes from creeping into them. The pictures on Len's desk—a wife and two boys—stared out at them both from all sides of a plexiglass cube.

"I'm not afraid of controversy," he said after an endless pause. "Controversy's good. It keeps the money flowing, and that keeps us alive. But you've got to be responsible. You can't just start saying things because they're fun, or because they get somebody riled up. We've got advertisers, and we're responsible to them."

She nodded soberly.

"I have people above me. I have to answer to them."

She nodded some more.

"There are people out there who want to destroy this country. You've got to take this thing seriously."

She nodded more soberly still. She left a long, sober pause. A person could get damn near lemonized in a pause like that.

"I appreciate your integrity, Len. I count on it. And I know you're in a tough position here. But honestly, I think I'm onto something, and the reaction we're getting is like a compass needle pointing north. Do you know I've been getting hang-up calls at home all afternoon? On an unlisted number, Len. How many individuals can ferret out an unlisted number that quickly?"

Another pause, which Annette tried to inject with her own intensity, although it ended up as sober and uncomfortable as the ones before it, and it went on longer. She should say something about the calls coming from an unidentified number, because that seemed significant, but she couldn't figure out why, and Len wasn't the kind of guy to help you think through a half-understood insight. Something started shaking under the high point of her rib cage, a kind of fluttering where nothing had ever fluttered before.

"All right," Len said at about the moment she was ready to shriek. "I'll let you on the air with this, but only as a question. Understood?"

"Understood."

"You're not an advocate—you're asking a question."

"Absolutely."

"No axe to grind."

"None at all."

"And I want to make it clear, just between us: I don't like it."

"Of course not."

"It's only because . . ."

She waited while he searched for a reason and looked unhappy about the process.

"I'm only agreeing to this because the world's gone insane. If people want to believe this crap—well, we're in business here, and a market's a market. That's democracy. But I still don't like it."

He closed the folder. The meeting was over. She stood, thanked him, touched a vibrating hand to the doorknob.

"You don't know how close I came to letting you go."

"I understand. Believe me."

Another silence. He didn't know how close she was to shrieking.

"Let me ask you a question."

"Sure," she said. What was she supposed to say? No? Fuck you? The man was her boss, for Chrissake.

"You genuinely think it could've happened?"

"The war you mean? Could've not happened?"

"Right."

She hesitated, not because she wasn't sure what to say but so she could find the right tone to say it in.

"I think it's a possibility."

The tone came out of a 1940s movie: Great American Individualist Defending Unpopular but Soon-to-Be-Justified Position.

Len looked at her hard, as if he thought he'd be able to read something beneath the surface, and she had the odd, defiant feeling that she could make herself into nothing but surface, so let him look all he wanted.

O.K., it's time to ask: did she really believe Vietnam could have not happened?

Yes.

Probably.

Absolutely.

This isn't a simple question, and it's the wrong question anyway. She was caught in her own momentum, and if that wasn't quite the same thing as belief, she was moving too fast to notice the difference. People were reacting. Michael had been damn near in tears when he called. Did anything else matter? How could she not be on the trail of something real and important?

And what's the definition of *real* anyway?

Len gave up trying to locate Annette's depths and favored her with a tight little nod. He was as out of proportion behind his desk as a fourth grader on a plow horse. She thanked him again, told him again that she appreciated him. What the hell was the signal, now that the folder was closed, that she could scuttle out the door? She smiled, unsmiled, thanked him again—what was she thanking him for anyway?—and turned back to the door so she could flee before her mouth went completely out of her control.

For the first hour of the show, Annette was under attack. How could she say and death and blood and served my country so people like you could blah blah blah and so forth.

"All I'm doing is asking a question," she told them, repeating the phrase like a prayer: god keep me safe from all evil and the management. "I'm raising a disturbing possibility, and if there's nothing to it, why are people getting this upset? You have to ask yourself that."

Then the weight shifted a little: another veteran in tears; a high school girl who should've been asleep at that time of night; a man with the voice of a bull who claimed the North and South Vietnamese governments were both in on the conspiracy, that it was orchestrated by a CIA man named Conan, Conayne, Ptomaine—she couldn't quite catch it, but it was something along those lines—and possibly by Ho Chi Minh himself. Another man, who said, "Personally, I think you're nuts, but you know, you'll make your fortune out of erasing this war."

He sounded so friendly about it that Annette instinctively counted him with the supporters. She hummed into the mic and her brain confirmed her instinct: definitely a supporter.

"Because here's the thing," he said. "America's never been comfortable with Vietnam. World War II? We know what we did, and we like it. Korea? No problem. First Gulf War? Amnesia. Iraq War? We were lied to so it's not our fault. Vietnam though . . . That one bothers us. First off, we lost. We don't like that. Second, we had a national nervous breakdown over it: riots, flag burnings, draft dodgers. Third, we did some very nasty things over there and had the bad luck to find out about them. My Lai, napalm, cluster bombs. Agent Orange."

He paused, either for air or for emphasis, and Annette should have snatched the conversation back, but she hadn't been listening. Everything he'd said after "make your fortune" had been background noise.

What a lovely, old-fashioned phrase that was. The words every girl longs to hear.

"So there it is," the caller said into her silence. "We don't like this war. And now you come along and tell people it never happened? Hell, it's perfect. They'll probably run you for president."

"Great idea."

Annette punched the next button and drew a vet who told her she'd saved his life.

"Literally," he said. "Saved my life."

And then he hung up, leaving her to figure out a transition to the next call, because what do you say when someone tells you that? "Gee, that's nice"?

On the other side of the glass, Nick was subdued—no grinning, no sign-language cheers, no hand-lettered Annette for

President sign. When she ended the show, she still had a full bank of lights.

"Line three is some guy wants to talk to you off the air," he said when she pushed open the studio door.

"Not my father, is it?"

Nick shrugged.

"Didn't say so."

"Figures."

"Claims you want to talk to him, though."

"I do, huh?"

"If it's not your father, tell him you're busy and anyway you love only me."

She took the call in an empty office. Someone's kid stared out of plexiglass on the desk, a boy with a grin that would make any teacher dive for cover. Something about family photos on people's desks made her claustrophobic. All those combed, smiling children. All the laundry it took to get them that way, and the yelling and the cooking and the cleaning. Growing up had been like living with a head cold for eighteen years, and now that her sinuses had finally cleared, Annette was in no hurry to see if it was any easier to breathe on the parent end of the relationship. Len's kids probably hid under their beds when they heard his car in the driveway.

Line three was the man with the bull voice. Frank, her computer screen had said. She kept her voice tight and businesslike. Listeners weren't supposed to present themselves after hours, and either he picked this up from her voice or he knew it beforehand.

"I'll get right to the point here. Certain things can't be said on the air. What I want to tell you is this: I admire your guts, saying what you've been saying, and I think I can help you."

Annette opened the center drawer of the desk and turned over the pens and pencils that lay in the tray like trimmed logs after a clear-cut.

"And how could you do that?"

Never mind why.

"Information. Facts I have access to that you may not."

Annette rummaged through the paper clips. Whoever's desk this was, she'd left no trace of a personality. Annette was sure, somehow, that it was a woman's desk, although she'd never noticed who sat there during the day, and she didn't see lipstick or tampons or anything like that in the drawer. She separated a single rubber band from a tangle and stretched it. She wasn't exactly thinking about this man's offer, but she was weighing it, getting used to its heft. Here he was, the stranger her mother had always warned her against, offering candy if she'd get into his car, and there was nothing for her to decide. It wasn't the candy she wanted.

Move over, buddy, I plan to drive this car.

"I'd be glad to look at anything you want to send me."

She gave him the station's address, and he accepted it without insisting they meet. She was relieved. She was disappointed. It was hard to tell what she was. A professional should probably want to meet her sources. She had two seconds of stone-cold understanding during which she knew just how far she was from being a professional, and then she pushed it away. She knew where that led. She shut the desk drawer, turned away from the plexiglassed kid, and joined Nick and the moths on the front steps.

"Jesus, Nick, give me a beer."

He flipped open the lid on his cooler and handed her one—not ice cold, but cool enough.

"Weird caller? You want me to get rid of him if he calls again?"

"Huh? No, he's o.k. I wasn't thinking about him."

She sat on the opposite side of the door frame from Nick and leaned against the building. The air was thick and warm and comforting after the station's air conditioning. Tomorrow would be hot. The moths did their flit-and-swoop routine through the floodlights. Nick did his who-was-the-caller routine, his what-did-he-want routine. Not that he'd done it before but it had the feeling of a discussion they'd had a hundred times already. The kind of discussion her parents had morning after morning over their bran flakes until her father couldn't do it one more time and walked out. And she answered Nick the way her parents had answered each other, giving away as little as she could without changing the topic. Maybe some piece of her mind was still staring at the plexiglassed son and thinking how little she knew about journalism. Maybe that same piece of her mind was scared. Maybe it was scaring the rest of her. Who knows. She couldn't afford that kind of insight if she was going to get anywhere in the world. She told Nick as little as she could because it was something she knew how to do. Eventually he gave it up.

"You could come by my place," he said. "The beer's colder."

"Yeah, and you've got clean sheets on the bed."

"No but I could probably find some if it makes a difference to you. It's not like it's a religious issue or anything."

"Sure, Nick, that's what's been stopping me."

They stared out at the parking lot and sipped their beers. Nothing happened worth noting. Nothing that hadn't happened so many times that it had turned into background, into nothing at all.

"How long do you suppose it's going to take me to get out of this godforsaken state?"

Nick shrugged.

"Where do you want to go, really?"

They'd had this discussion before too.

"Anywhere. You name it."

"This isn't a bad place if you'd give it a chance."

"It's the end of the earth, Nick."

"Why don't you come fishing with me next weekend. We'll go up by Brainerd. It's pretty."

"I hate fish. I hate pretty."

Nick sipped his beer placidly. If she came back in twenty years, he'd still be there, drinking in the parking lot, listening to the cars on the freeway, communing with the moths. The thought was oddly comforting.

"You want some soy nuts?"

Nick held a packet toward her, and she shook her head.

"They're good."

"Nick, I hate good."

Annette turned the bedside light off and couldn't remember if Nick had laughed. What if he thought she really did hate good? Something had been out of whack between them lately. She'd been . . . what? Caught up in herself, maybe. Caught up in her unidentified caller, in Len, in this Vietnam thing. She hadn't thought about Nick, and maybe he needed something from her. Time. Attention. Sex. Maybe she really should sleep with him. Maybe, maybe, maybe.

If she couldn't stop thinking, she'd be up all night. She turned the light on and read until the words papered over all thought.

CHAPTER 4

 On Thursday night when Annette and Nick left the station, a Jeep sat in the parking lot, and a man stood leaning against it. He detached himself from the fender, lumbered toward them, and stuck a hand into the air.

"Stan Marlin."

Annette shook the hand because it was pointed at her, and because Pavlov had done those experiments with the dogs, and because it was impossible not to, even though inside her head a panicky voice very much like her mother's was asking who Stan Marlin thought he was anyway, and what he was doing here.

"I'm looking for Annette Majoris."

She flipped through the voices on file in her memory and came up with his: the off-the-air caller from last night. He had a body to match the voice—bull neck, top-of-the-barrel chest, middle-of-the-barrel gut.

Nick moved up protectively beside her, although it was beyond her what he thought he could do if she really needed protection. She grinned, not to tell either of them anything but for the sheer absurdity of it. Put the two of them on one side of the scales and her on the other and they'd outweigh her three-and-a-half to one but she felt stronger than either of them. Stronger than both of them taped together. She didn't usually feel that way off the air, but she could get used to it.

"You were going to send me something," she said.

"I thought it might be better if I brought it. You know how the mail is—throw something in the box in June and call to see if it got there by December. Standard governmental efficiency."

Annette nodded—what the hell, why not?—although she'd never had any trouble with the mail, and he produced a folder from the passenger seat of the Jeep and held it up on display, not ready to surrender it yet.

"This is preliminary," he said. "A few things I've been able to put together. I have to tell you, I don't think of myself as naive, but what all this points to—it's unbelievable. I've got to hand it to you, if it hadn't been for you, I never would've thought to look into it."

She grinned harder and he gave the folder a tight shake—saying good-bye to it, maybe, or warning it to behave—and handed it over.

"Like I said, this is just skimming the surface, but there's some good stuff in there. Damning evidence. Absolutely mind-boggling. Give us a little time and we'll uncover it all, every bit of it."

Annette accepted the folder without taking her eyes away from its source.

"Fred," she said. "Or Frank. You said your name was Frank."

The man's face was blank for a second, then the name registered.

"On the phone. Right. I'm sorry about that. I didn't know if . . . We're talking about a government gone wild here, and citizens may think the government's changed—hell, even the government may think it's changed—but it's still the government, and it's prepared to defend itself against the likes of you and me. Until I knew a bit more about what I was dealing with . . . Hell, I don't know why I gave that name."

He laughed.

"People do that. Invent names."

She glanced at the folder.

"I'll look through this."

"I left my number in there. You can get in touch if you want to. I'll have something more substantial for you soon."

He stuck his hand out to Annette again, then offered it to Nick, in all his cowlike bulk.

"Mr. Majoris?"

Nick took the hand without disagreeing.

"Nick Carlson," Annette said, leaving Stan to fill in the relationship for himself.

The man turned his bull head back to Annette. What sin had she committed in her life to be exiled to the Midwest and surrounded by bovines?

"I don't want to impose myself," the man said. "Turning up like this. Middle of the night."

He looked at the fringe of trees, seeing the same dangers there that Nick saw, making sure she didn't mistake him for one of them, but he didn't leave. He seemed to be debating whether it was safe to tell her something, or too early, or bad manners. He looked back at her and shook his head, which meant something or other but who could tell what.

"You strike me as one extremely sharp lady," he said, "and I don't want to frighten you, but you've stirred up some forces here that even you can only guess at, and I want to tell you that if you need protection, anything of that sort, we're prepared to offer it."

Annette shook her head: no, thanks anyway, but no protection tonight. No onions either, if you wouldn't mind. No pickles. No ketchup. Hold the burger, too, while you're at it. She watched him climb into his Jeep. Only when his taillights were disappearing behind the lilacs did the questions she wanted to ask announce themselves at a shriek inside her head: what the hell forces was he talking about, and what was he trying not to frighten her about?

★

She didn't look at the folder that night. It was late by the time she got home, and she'd had a beer with Nick. Right—when wasn't it late, and when hadn't she had a beer with Nick? O.K., she wanted to sleep. And the folder bothered her. What the hell, why not admit it? It scared the shit out of her. After Stan drove off, she and Nick had laughed away the spookiness of a listener tracing her to the station as if hearing her voice gave him ownership of her time. Protection, yet. Preliminary folders. What a self-important jerk. She even ate some of the yogurt-covered raisins Nick offered her. They were foul, and even worse after a mouthful of beer, but accepting them gave her a sense of connection to Nick, and something to think about that didn't involve wars or listeners tracking her down or the idea that she might need protection. She drove home with the CD player blasting Perry Como, who she'd be the first to admit was sappy and in the worst possible taste, but there was something soothing about all that sap, and who'd know the difference anyway—she only played him when she was alone. But not even ole Perry was enough to settle her down tonight. At the edge of her mind, she pictured the moment when Stan's taillights had flickered behind the leaves of the lilacs and whatever he'd said about stirring up some kind of forces exploded into questions she didn't have answers for.

She woke up the next morning with Stan's visit still gnawing at her and moved from the newspaper to the computer and from the computer to the newspaper. She walked to SuperAmerica for coffee and a muffin, carrying them past the pumps, past a puddle of spilled gas, but by the time she got them home, Stan's unnamed forces had settled into her stomach and expanded, taking up the entire space where she'd planned on installing the muffin. To make herself feel less foolish about buying it, she ate a couple of pinches and crumbled the rest, picking out a blueberry or two while the coffee grew cold.

It wasn't until the hang-up calls started again in the afternoon that she remembered the folder, and suddenly the calls weren't half as much fun as they used to be. In fact, they scared her. It was one thing to know you'd gotten under someone's skin, and it was something else again to think you'd pissed off powerful forces somewhere. Still, as long as they'd made her lousy mood worse, she had no reason not to look at the folder.

She retrieved it from the scattered newspapers by the apartment door, unplugged the phone, and stretched out on the couch.

Each sheet of paper inside the folder was dedicated to a single topic, even when it didn't hold much information, as if Stan-Frank really did mean to go back and fill them all in. She must be living right. The man was a gold mine.

"According to v.a. psychiatrists," the top one read, "700,000 Vietnam vets suffer posttraumatic stress disorder, which they define as panic, rage, anxiety, depression, and emotional paralysis. That's a higher % than suffered shell shock in wwi or battle fatigue in wwii. [Find comparable numbers.] Can this be accounted for by anything other than the implantation of false memories? How many suffer from disorders too subacute to register on v.a. scale?

"Average age, Vietnam solder, 19.

"Average age, wwii soldier, 26.

"Why the sudden preference for the younger, more malleable soldier?"

Interesting but not conclusive. She flipped to the next page.

"Reporter Stanley Karnow states that despite the 'bombings,' Hanoi, Haiphong & the surrounding countryside are 'almost completely unscathed' & 'appear to have been barely touched.' By comparison, Langson, which was destroyed in the border war w/ China, is largely rubble."

Ha.

The next page was a timeline of sorts.

"1945, U.S. parachutes a team into Ho Chi Minh's jungle camp, finds him nearly dead of malaria, dysentery. U.S. medic saves his life. U.S. supplies Vietminh with rifles, mortars, grenades & trains Vietminh solders. Gen. Vo Nguyen Giap tells a Hanoi crowd to regard the U.S. as a good friend.

"1947, French Communists support French military actions against Communist Vietminh. Moscow shows no interest in Vietnam insurgency. Has a deal been cut this early, so they know the effort's a sham? Or is this lack of support what drove the N. Vietnamese, later, to cut a deal w/ the U.S.?"

There were a dozen more pages like that—bits of information studded with questions. Well toward the back was one labeled Martha Mitchell.

Who the hell was Martha Mitchell?

As if he'd heard the question, Stan-Frank gave her the answer: the wife of Nixon's attorney general, known for calling reporters late at night and, presumably, drunk on her highly placed ass. Spilled the beans on Watergate. Also on Vietnam, although who'd believe a drunk? Well, one columnist at the New York *Post* did, as it turned out, a guy named Albert Harvey, and the paper was all ready to run his column when they got a call from we'll-probably-never-know-who and pulled it—filled the hole with some piece of fluff about a small-town dog show in New Jersey.

Harvey drowned off the coast of Long Island not long afterwards. Martha Mitchell was dead. The editor who'd pulled the article had the sense to keep his mouth shut until long after he retired, when he told the story to his nephew, who Stan knew through some organization he was part of. Annette could meet him herself if she wanted.

The last page was a note, apparently to her although it wasn't addressed to anyone, acknowledging the sketchy nature of the material and promising more. It ended with his home phone number (he had no cell, it said, and if she had one she should get rid of it; they were too easy to tap). Then he tacked on another warning about forces that would want to silence her, but somehow it felt different than it had a few minutes ago. If Stan-Frank was ready to do her research, she could handle anything. They wanted to silence her? Hell, let 'em try.

To prove she could handle whatever she'd stirred up, she plugged the phone back in and picked up a call from her mother.

"Are you having trouble with your answering machine?" her mother asked. "I called several times, but it just kept ringing. I even had the operator try. I thought I might be getting a wrong number somehow."

"I unplugged it. I had some work to do."

"Someone could be trying to reach you."

"If it's important, they'll call back."

"Annie, that's inconsiderate."

Annette moved to her computer, wedging the phone between ear and shoulder while her mother expanded on all the ways and reasons it had inconvenienced her. Her, her, her. Annette called up a solitaire game. The depression was gone. She moved a three of diamonds onto a four of clubs and waited for her mother to take the conversation in some other direction.

Why didn't she want to explain about the phone? Does it matter? Fine, she was too old to report on her day at school. And her mother would fuss—Annette didn't know what she'd say and she didn't want to find out, but she knew she'd take all her diffuse worrying and focus it on this target. If she heard Annette at all. Talking to her mother was like talking to the TV sometimes. Besides, it was a habit, not telling her mother things—a kind of power she wasn't ready to give up.

Years ago, after Annette's father remarried, from behind the safety of his new wife he'd invited Annette for an agonizingly long weekend during which he'd told her that not arguing with her mother was the surest way to make her stop talking about any subject other than herself. He delivered this information with all the ceremony of a priest passing on the tribal wisdom. He didn't know Annette well enough anymore to understand that disengagement wasn't one of her gifts. Maybe he never had known her well enough, but she tried it now, holding herself carefully blank as she moved the jack of clubs.

Her mother kept talking. Maybe Annette was supposed to recite some silent incantation that her father had withheld from her. That would be just like him, to give and withhold at the same time. Or maybe it wasn't working because the topic wasn't really the phone but Annette's mother and how she'd been inconvenienced. Annette hit undo and the jack snapped back to its old spot. She hit it again and the three moved off the four. If she hit it enough times, maybe the computer would unwire itself, jump into its cardboard boxes and styrofoam packing forms and ship itself back to the store. The store would return her money. Which would be helpful right about now. She was about to change the subject to money, but then magically, miraculously, her mother moved on of her own accord, telling Annette about her job and a trip to the Czech Republic to meet with someone or other. It washed over Annette like the draft from the air conditioner, comfortable and annoying at the same time. Her mother had taken a new job in January. She was in charge of marketing for a company that made sports and exercise equipment, which meant she traveled a lot and took people to lunch and hated exercise. It meant she made more money, but it also meant she spent more. People expected a certain level of style from her, she said, and she'd had to buy something or other for the trip—Annette missed what it was—because she couldn't afford to disappoint them. The details swam past Annette like shoals of fish, but there was that topic, money, again.

After something between five minutes and half an hour—time stood still while Annette moved cards and mashed the phone against the cartilage of her ear—Annette broke in to ask if she could borrow a few hundred bucks. She hated to ask, but she was close to maxing her cards out, and yeah Mom, she knew she shouldn't have, but there it was, she had, and the payments were due, and she wouldn't have to borrow money forever. She had her eye on a couple of stations—Boston, D.C., Atlanta—that would pay real money. Something would open up soon. They worked out a repayment schedule. Her mother was big on job prospects. She was big on repayment plans, and as serious about them as if Annette had been keeping up with the schedules they'd worked out for her earlier loans. It was nickel and dime stuff, and Annette had every intention of paying it back, but it would have to wait till she could do it right. She imagined herself flying home, laying a stack of hundreds on the coffee table, fanning them out with one hand like playing cards, showing how many more she was paying back than she actually owed. Twice the amount. Three times the amount. Christ, what *was* the amount? Why be stingy? She'd lay a round ten thousand on the table—payback plus interest plus proof that she was grown and loved her mother the way an adult could afford to.

They hung up, and Annette picked up the folder again, leafing through what she'd already read, packing anything that might be useful into her memory. Martha Mitchell. Remember Martha Mitchell. Do not confuse Martha Mitchell with Martha Stewart. She got three more hang-up calls from the unidentified number, then a man telling her she was a lying bitch and she'd better watch it.

"Oh yeah?" she asked. "Watch what?"

"Just watch it. You understand?"

He hung up too soon to hear her say that she understood but she doubted that he did. The voice didn't match any of the ones that had stored themselves in her memory, but that didn't necessarily mean anything. She didn't have total recall. She unplugged the phone and said, "There, asshole. What're you going to do now?"

The answer was, he wasn't going to do anything. They were phone calls, nothing more, and standing up to them felt good, even if it wasn't as satisfying as doing it in front of an audience.

CHAPTER 5

Annette stalled a few days before she called the number in the folder. She wanted to give Stan time. She didn't want to seem anxious. Which is another way of saying that she was anxious. Where else was she going to get information? She wasn't a journalist; she wasn't a historian. She was a personality, and one with no budget for a research staff.

Which brought her to Stan, who either had his own budget or didn't need one, and who asked her to meet him at a Perkins. Haute cuisine among the antigovernment set, she presumed. Fine. No goat cheese, no fresh basil, and she'd pay for his research by not acting like she expected them.

He was installed in a booth by the time she walked in, with his big hands resting on a new folder and his head bent over, studying the contents. He'd once had a widow's peak but all that was left of it now were a few strands of hair, like faint traces of sandbar in a rising tide of scalp. For a split second, that loser feeling broke over her wordlessly. It didn't have time to gather words, just hit her with a do-the-world-a-favor-and-stick-your-head-in-the-sand-until-you-suffocate feeling.

Not now, she told herself. *You're on the air,* and she shoved the feeling away.

Stan closed the folder and waved the waitress over before Annette could slide all the way into the booth.

"What say you bring us coffee right away and we'll order later."

He turned to Annette.

"You drink coffee?"

She did. Which was good, because the waitress had left already.

Stan passed Annette the folder after giving it the same quick shake he'd given the first one.

"You can look at that when you have time. I've got a couple of people working with me on this, so we should be able to turn things up faster now if there's anything out there *to* turn up." He hesitated. "I hate to say it, but I think there will be."

"There will, don't worry about that."

The waitress came back with coffee and Stan handed Annette a menu as if he'd researched the restaurant too and brought a menu from home—one that was more complete than anything the restaurant would circulate. If they had goat cheese hidden away in the kitchen, he'd find out about it. And he'd think they were effete New York snobs for harboring it.

"Maybe we'd better order."

Annette ran an eye down the menu and settled for two eggs over easy with toast and bacon. It was the least imaginative thing she could find. She hoped he approved.

The waitress took notes and left. Maybe she'd turn the notes over to a spy agency working undercover in the kitchen. The forces Stan said she'd stirred up, keeping a close eye on her eating habits. Was it illegal yet to eat eggs that weren't cooked until they were hard enough to bounce?

Annette had made several decisions about what to say to this man, but now that she was here she couldn't remember what they were. She hadn't expected this: that his presence, his body sitting across from her in a booth at Perkins, would throw her this way. Part of it was a queasy conviction that he was attracted to her, although he hadn't made any of the obvious moves: no fingers lingering on the menu when he passed it to her, no eyes leaving a slime trail as they slid across her body. That would at least have been clear. This was unnerving somehow, and repellent. Christ, the man was older than her parents. Plus, he was losing his hair and thought Perkins was a classy place to meet.

So yeah, she was off balance a little. Maybe it was the Minnesota Nice thing, even though this was work and she should be able to shelve all the emotional stuff when she was working. But she didn't want to offend him. She didn't want to run him off. Which meant that instead of starting the conversation wherever she'd meant to, she started it someplace else, with the vague feeling that she was making party conversation with someone she didn't know and might end up wishing she hadn't met.

"Are you a vet yourself?"

She might as easily have been asking what sign he was born under.

"Four-F." He tapped his chest. "Some technicality about the heart, although it's never slowed me down any. Thought it was the end of the world when they wouldn't take me. Wanted to serve my country. Serve it, hell—wanted to die for it."

He shook his head. She had a feeling he'd told this story before, and that he always shook his head there.

"I was young, idealistic. Naive. Didn't know the difference yet between my country and my government."

He leaned forward in a way that wasn't about sex, she hoped, but still said this was just between the two of them.

"You know what made me understand the difference? It's a small thing, but here's how it happened. I bought a house, not a big place but nice, and I wanted to redo the bathroom, add a sunroom in the back. Well, all of a sudden I'm tied up in permits, inspectors. They have a different inspector for every color of paint. And it's not enough I'm remodeling my own house the way I want to for my own use, I've got to add this because it's code and that because the hot-water-faucet inspector thinks it's safer. And who pays for all these changes they want? Well, gee gosh, I guess I have to do that. With my money, on what's supposed to be my property."

He pulled back to his side of the table and lifted his coffee cup as if it proved his point somehow.

"I practically moved into the government center, I spent so much time there. I tell you, it got to where they'd start to weep when they saw me coming. I lost money fighting with them, even though I got my way on a couple of things, because my business just about went to hell—it took me a year to get it back on its feet after that—but I learned what government means in our lives, and I'm telling you, it's not our friend. Anyone tells you it is, you put your hand on your wallet and back slowly out of the room."

He nodded and drank his coffee, circling the cup with one hand and pointing the empty handle toward Annette.

"That's when I started looking around. Taxation. Driver's licenses. Hell, dog licenses. Next they'll want to license cats. Fish. There's gun control. Land use. My god, they've got us so tied up in red tape and environmental hysteria, a landowner doesn't own his own land anymore. Can't improve it unless he gets Snow White and all the seven dwarves to sign forms in eight-tuplicate for him. And don't even get me started on what a businessman puts up with. You've got the environment, the minorities, the city, the county, the state, the feds, the spotted owl—everyone's got a better idea than you do on how to run your business. It's a miracle we've still got an economy."

He'd leaned forward again as he talked, wrapping the cup in both hands and aiming the handle at her. He seemed to notice it and think it might be threatening, because he set it down.

"I thought I had a pretty clear idea what the government was capable of, but I have to tell you, what you're suggesting shocks me. Genuinely shocks me."

Annette smiled: modesty, sympathy, agreement. Shock, of course. She was doing fine. She hadn't offended him yet.

The waitress was approaching with their food, and he stopped talking until she left. As if what they were talking about hadn't already been on the air. As if the waitress really were reporting to the bad guys in the kitchen.

"You talked about forces I might stir up."

She'd tried to sound casual—what's your sign, and oh, do you think anyone might decide to kill me or anything?—but she wasn't sure she'd succeeded. She poked at her egg. The yolk was hard nine-tenths of the way through, heavy on the *over* and light on the *easy*, but she wasn't sure if Minnesotans were allowed to complain about their food or if only New Yorkers did that. It didn't matter anyway, since the waitress had abandoned them.

"No *might* about it. Anything this big, we're talking major elements with a stake in keeping it quiet. Army, Navy, Marines, CIA—hell, and that's just our own government. We're probably talking about foreign governments too, plus the U.N. and everything that flows from that."

He shoveled a wedge of pancake into his mouth as if thinking about enemies made his food that much sweeter. Annette set her fork down and tried to think of something she could do with her eggs that didn't involve eating them.

"I don't mean to scare you," he said.

"No," Annette said. Of course not. Don't give it a thought.

"You haven't had anyone following you, have you? Watching you, showing up in odd places?"

"Not that I've noticed."

"From here on out, notice. Safest thing to do is exactly what you've been doing. Make yourself as public as possible on this. Talk about it on every show. Don't back down. If they can't make you disappear quietly, I don't think they'll touch you."

That made sense. Or if it didn't make sense, it was still convincing. It was her job to rattle cages, after all; she couldn't run for cover every time a cage occupant growled. She poured ketchup on her plate and dipped a forkful of egg in it. It didn't taste good, but then she hadn't expected it to.

"Let me tell you about the organization I work with," he said. "Because I believe this is a group that can bring America to its true moment of greatness."

Annette had to listen a long time before she found an opening. "I'd like to meet that editor's nephew," she said.

Annette had parked the car behind her building and turned off the engine before it hit her: this Vietnam thing? This so-called war? It terrified her. She'd gone for a stroll around the block and found herself doing a high-wire act. And her safety harness had been shipped to New Jersey by mistake. She let her fingers slide down the steering wheel and sat in good-girl pose, hands folded in her lap, reminding herself that she was only doing her job. They'd hired her to shake things up.

Right, and if she shook so hard that crockery got broken, Len would blame her.

She stared out at the parking lot without seeing it and thought of the vets who'd been calling her. Michael with the break in his voice. The other guy—the one who said she'd saved his life. What would happen to them if she dropped the issue?

There was no point in thinking about it. She couldn't back out anyway.

CHAPTER 6

 Over the next few weeks, Stan sent Annette a packet of information every few days, although never by mail. Mostly they were hand-delivered and waiting stampless for her at the station, but one morning, still wearing her bathrobe, she answered her apartment door to a geeky-looking guy in camouflage pants, who offered her a folder.

"How'd you find me?" she asked.

"It's from Stan," he said, as if this answered the question.

"Yeah, but how'd you get this address?"

"Stan gave it to me. It's on the folder."

"It's not listed," she yelled at his back as he shambled down the hall toward the elevator.

Whatever Stan's eccentricities were, though, the information he sent was good. It was more than good—it was fantastic. It was beyond anything she'd dared to dream of, and she sorted through it, selecting, repackaging, memorizing, until it flowed out of her as naturally as the opening lines of her show. Once or twice she asked herself what she'd do if all of it turned out to be wrong, but that wasn't a question she could afford, and she pushed it aside.

Then Stan hand-delivered the nephew. She walked out of the station one night to find Stan leaning against his Jeep with the kind of man Annette wouldn't have noticed if she'd passed him three times in a suburban mall—fortyish, his cheeks slipping downward into early jowls, wearing some kind of synthetic slacks and a knit shirt.

"Curt Pearson," Stan said, waving a hand toward him. "Nephew of the editor who pulled the Martha Mitchell column."

Annette shook the man's hand, and her own hand didn't pass through his, which wasn't enough to prove he was real, but it did help.

"You're from New York, then?" Annette asked.

"Wisconsin. My uncle was kind of the black sheep, moving out there like that."

O.K., she couldn't prove anything by testing his knowledge of New York.

"And he worked for the *Post?*"

"Forty-one years."

He wasn't what you'd call talkative, and Annette had to lead him step by step through the story Stan had written out for her, but he told it convincingly—not overeager, sure of himself without seeming rehearsed. Said his uncle had told him the story late at night after his mother's—the editor's sister's—funeral. They were sitting in his mother's living room going through old photographs, and the nephew didn't say that a kind of quiet—a kind of trust—had grown up between them, but Annette imagined it that way all the same. Maybe they'd had a couple of drinks. The nephew asked the uncle if he'd ever regretted moving away, and his answer—which the nephew took to be yes, although the editor never exactly said that—eventually led to this story, which was all about regret. Not to mention fear.

"I don't suppose he saved the article, did he?"

"Don't know. We've got his papers somewhere. No kids of his own, you know. It all had to go somewhere, and it seemed kind of rude to just throw it out."

"He'll look," Stan said.

"And you'd be willing to call my show and tell me this on the air?"
The man shrugged.

"Don't see why not."

"I'd have you on as a guest but my station manager . . ."

"He understands," Stan said. "Probably better this way."

It probably was. If his story fell apart, it didn't belong to her.

At home, Annette Googled the uncle, and he really had worked
for the *Post*. He really was dead. So was the columnist. What she
couldn't find a way to check was whether the guy she'd met really
was a relative, and for a blind, screaming second, her body lost its
belief in Stan and all his information. It was like waking up as a
dog, with her head out the car window, the wind pounding at her
so hard that her eyelids rose an air-conditioned millimeter off of
her eyes. *This is all wrong*, her body screamed. *Someone's going to
get hurt. It will all end in tears.*

She took a slow, steady breath.

I'm only asking a question, she told herself in the most reliable
voice she could get hold of. *It's the vets who say I'm onto something.*

The wind slacked off. Her eyelids embraced her eyes and
warmed them. It was only a question, and it offered people peace.
Surely that had to be good.

When the nephew called the show a couple of days later,
his voice was as flat as it had been in person, as if he was calling to say the water would be turned off in the building
between nine and noon, but he was clear, he was easy to follow,
and he was quotable: Martha Mitchell, Vietnam, there was no
war. "You're going to think I'm out of my mind when I tell you
this," Martha was supposed to have said, "but there is no war.
There is no enemy. Just a nest of lies no sane person can find
his way through."

Annette began to open her show with the information Stan fed her. She leaned into the mic, her voice low and intense.

"Ladies and gentlemen, boys and girls, everyone else in between, you're listening to *Open Line*, I'm Annette Majoris, and it's just you and me here tonight—no guests, no experts to get between us—and on this particular night I want to welcome you to the heart of darkness, to the disturbing and mysterious world of what went wrong with the greatest country in the known world."

She paused for half a beat and raised her eyebrows at Nick, who was chewing on a carrot. He signaled with a nod that he was listening, but his eyes didn't tell her she was wonderful or that he wanted to sleep with her—or that he wanted to claim he wanted to sleep with her. Well, to hell with him; she was wonderful anyway. She was about to be more wonderful. Assuming, of course, that she didn't get fired. She shifted her gaze to the mic.

"I'm going to open up the lines for calls in a few minutes, but before I do that, I want to talk to you uninterrupted about some information I've found recently that scares the pants off me.

"If you've been listening to the show lately, you know I've been asking questions about whether the Vietnam War really happened, and more and more evidence has been turning up. But people have been asking me what the government would gain by faking a war. I haven't known how to answer that, and it's a damn good question. I mean, come on, it's got to be easier to fight a war than to fake one."

She uncapped her bottle of Evian although she wouldn't be able to drink from it until she took the first call. Her mouth was as dry as an old sock, and inside her skull a tiny version of Len's voice was boring its way through the bone like a dentist's drill, reminding her only to raise questions, not to make statements, reminding her that she hadn't studied journalism and therefore knew nothing. She'd barely started talking and here he was already—or here his dentist's-drill surrogate was—going nuts.

What the hell. He was making *her* nuts, why shouldn't she see to it that he suffered too?

"Well, I've found some information that might explain what the government thought it would gain, and I want you to hear it and make up your own minds about what it means, because hey, that's what democracy's all about, right?

"O.K., we're going back to the 1950s here. You know the fifties, the golden era, when men were men and women wore aprons. When the families had values and the streets were safe. When the government was your friend. When America was really America. Any high school students out there, you ought to be in bed by now, but before you go, write that down. If they ask about the fifties on a test, that's what they want you to tell them.

"But what I'm going to tell you about is another side of the fifties, the part they don't want you to know, so if you take notes on this one, kids, leave them home. Remember, don't try this at school.

"Fine. Here we go: Project Sunrise. Nice name, isn't it? Hopeful. Sweet. Well, hang on to your hats, because Project Sunrise was based in Area 51, in the Nevada desert, and this is a piece of ground so top secret that it's still fenced off. If you're driving past and decide to stop and look at the fence, all of a sudden a couple of very polite soldiers'll drive up and ask if you're having car trouble, and you'll be on your way so fast and so politely you may not even notice you just got told to move along on a public American road that you pay taxes for. I'm not sure, but I suspect that if you laid out a picnic and insisted on staying to finish it, you'd get arrested for malicious condiments.

"So Project Sunrise is secret. What was it, and how do we know about it? First question first: it was an experiment in mind control, and it was run by the U.S. military using its own soldiers as guinea pigs. You don't believe the government would do that? You ever hear about the atomic veterans? A group of soldiers. Their officers told them to line up and watch the birdie, then they dropped an atom bomb and studied these guys to find out about the effects of radiation on the human body. It happened. In the fifties. It's public record. Except of course for the years when they claimed it never happened.

"Next question: how do we know about Project Sunrise? We know because the boys controlling the minds weren't good at it yet. They made mistakes. Word leaked out. We don't have time for me to tell you everything that leaked, so I'm going to stick with one source, a retired Army nurse named Glenda Martinez."

Annette looked through the glass. Nick had stopped chewing on his carrot and was watching her like she'd grown antlers. Whatever he thought of her, though, she had his complete and slack-jawed attention, and if she'd pulled Nick out of his sulk, she had them all, her whole invisible audience.

"In 1962, Glenda Martinez wrote her sister a letter and told her sister to open it only after she—Martinez—died, and what she did in that letter was describe her work inside Area 51 between 1957 and 1960, and if you ever read the actual text, you can hear how scared she was to put it on paper. She told her sister three separate times never to let anyone know about the letter because it was too dangerous.

"What did she say? That for three years when the country wasn't at war anywhere, she was caring for cases of battle fatigue in Area 51—what we'd call posttraumatic shock victims. She was taking care of soldiers—new cases, not holdovers from Korea or World War II—who had strange, fragmented memories of doing horrible things in battles, but they were never sure where the battles had been, or when, or even who they'd been fighting. Some of them thought it was the Chinese or the Koreans, some said it was the Russians, and some of them thought it was Americans—even their own families. And get this: some of the soldiers also had physical wounds, as if they really had been fighting. The staff never talked to each other about what might have happened to the men, but Martinez wondered if they hadn't actually been set against each other.

"The staff, apparently, wasn't in much better shape than the patients. Very polite armed guards escorted them to and from the hospital, and they were told quite a bit less politely that they'd be charged with treason, every last one of them, if the outside world caught wind of anything that went on inside Area 51.

"So that's the letter. Two weeks to the day after she wrote it, Glenda Martinez took her own life. Or seemed to have taken her own life. Less than six months later, her sister was dead.

"Final question: why would the government want to do this? I still don't have a solid answer for that, but it may have been to see how far they could push a soldier. Would he do things he thought were wrong? Would he shoot American citizens? Would he kill his own family? Could he be used that way if necessary? Or it may have been because if you want to stay in power, mind control's a dandy thing to have and they were seeing how well it worked.

"So there it is, kids: implanted memories of battles that couldn't have happened, a supersecret project that turned out mental and physical wrecks, and we're still back in the fifties, before, as anyone will tell you, the government got out of hand and moral decay set in.

"I'll give out the phone number and start taking your calls in just a minute here, but before I do, I want to tie this into what we've been taught to call the Vietnam War. I won't take the time to cite chapter and verse on this tonight, but other sources hint that Project Sunrise was getting too big for Area 51. The Pentagon couldn't keep cranking out soldiers who'd fought in wars that everyone knew never happened. It needed a war the public believed in, and it may have found that in Vietnam. Kids; boys and girls; men and women; citizens of this proud, beleaguered nation: I don't want to believe this any more than you do, so I'm going to give out the phone number now and ask you to call and convince me that this is all my imagination."

★

And they called. Of course they called. Ever since she'd been talking about Vietnam, callers had jammed every line the station had. When the lines were full, they hit their redial buttons until they wore the lettering right off them. If they were in their cars and didn't have cell phones, they drove to all-night gas stations, pushing strangers out of the way to get at the pay phones first, and they rained down on her like manna—whatever that may have been—from heaven. And she was perfect. With the guys who called all pissed off because none of this mattered in the post-9/11 world, she was patient. The world had changed, the enemies had changed, the faces in the White House and in Congress had changed, but the new guys had inherited this technology when they inherited the machinery of government. How many politicians would hand that back? And if government was capable of a deception like this, then how were we to know what was real anymore?

"Let me put it to you this way: think about Saddam Hussein. Think about the weapons of mass destruction. Think about Colin Powell's weapons-of-mass-destruction show-and-tell at the United Nations Security Council. You remember back that far? Convincing, wasn't it? Now ask yourself how much it's worth to be sure of anything."

Bull's-eye.

And with the angry ones, the logical ones, the ones who tried to convince her that Project Sunrise hadn't happened and the Vietnam War had, she was full of regret. She wished she could believe with them, but there was this bit of evidence, and that one.

Martha Mitchell. Poor drunken, terrified Martha Mitchell. And a reporter from the *Rocky Mountain News* who spent an evening getting monumentally drunk with an officer who worked on Project Sunrise and told him, in a drunk's confidential idea of a whisper, that the project had outgrown Area 51 and scared him half to death. Everything about it scared him. He told the reporter, "You'll hear about it pretty soon here, only you won't know that's what you're hearing about; you'll think it's something else. God help us, no one'll know what it is." And then he wept.

When the reporter tried to call the man the next day to make sure he'd gotten home safely, he was told there was no such person—never had been, never would be, and please be so kind as to not call back.

And there was more. A secret commission, three of whose members died before it could complete its report. A colonel who joked with his wife over breakfast about how he was supposed to go out and start a set of rumors that Area 51 was being used for the secret study of a flying saucer and the aliens who'd piloted it. He showed her a nest of wrinkled cash lying loose inside a bowling ball bag.

Six hours later he was dead in a single-car accident. The bag was gone, the money was gone, and the rumors were still circulating.

The callers weren't all with her yet, but they were listening. And most of all, they were calling. Some of them were weepy, frightened, not sure what they believed. One vet seemed to remember an underground chamber, a light broken up by something like slow-moving fan blades, bits and pieces of battles, carnage, war. It made no sense to him—his memories of Vietnam were clearer and more coherent than these—but it was keeping him up nights, and maybe this was what she was talking about. Bit by bit she drew it out of him: the damp walls of the chamber, the crushing fear. Was there a voice? A face? He couldn't remember either but maybe a voice. Possibly. Could he remember what it said?

"Honey," he said, "I might be able to do that if I worked at it but whatever it's got to say, I don't want to hear it. You understand what I mean?"

Of course she understood. It was her job to understand.

★

She ended the show with a disclaimer for Len: she had no axe to grind. She was only asking a question, trying to make sense of disturbing information as it came to light, asking her listeners to work through it with her. She doubted Len would hear that part, but she could quote it at him when he complained about one of the times when her voice forgot to rise at the end of a sentence to turn it into a question.

She settled beside Nick on the steps and accepted the beer he held out to her. Now that she was off the air, Len's voice was back in her head, dentisting away, and she was on the edge of a killer headache when she should have felt triumphant, damn it. She'd been good tonight. Great. Brilliant. Inspired.

She pushed the tab into her beer and drank.

"So. Did I have 'em going tonight or didn't I?" she asked.

"You had 'em going," Nick said, but he wasn't enjoying it the way he would have once. It was a fact, and he admitted it because he was honest, and because she'd forced him into it.

"C'mon, Nick, gloat with me a little here. I was good tonight."

Nick nodded ruminatively, the way cows would nod if they cared to, reminding her that she wasn't in New York, that Minnesotans hate controversy, even if they were paying her to create some. Reminding her how small her audience was—a handful of suburban insomniacs, the cooks in the all-night diners, twelve cab drivers on the night shift, fourteen unsleeping manic-depressives in their manic phase. Reminding her that Nick, damn it, was supposed to be her friend, the one person she could count on.

"C'mon, Nick, what's the matter here? I thought you'd be glad for me."

"I've never known anyone like you," he said, as if this somehow answered what she'd asked. "And I like you. You know I do. But this Vietnam stuff . . . I mean, I can take a joke as well as the next guy, but don't you think it's getting out of hand here? You know, what are you doing with this stuff?"

"What am I doing?"

"Yah. You know, what're you doing?"

"I'm doing a radio show. What do you think I'm doing?"

He shook some corn nuts into his hand and fed them one by one into his mouth. Annette looked across the parking lot and into the moth-stitched night to keep from following the workings of his jaw, but she heard the nuts crunching anyway and imagined them forming a paste inside his mouth, imagined him storing the paste in one of four stomachs so he could chew it again later. She wanted to scoot to the far edge of the steps, but she'd still have heard him chewing. At the same time, and in almost equal measure, she wanted to lean her head on his shoulder and beg him to like her again.

Or did cows have three stomachs?

Screw it. She already knew more about cows than she wanted to.

"What I mean," he said. "You're getting kind of spooky, you know? You don't believe this stuff, do you?"

She took a deep breath.

"I'm asking . . ." she began to say.

"I know, you're asking a question is all. But do you believe it?"

"Len gave me orders not to believe it."

"Hey, I'm not Len. You're not on the air."

"Yeah, Nick, I do. O.K.? I think it probably happened. If I didn't believe that, I couldn't go on the air with it night after night."

Which was the right answer for the time, place, and person. It was what Nick needed to hear. It was what she needed to hear.

"Jesus, you're crazier'n they are."

Annette didn't ask who *they* were. Stan and all his friends and acquaintances, maybe. Her callers. What did it matter who *they* were? She set her beer down and stood up.

"It's good to have friends," she said.

She turned away from him and walked to her car, willing him to call after her, to say something more. The entire sounding board of her back was tensed for it. She didn't need an apology. She'd have been happy to keep arguing, but when he didn't say anything she had no choice but to unlock the door and drive home.

Before she reached the freeway entrance, she'd ejected Perry Como. He was grating on her nerves tonight.

Annette settled into the visitor's chair and stared across Len's bare desk, watching him flip through pink message slips. She tried to remember exactly what she'd said last night so she'd be ready to defend it, but the whole show came up blank, and her mind presented her with observations about the desk instead: the Russian steppes, sweeping uninterrupted to the horizon. Hell, the Battle of Stalingrad could have been fought on that desk. It was big enough.

"This isn't what I expected," Len said finally, "but you're picking up advertisers. You offend people, but you're picking up advertisers."

Annette nodded soberly. Len was the only person in her life with whom less really was more.

"You're walking a thin line here, you understand that? Advertisers or no. So be careful."

Annette nodded.

"I don't have to spell out what I mean by that, do I?"

Annette hadn't a clue what he meant, but she shook her head. All right, she had several clues, but she wasn't sure they were the right ones. He meant more of the same, she figured. Questions were O.K. but conclusions weren't. She half suspected he had some new thin line in mind, but it was probably better not to know. That way if she crossed it, she could say he'd never spelled it out.

Len flipped the folder closed.

"I could've told you this on the phone, but Kathi says she can't reach you anymore, not even your answering machine."

"Hang-up calls. All the time now. Some guy telling me to watch it. I leave the phone unplugged most of the time now. Len, I can hardly pick it up to call out."

Len grunted like he figured it was her fault.

"Get a different number. Get a cell phone. Get two cell phones. I don't care what you do—we've got to be able to reach you."

Annette nodded. She hated cell phones. Every seventh grader in the country had a cell phone. And they called her attention to how few people called her, and how few people she could call.

"That's it?"

"I told you, I could've talked to you on the phone, but I couldn't reach you."

"I didn't mean that. I was just checking."

"Yeah, that's it."

Annette stood. She had an impulse to back out of the office bowing, the way you did with royalty.

Hell, what did she know about royalty?

"Thanks for letting me know," she said.

She turned her back on him and cut a path to the door along the shortest possible path between two points, managing not to trip on the carpet.

Annette opened her door to find another of Stan's packets, thin this time, just a few typed pages with the antique look of a carbon copy. She parked herself at the table to read it. She should buy a desk. It would make her feel businesslike.

What she had in her hands, she realized a sentence or two into it, was the Martha Mitchell column—the actual damn Martha Mitchell column. The uncle had saved it.

It wasn't a great column. The writer went into a space-filler of an opening about the nature of late-night phone calls, but old Martha had actually called this guy—gotten him out of bed and filled his telephone-ear full of Project Sunrise and Richard Nixon being reviled for a war that wasn't real, which was tearing him apart, and wasn't that a nice little bit of irony.

"I'm not supposed to be saying this," she'd said, "and you're not supposed to be hearing it, but it's true all the same. There is no war, just something much, much scarier."

Well, holy shit.

Annette looked out the window, letting the full impact hit her. Then she looked back, but at the paper this time instead of at the words. It had a convincing, lost-in-the-attic look to it, with small bends and tears at the edges.

She'd open her next show with it.

She set it aside, plugged the phone in, and dialed her mother because Martha Mitchell or no Martha Mitchell she still had to call. Her mother left messages for her at the station these days: call me Wednesday at three fifteen. Call me Friday at seven. And Annette did, scheduling her life—such as it was—to keep her mother from fretting.

"They're only hang-up calls," she told her now for the twelfth time. "They're a nuisance but nothing more than that."

"It's stalking is what it is. There's someone stalking you."

Annette remembered clearly that she'd once wanted her mother to understand what the hang-up calls were like. What she couldn't remember was *why* she'd wanted that. She moved the nine of clubs across the screen to the ten of hearts. She'd been playing this game for months and hadn't won a hand yet.

"No one's stalking me."

"You don't know that."

Annette sighed audibly.

"Don't laugh this off. You're a public figure. People get obsessed with public figures. Look at John Lennon. Look at Jim Brady."

Annette's mother had a thing about Jim Brady. Annette never had been able to make sense of it.

"No one got obsessed with Jim Brady."

"He got shot, though, didn't he?"

"Which goes to show you."

And so on, to the considerable benefit of Annette's long-distance carrier. Annette wasn't sure which rubbed at her nerves more, the hang-up calls themselves or her mother going on about them. She'd taken to checking her car before she got in it: a quick glance in the back seat to make sure no one was crouched there, another glance underneath to see if anyone was lying flat on the pavement, waiting to grab her ankles. Every time she walked through a door she looked in both directions. Foolishness, all of it, and she knew that but she did it anyway, out of superstition as much as anything else.

She wasn't sure how she'd know the difference between someone threatening on the far side of the door and someone minding their own business, but she hoped it would be clear if the time came.

She would have mentioned the Martha Mitchell column but thought it might be a good idea to keep it to herself till she could go public with it, just in case.

She didn't ask herself in case what.

Nick pointed and she was on the air.

"Ladies and gentlemen, birds and bees, nuts and bolts, you're listening to *Open Line*, I'm Annette Majoris, and you've heard this part before, so let's skip it. Last night I told you what I learned about Martha Mitchell. Tonight we're doing the Bemis papers. You never heard of the Bemis papers? Well, folks, there's a reason for that.

"Benjamin Bemis. Expendable member of President LBJ's staff, sent as a liaison to we'll-never-know-who-exactly because all Bemis called them in his surviving papers was the Ghouls on the Ground. We can safely figure that they were the bad guys. What we do know is this: he kept a diary, he wasn't supposed to, and that carelessness may be the reason he died in a small-plane crash. We also know that parts of the diary survived—not all of it, just fragments, loose pages, bits and pieces, stashed first in his parents' attic and then in his brother's.

"So what do the fragments tell us? That the president was afraid of what was happening in Vietnam. 'If this'—and I'm cleaning it up a little here— 'stuff ever leaks out,' Bemis quotes him as saying, 'there ain't a paddle been made that's big enough to get us out of the creek.'

"He also wrote about mind control, the illusion of a war, Johnson's fear that too many people knew what was really going on and that someone would get careless. Bemis doesn't give us details about what they were hiding—he may not have known them; he was low on the food chain—but three things are clear: there was no war—no, let me restate that. He believed there was no war; LBJ was scared; and Bemis was scared.

"So there you go. That's what we hear from Washington. Now let's hear from you, the citizens, the real people of this country. Pick up that phone and talk to me."

Her first caller was a vet with bad dreams, lousy sleep patterns, and vague memories: damp walls, darkness, light so bright he was blinded—all of it terrifying, although none of it sounded that bad. It seemed like there must be something else, he said, something just out of reach, that made it so awful. If he could only remember what happened, it would be o.k. It was the not knowing that tore him apart.

Annette leaned into the mic.

"George, listen to me. You may not be able to remember, and that's all right. If you can accept that, you can live with this. Are you listening, George?"

"Yeah. I'm listening."

"Good. Are you willing to try something? Do you trust that I won't do anything to hurt you?"

"I guess so. Sure."

"That's good. Listen now. Take a deep breath. Relax. Close your eyes. We're not going to push this any further than you can comfortably go, o.k.?"

George made a sound that would do for an o.k.

"I want you to imagine yourself back in the dark."

She waited a second. It went against her instincts to leave dead airtime, but she had to. Focus on the caller. Give him time to experience this. Besides, going against the grain like this was dramatic. She flattened her voice out and made it quiet, so it wouldn't break the spell.

"Now I want you to imagine taking one hand and placing it on that damp wall. What's it made of?"

She paused.

"What's under your fingers, George? Concrete block? Plaster? Dirt and rock?"

Another pause. It was killing her.

"Mud," he said. "Mud and rock."

His voice hurt to listen to. He'd dragged this tiny shred of information across fields of broken glass, and it came out scraped and raw.

"It's o.k., George. It's safe to remember that. Just keep your hand there and feel how damp it is, how uneven. It's mud and rock under your hand, but you're safe and it's O.K. to remember this. You feel safe, George?"

"I guess."

George's voice shook.

"You want to go a little further?"

Dead airtime.

"I guess. Maybe a little."

"We won't go far. Just keep your hand on that wall and watch while a door opens, O.K.? First there's a little light, then there's so much light that it just about blinds you but it's all right, George— you don't have to look at anything right now, you can close your eyes and walk out the door. You can walk until you're outside. Are you outside yet, George?"

A pause. She loved him, she realized. Loved him purely. She'd never known what that phrase meant before, but here she was, holding nothing back and unafraid of where it would lead her. If she could live her entire life in this moment, she would be happy.

"Uh-huh," he said. "I think so."

"Can you feel the air on your face?"

"Uh-huh."

"Is it warm or cold?"

A pause.

"Warm. It's warm."

"Good. You're still safe. Stay with me. Now I want you to reach one hand out and tell me what you feel."

Dead airtime.

"I don't know. Stuff. It's—I don't know."

His voice changed, marking a quick trip back from wherever he'd been.

"I can't do this."

"Hey, you did great. You felt something, didn't you, and it scared you. Can you remember what it felt like?"

"Kind of."

"Rough or smooth?"

"Smooth mostly. It was smooth."

Relief poured into his voice at the manageability of the question.

"Did it feel like a plant or an animal, or something man-made?"

The pain came back to his voice.

"Plants. It was plants. A whole jungle full of plants."

His voice broke open for a sob and closed up for the words again, which came with a kind of triumph.

"A jungle. I swear it. It doesn't make any sense but I swear that's what it was."

"That's o.k. It doesn't have to make sense yet—just trust the memory."

He gave a shaky laugh, and she began the process of a gentle disconnect: reassurance, an invitation to call back, to let her and her listeners know how he was doing. The final punch of the button. The empty spot where George had been. She didn't glance at Nick because his face didn't tell her anything she wanted to know anymore.

It was almost scary how good she was. She punched the next button.

"Gary," she said. "Hey. You're on the air."

"I'm on the air," Gary repeated. "Good, then. We're going to do this."

He drew a breath and launched himself into the unknown. He'd been in Vietnam, he said, his voice hesitant and light. He didn't remember underground chambers or anything like that, and he didn't dream about them, but the thing was . . .

He paused and Annette waited, giving him space.

"This is embarrassing, o.k.? I never told this to anybody."

He stopped there, his secret dangling in front of her.

"It's fine," she said. "Whatever you remember is fine."

"What happened . . . I don't know how to tell you this. It's . . . the first time I went on patrol? I got so scared I shot up this family's chicken, and I mean I didn't just shoot it, I shot it up so bad that by the time I got a grip there was nothing left but blood and feathers and this one little kid screaming like I'd just killed his mama and I still . . . I don't know. It bothers me. That's what I dream about. I mean, I saw worse things than that. I *did* worse things than that, but it still, you know, it kind of haunts me."

Another pause, but when he came back, his voice had more solidity.

"So here's what I'm trying to tell you: I don't understand this whole business with the underground chambers and the implanted memories, because, come on, who'd bother to implant that poor chicken?"

"Hard to say, Gary. Maybe someone had a sick sense of humor. Maybe they wanted you to imagine a human being and your unconscious wouldn't let you, so you substituted a chicken."

"You think?" he said.

"It's possible."

"Because if . . ."

He broke off and started over.

"Because if you could tell me that chicken wasn't dead. If that chicken never existed or if it went on to raise itself a whole family of little chicks . . ."

He exhaled into the phone, the exhausted sound of a soul's surrender.

"I'll tell you, I don't even care if you're wrong. I for one am going to sleep better."

Another pause. When he came back, his voice was stronger, as if he'd made up his mind somehow.

"I don't think people understand what it was like for us over there, but I can tell you this much: if none of that stuff ever happened, I'm a happy man."

And he hung up, leaving Annette to thank an empty line for the call.

★

Nick dodged her eyes when she pushed through the studio doors.

"Gotta get home tonight," he said in the direction of the mixing console. "Trying to cut down on the beer."

"Your lonely bed calling to you?"

He brightened at this and for a second she thought he'd invite her to join him in it—she even considered accepting—and for that second they were friends again, and then suddenly they weren't; he'd slipped away, although he'd have denied it if she'd asked him directly. And that was a Minnesotan for you. Everything was fine—it was just that he didn't talk to her anymore. So fuck him if that's how he was going to be. She had beer in the refrigerator, and she could sit home and drink it in comfort. It was getting too cold at night to sit on the steps anyway.

If she'd known George's number, she'd have taken it home and called to ask if he was all right.

CHAPTER 7

 Ever since Cal Anderson took the Minnesota Constructive away from him, Stan had been campaigning to take it back, and he could have had it by now if he'd wanted to do it the easy way, the sloppy way. The national network of Constructives had been set up so that the state organizations would change with the times and resist permanent capture by any single personality. That was their strength. That was also their weakness. Stan had the support to take it back, but he wanted to do it decisively, and for this he needed time. Otherwise Anderson would tie him up in motions and challenges for the next two years.

Stan's campaign took him through the kitchens and living rooms of Constructive members in the suburbs and the farm towns and the former farm towns surrounding Minneapolis and Saint Paul, and into the cities themselves to talk with members trapped there by houses they couldn't sell, or that they might have sold if they could have afforded something better once they did sell them; members trapped by bad luck and worse taxes, by a government that didn't give the individual room to take any initiative, although some of them, to tell the truth, didn't look like they had much initiative left in them, but he talked to them anyway: he'd stumbled onto the most massive cover-up any government had ever undertaken, something John Q. Public needed to know about. And the thing was, John Q. was already finding out. What was missing was the Constructive to give John Q. a larger context. Vietnam might sound like ancient history in this age of roadside bombs and Arab terrorism, but if Annette's callers were right and the government really had been experimenting with mind control, then who could say what else they'd done, or what they might be doing right this minute. The simple fact was, the Constructive was poised on the brink of history with this, but Cal Anderson, for reasons Stan couldn't explain, was determined to go on with business as usual. Maybe it was because Anderson wasn't the one who'd unearthed the cover-up, so he thought Stan owned the issue. Maybe it interfered with his own agenda. Maybe other forces were at work, although Stan never let people draw him into guessing what those might be. A lot of people liked Anderson. There was nothing to gain by slandering him. He had to let Constructive members draw their own conclusions. So Stan drank the coffee that women brewed for him and the beer that men brought from their refrigerators. He drank iced tea and hot tea and Coca-Cola, and when he got up to leave, people grasped his hand, hanging on to it as if his touch could heal. At night, he had more trouble than usual shifting out of his public self so he could sleep. His brain leapt from fact to incident to conversation to possibility, counting converts and votes and allies. And when it wasn't counting, his brain was making him picture Annette in ways he didn't want to picture Annette. He wasn't the sort of man who let his hormones drive his brain, but all the same an image of Annette came to him at night and with one hand he pinned her wrists and with the other undid the buttons on her blouse while she writhed, first to get away from him and later, when she'd realized she not only couldn't get away but didn't want to, to rub against him while he peeled her blouse back from her shoulder and bit down hard and steady on the cords at the side of her neck until she cried out.

He couldn't stop imagining the scene and couldn't get rid of the idea that it would play across his face like a movie the next time he saw her, horrifying them both and wrecking everything he was building.

And then, an hour after he finally did get to sleep, the liquid he'd poured down his throat that evening woke him up, announcing that it wanted out, and halfway down the hall his brain leapt awake—counting, picturing, unbuttoning—and he had to start the process of shutting it down all over again.

He began to dread bedtime, and it took all his considerable self-discipline not to knock back a few shots of bourbon with Flambard and guarantee himself a decent night's sleep.

The showdown with Anderson was scheduled for October. If he waited any longer, he'd lose momentum; if he moved it any sooner, Anderson would have momentum of his own left. But the waiting was killing him. At night, while he struggled to subdue either sleep or Annette, he mapped out how much longer he could campaign on this issue before even Anderson was bright enough to steal it out from under him. Each time he ran the calculations, the answer came out different, but the problem stayed the same, chasing him all the way through September.

Rumors drifted back to him. Anderson's great joke was that the Vietnam War was real enough but that Stan wasn't—he was only trying to make people think he existed. That was early in September. By the end of the month, Anderson was telling his people to expect a physical attack, even an assassination attempt, and this struck Stan as something worth losing sleep over. He used to think Anderson's group was too busy courting respectability to try violence, but if Anderson was scared enough, he might just launch a preemptive strike and convince himself it was self-defense. Stan upgraded the security on his house and installed an alarm on his Jeep. He'd been meaning to get a car alarm anyway, what with some of the neighborhoods he was parking in these days. He thought about forming a security detail—nothing formal, just a few men willing to keep their eyes open—to protect either him or Annette, but the thought never survived until daylight. There was always a reason. Sometimes two. Anderson wasn't worth taking that seriously; Stan could take care of himself; Annette would be frightened; protecting Annette was too appealing to be a good idea. And with Flambard living at the house . . . He didn't look like much, but he'd been training with a militia when Stan first met him, and even if Stan never told him so, he felt better knowing that Flambard slept with a pistol by his bed. And who knew what he kept in the closet. He could have a tank in there. He had a constitutional right, didn't he? It wasn't anything Stan needed to know about in detail.

So the days passed and nothing happened except that rumors continued to flow toward Stan like water running downhill, and he took them as a sign that he was winning. Why else would news travel to him from every corner of the Constructive? The rumors sketched a picture of Anderson losing his charm, making threats against Stan, drawing his inner circle around him as if no outsiders could be trusted.

Two weeks before the vote, the rumors asked why two grown men were living together, why Stan had opened his house, rent free, to a man two decades younger than himself. They didn't say Stan and Flambard were dressing in high heels and lacy bras and chasing each other from couch to mattress, just tossed the question out like poisoned seed for a flock of pigeons that was plaguing the neighborhood.

"He's security," Stan told people, knowing the answer wasn't interesting enough to travel far, and knowing the question had thrown him. Him and *Flambard?* Men didn't *do* that kind of thing. Not with each other. It took him a couple of days to pick up the phone and launch a decent counterattack: if Calvin Anderson could accuse two patriots of such a thing, that showed his desperation, and didn't any American have the right to open his house to a fellow American without facing dirty-minded rumors? And not just a fellow American, a fellow American patriot who had been in need, materially and emotionally, when his wife chucked him out. A man he'd be proud to call a comrade if the goddamn Communists hadn't gone and wrecked the word.

Maybe it was Anderson who had a problem that way if he thought about sex every time he saw two men maintaining a friendship, and that one circulated far enough that it came back to Stan with the *maybe* lopped off.

On the Saturday the Constructive was scheduled to vote, Stan drove to the rented hall alone. Not because he was intimidated by the rumors, he told himself, but because he wanted to get there early. He had a half-formed sense that the Anderson camp might do—well, something, although he couldn't think of any dirty tricks that would be useful at this stage. Still, maybe someone on the other side could.

The only person in the hall when he walked in was old Ray Garlin, setting up folding chairs. He'd been one of Anderson's people until a week ago, when Stan dropped by his house to talk. Ray was retired. He'd once told Stan what he used to do, but Stan couldn't remember now. Something involving a khaki work shirt and pants, because the habit of wearing them had taken such deep root that Stan had never seen him in anything else. Stan shook Ray's hand and helped carry chairs from the rolling carts, unfolding them in rows, matching himself to Ray's pace for fear Ray would interpret anything faster as a criticism. Besides, it wouldn't hurt to be seen pitching in when people walked through the door.

The two of them didn't say much to each other, just unfolded their chairs and went back for more. Ray had never been much of a talker, and Stan had run out of sociability. He was tired. And the room was depressing: high windows that let in only enough light to show how unloved the place was. Tan walls, tan linoleum dimly flecked with red and gold. Brown drapes covering the farthest ends of the stingy windows, blocking out a bit of precious light. It all spoke to Stan of how small the Constructive was thinking, renting a hall for meetings instead of setting up an office where people could find them.

Then the members began to drift in. They stopped to trade jokes with Stan and tell him they were with him, and he thanked them and leaned on the unopened chair he'd been carrying. The men shook his hand, the women kissed his cheeks, and he forgot about Anderson and his dirty mind. By ten minutes to the hour he glowed from the accumulation of goodwill and lipstick that had rubbed off on his skin and he'd damn near given himself whiskerburn.

The chairs filled up and he and Ray unfolded more. When Flambard got there, he pitched in—Stan couldn't ask him not to—but then so did a couple of other men close to Stan, all of them self-important in this low-level job Stan had drawn their attention to. Only Ray had nothing more on his mind than setting up chairs.

At five past the hour, Anderson swept in with a fistful of followers, the last of the faithful, clenched around him as if they were the Secret Service and he was the president. A wavering Constructive member could no more have cut through that cordon to discuss his doubts with Anderson than David Koresh could have walked into Clinton's Justice Department to drink a can of Coke with Janet Reno.

All that was missing were the black helicopters. Stan was looking at genuine fear.

As he was about to pass Stan, Anderson checked the flow of his following and turned. Stan gave Anderson a second to come toward him, and when he didn't, Stan crossed the linoleum himself, hand outstretched.

"Good to see you here. No hard feelings, I hope."

Anderson stared at him, stone-faced, without lifting his hand to take Stan's. Something had gone wrong behind Anderson's face—had turned suspicious and mean—because this was a different person than the charmer who'd taken the Constructive away from Stan a few months before, as if without the public flow of love, this was all that survived. Stan was contemplating his own hand, wondering how to get it out of midair, when Anderson turned away and stalked to the front of the room. His Secret Service turned with him, almost tripping on each other in their hurry to get away with their dignity in place. That freed Stan's hand to drop to his side and Stan himself to laugh loud and naturally until Anderson called for order and opened the meeting.

It didn't bother Stan that Anderson got to run the meeting. It was like letting someone's kid honk the horn on his Jeep; it made the kid happy, but Stan was still the one jingling the keys in his pocket. He smiled with the clean joy of someone whose head was about to receive the crown. Hadn't his whole life been grooming him for this job?

CHAPTER 8

 Stan stood in his living room and stared at the phone. It wasn't like him to dither over a phone call, but here he was, dithering like a teenager afraid to ask a girl for a date.

The date—the potential date—in question was Walter Bishop of the Bishop Milling fortune, and what Stan knew about him was this: he'd been more or less born into the upper ranks of the Republican Party and he'd become a major donor and a confidant of the governor's, aligned with the property-rights wing. But a Constructive member who was a contractor had spent some time straightening out problems in a crew that was working on an addition at Bishop's house, and he'd gotten an earful of Bishop's phone calls. The man was restless in the Republican Party, tired of the way, now that it controlled the government, it was making government bigger, stronger, and more intrusive. And he was fascinated with Annette's take on Vietnam. He didn't know it yet, but he was dying for Stan to ask him out.

Which is precisely what made the call so important. A guy like this could open doors Stan didn't even know the location of. Instead of watching the Republicans skim members from the Constructive, the Constructive could skim off the Republicans. So Stan didn't want to ask for a date when he had a sprig of parsley stuck between his teeth. He paced his living room, turned into the kitchen, and paused at the sink, staring out the window at the silver stain in the driveway next door, where three years ago one neighbor kid had thrown a can of metallic paint at another one. He hardly noticed it anymore and shouldn't be noticing it now— he should be figuring out what to say—but every time he got past "Hello, Mr. Bishop?" his mind wandered off somewhere.

Right now it was wandering to the ping-pong game his stomach was playing with his breakfast.

A minute or two later, he wrenched himself out of his trance, picked up the phone, and dialed.

What if he got an answering machine? He almost hung up to give himself more planning time, but a man's voice answered before he had the chance, and some switch in Stan's mind flipped itself to the right setting, and he was perfect. He introduced himself, mentioned the Constructive, and said he worked with Annette Majoris.

"You're kidding," Bishop said, sounding like a love-struck twelve-year-old. "You work with Annette Majoris? Really?"

★

On the day of his meeting with Walter Bishop, Stan stopped home at noon to pack himself into his suit. It was a measure of how important the meeting was, and how uncomfortable he was about it. The damn suit sat on him like the canvas top on a covered wagon. And that's what it might as well have been, because when he got to the restaurant, there sat Walter Bishop wearing the Ferrari of the suit world and looking like he wore that sort of thing every morning at breakfast. Without worrying about dropping the toast butter-side-down on his pants.

A waiter handed Stan a menu, and Stan accepted it gratefully. It was a road map in this highly foreign territory. You'd think he'd never been in a restaurant before. He dropped his eyes to the paper, but it was written in an elegant script that, yeah, sure, he could have read if he'd thought to put his reading glasses in his suit jacket or if they'd been willing to turn the lights up, but of course that wasn't something he could ask them to do, and it made him feel like he'd been handed a note saying his sort wasn't welcome here.

"What is this, French or something?" he said.

Bishop smiled, although not quite as if they were sharing the joke. Even when he wasn't smiling, Bishop radiated energy, good cheer, good health—a bit more of each than his skin seemed comfortable containing. He looked like the effort of keeping them in would split him open any minute, and Stan found it intensely annoying.

"The part that isn't English," Bishop said.

Great start. Stan set the menu aside and launched into his pitch. It was premature, but at least it got him away from the menu. He talked about the Constructive, the nation's metastasizing government and its matching deficit, the so-called war, the Constructive's web site, its thousands of hits, Annette and all her listeners. He said the Constructive's task was to push the boundary of the political safety zone but not shatter it, which would expand the room that people like Bishop operated in. It was the perfect mix of excitement and responsibility. In spite of which, he was having a hard time keeping it from going flat in the presence of all this dim lighting and these waiters who looked more comfortable in their starched shirts than Stan was in his starchless one. Stan respected money; it wasn't that. He didn't resent the people who had it, or at least no more than any other American resented people who had more than they did. What he resented was handwritten menus in languages no American could be expected to understand.

"I've been following your girl Majoris," Bishop said. Now that he had control of the timing and setting, he sounded distant and adult about her—an interested observer, not some poor jerk fantasizing about the buttons on her blouse. "She's cheeky. I like her."

Stan agreed. She had a great presence. Her following was growing more quickly than even he had predicted, although he'd known she'd catch on. The waiter appeared with his pad and interrupted his momentum. Stan glanced at the menu.

"I'll have the chicken," he said.

There had to be chicken on there somewhere.

It took Bishop longer to order. He had to discuss mustard sauce, Béarnaise sauce, arugula. He had to ask about the wines, and pronounce them in French or whatever. Stan held his face in the best imitation of neutrality he could manage and waited for the waiter to leave.

"You're probably tired of people asking you this," Bishop said, as happy as if Stan had been chipping in on the French part of the conversation, "but I have to ask anyway. Your girl Majoris—you believe what she's saying?"

"I'll tell you the truth here: we've uncovered a massive amount of evidence. More than she's had time to raise on the air. I'm thinking I'll have to publish a pamphlet to get it all out there. But yeah, absolutely I think she's right."

"It's a disturbing thought," Bishop said.

"These are disturbing times."

Bishop seemed to think about that for a few seconds, and if he hadn't looked so damned smug, Stan would have felt better about the progress he was making.

"It's hard to accept," Bishop said finally. "I'll tell you the truth, I've been following her show, and she's good. She's very good. You don't want to believe her, but I'm afraid I do. I'm beginning to. I'd really like it if she was wrong, but the thing is I think what she's saying deserves a wider audience. It would be good for the country, hearing what she has to say."

The waiter brought a bottle of wine, poured Bishop a thimbleful, was rewarded with a nod, and poured the rest, totally interrupting the flow of the conversation.

"I assume that at some point you're going to want to talk about money," Bishop said when the waiter had left. "Would that be correct?"

Stan felt himself blush in the dim light.

"You got me there."

"Don't be embarrassed. It's one of the things people come to me for. So let me ask you this: what about yourself? No one likes to talk about what they get paid, but what kind of paycheck is the Constructive able to give its spokesman?"

Stan felt more heat rising to his face.

"I had a package delivery business I sold a few years back, and I did it so I'd be free to do what I want with my time."

An extra measure of good cheer worked its way through the skin of Bishop's face. Stan was pretty sure he was being laughed at, but it did no good to know that, and he pushed the thought away.

"Is that another way of saying the Constructive doesn't pay you?"

"It's not a job a man should take for the money."

"People don't respect what they get for free. That's the first law of human nature."

He beamed at Stan. It was the round damned cheeks that did it. They made him look like a cross between a smug chipmunk and a third-grader. Stan couldn't afford to dislike the man, though, and it wasn't fair anyway, dismissing him because he had round cheeks. Right and convenience converged here, and Stan resolved to like him.

"The immediate problem is how to keep the Vietnam issue from being marginalized," he said. "That's what I wanted to talk with you about. We can worry about me another time."

"I'll tell you what," Bishop said, holding his wine up to eye level so he could admire it, and for a second or two he didn't tell Stan anything. When he pulled himself back to their conversation, he started over.

"I'll tell you what. If you want this to go mainstream, you need money. Nothing brands an organization as a fringe group as fast as running it on the proceeds of garage sales."

He set his wine down without drinking.

"I think we both understand why I'm not about to join your organization—I have a different role to play—but I do see a need for it. You're right at the edge of the national conversation. You expand the range of what the rest of us can talk about."

Stan nodded. It was exactly what he'd told Bishop earlier and from the fullness of his heart, he forgave Walter Bishop his chipmunk cheeks.

"If you're up to it, I can introduce you to people who have the ability to move the Constructive out of its nickel-and-dime days, but if they're going to take you seriously, they're going to have to know you're worth something. You'll only have one chance at this. These aren't people you have to convince about your message. They understood the individual's right to his property before the Constructive had its first two members, they're none of them friends of big government, and they've noticed a certain—I don't think *betrayal*'s too strong a word—a certain betrayal of core values here. They know what a runaway deficit means. You don't have to tell them that. What you do have to convince them of is that you're not just one more bunch of extremists—that you can really accomplish something."

He held the wineglass in front of one eye like a rose-colored monocle and radiated good cheer through it.

"If I put together a group of them at my house, can you get your girl Majoris to come?"

CHAPTER 9

The invitation to Walter Bishop's house surprised Annette. Stan didn't strike her as a social kind of guy, but if he was going to invite her to a party she'd expect it to be a fifth of Jack Daniels and a tray of cold cuts from Cub Foods. But here he was rubbing wineglasses with a major advertiser. She had to give him this: he continued to surprise her.

For courage, she spent $230 on a new skirt—black velvet, slit up one side, and on sale for twenty percent off. She had her hair washed and styled. It cost money to hang out with old money. It cost just as much to hang out with new money, but that wasn't her problem at the moment. She blew sixty bucks on perfume—the smell of roses, not harsh like the cheap stuff but genuinely like roses. Subtle enough to cover the scent of all the strivers, the reachers, the have-not-quite-enoughs playing hide-and-seek in the branches of her family tree. Or at least she hoped it was, the same way she hoped the skirt was long enough to hide the grandfather who'd flunked out of prelaw and crawled home to Indiana to run the family hardware store, the great-uncle who'd written army manuals during World War II and recited them at family parties ever after, the other ancestors who'd made such a light mark on history that two generations later no one remembered what they'd done with their lives.

Just let me get through this one evening, she begged the universe without thinking to offer anything in trade for the favor and without asking herself who was out there to make deals. *Just this one evening.*

Stan picked her up like a date, and he took her elbow to lead her to his Jeep. It was embarrassing, a guy in his fifties wearing a suit that looked like he'd bought it for weddings and funerals, but he'd made a big deal of them showing up together, and she had no choice but to live with it. No sane human being, she told herself, would take them for a couple, and then a few minutes later she had to tell herself the same thing all over again.

The Jeep bounced her over every pothole and every line painted on the road like some old flatbed wagon, and they sank into their separate nervousnesses and said nothing to each other until they pulled up in front of a modern house in Deephaven, on the lake and set well back on a wooded lot, with the nearest neighbors out of sight behind the trees. She'd expected something ancestral, she realized. She'd gone to school with kids whose parents probably had as much money as this guy, but none of them had major food companies named after them. She told herself that it was just the name that threw her, that she could handle the rest of it, and she smoothed the velvet of her skirt and almost believed herself.

She could handle it as long as Walter Bishop understood that showing up with Stan was an accident, one of those things that happen to people sometimes. Not to him probably, but to other people.

The outside of the house was Hansel and Gretel meet Frank Lloyd Wright and they all get introduced by Donald Trump, but the inside dropped the German kids routine and went for impressive—big rooms; big windows looking out on a bare, late fall landscape, floodlit to show how much of it there was. Lots of clean lines, an uninterrupted view from the front door through the foyer to a huge fireplace on the far wall of the living room.

The man who greeted them was wearing enough money on his left wrist to pay off the lease on her car, but it was the other hand he extended to her, keeping the watch to himself. Not that she'd do any different if it were hers. He had nice hands and a smile overflowing with pleasure, like he really meant it when he said he was glad to meet her. Instead of a suit jacket, he wore a cashmere sweater over a white shirt.

"You have a great voice," he said, hanging on to her hand. "Is it O.K. to say that? I just love your voice."

"You could tell me that all day long."

He smiled at her. Smiled, hell. He radiated sex at her, that's what he did. She'd been wrong to fret about meeting him. He was just like anyone else, only more so.

"Maybe we should arrange that," he said.

"Maybe we should."

She gave him her best I'm-available smile, and he let her hand go. This was the first man she'd met since she left New York who she'd even considered being available to.

Which probably meant she'd meet his wife next.

What she met, though, were some half a dozen couples with no stray wives among them. They ranged in age from their stodgy thirties into their aggressively healthy sixties, and they rearranged themselves to make room for her and Stan, then proceeded to talk taxes and out-of-touch liberal elites and the need to seize the national consensus and break the back of big government once and for all while a sharp-looking woman in black slacks, a cummerbund, and a starched white shirt circulated with drinks and canapés, and Stan held forth like he'd memorized all the available facts on all the possible topics. Annette sipped white wine and looked interested. This involved keeping her eyes on the speaker. When someone new talked, she moved her eyes there. From time to time, she sat forward. If this bunch had called her on the air, she'd have said, "C'mon, Henry, Paige, whoever, is that all you've got in your life? What do you do for fun? Work up practice versions of your 1040 form, your schedule c, your double Q, your whatever the hell form people in your tax bracket use?"

Except these weren't the kind of people who called her show. They had other ways to make themselves heard. And since they weren't on her show and weren't radiating sex at her but were friends of the man who was, they scared her. They made her feel the way she'd expected Walter Bishop to make her feel, as if this were a no-smoking zone and she'd just flipped ash into their wine.

Stan went over pretty well, though, considering the suit, considering that he talked too much and had zero social grace. Sure they patronized him, but that was what he'd come here for: patrons. They listened to him. The men took up his points and explained them back to him in different words as if he wouldn't stand a chance of understanding them otherwise. During breaks in the conversation, Walter Bishop radiated at her.

Annette picked up her wineglass and discovered it was almost empty. She reminded herself not to get drunk.

"What the Constructive's trying to do is make America safe for democracy," Stan said a little too loudly, as if his audience stood just outside the living room windows, closed out of the good life with its feet on the frozen ground. "We want to give America back to the people who love it and who've invested in it. Nothing is more democratic than property. The ancient Athenians understood that, and they're the ones who invented democracy. Ownership is a sacred commitment, and when we first let government insert itself into that relationship, that was the beginning of the end of America's greatness."

Heads nodded. It went down well. Annette reached for her glass and found that the woman in the starched shirt had exchanged it for a full one. She raised it. *Sip*, she reminded herself.

Barely wet your lips. She set it down and smiled at Walter Bishop. He radiated back at her.

Around eight, Bishop herded them to the dining room. They moved like a flotilla, as if anyone who wandered off alone would be picked off by hostile caterers. Or maybe this guy didn't need caterers—maybe he had his own fleet of cooks, chefs, whatevers. She managed a solo trip to the bathroom but got no time alone with Walter Apparently Available Bishop, although the air between them was vibrating on a frequency that no one else seemed to hear. She held her hand over her glass at dinner when the wine was poured but accepted cognac after the meal, and Jesus, it slid down her throat like honey and lent everyone in the room a glow like stained glass. Even Stan's suit improved. Sure, the man lacked couth, but she had to admit he could get things done. Look where they were sitting. She sipped cognac and glowed.

One of the men said something about Vietnam and the word brought her back into focus: Vietnam. Right. She knew about Vietnam.

"What worries me is this single-issue focus," the man said. "I think the broader agenda tends to get swamped by that sort of approach."

That wasn't her concern. Stan picked up the question and answered it, balancing the broader agenda against the ability of a single issue to move people, and his voice was perfect this time. She sipped her cognac and floated.

★

Two days later, Walter Bishop left a message for her at the station: his name, his numbers—home, business cell, personal cell, fax—and "Loves your voice." She set it where she could see it during the show.

"The thing is," she told Terri from New Hope, "the government's abandoned us. It had a pact with the vets that it didn't fulfill and it's not going to do any better by the rest of us."

She pitched her voice into the mic and past Terri, riding the night air to Deephaven. Walter Bishop loved her voice. He was sitting by his fireplace at this exact moment, her voice blowing soft in his ear, promising him things no human in history has been able to deliver, but that didn't matter—all that mattered was that she meant every nonword of it.

"The vets are a kind of barometer," she said, "a lightning rod . . ."

Not a lightning rod—that was wrong. She shook her head to get rid of the image before she set any more weather equipment loose in the world: a thermometer, a rain gauge, a weather balloon.

"What I'm telling you is that if we speak up for the vets, we're speaking for America's forgotten middle class."

Terri's voice sounded black, and the thought jolted through Annette that maybe she wasn't part of the middle class, but she agreed with Annette anyway. That was the wonderful thing about the middle class: no one could resist it. Anyone said they were against it, they were against puppies, or kittens. They were advocating child abuse, desecration of the flag, abolition of the flush toilet. And it broadened the issue. Walter's friends wanted broader issues and here they were. Annette had never conducted a flirtation on the air before. It was delicious.

"So here's what I'm telling you," she told Terri, her voice low and sexy. "We've got a confluence of interests here. Confluence: that means 'flows together.' The enemy of my enemy is my friend—all that kind of thing. Whose tax dollars do you think the government spent messing up the vets I've been hearing from? Whose constitutional rights were abrogated so the government could conduct this experiment? Yours, mine, everybody's. Abrogated: I can't quote the dictionary on that one, but it means someone walked all over them. You see my point, Terri?"

Terri saw her point but still thought maybe she was spending too much time on this one issue. There was a whole world of issues out there.

"And there you have it, folks: the voice of compassion."

Annette punched the next button and Terri was forgotten. She'd never been there at all.

Walter Bishop, when they finally got hold of each other, wondered if she'd be interested in meeting the governor. It wasn't the invitation she'd had in mind, and it left her wondering if maybe she'd read his signals all wrong, but it did have the virtue of surprising her. And making her buy another skirt in case he remembered what she'd worn last time, and then of course she needed a top to go with it.

When he picked her up, he was wearing an overcoat that looked soft enough to rub her cheek against, the way a cat would. She hadn't traveled in Walter's kind of circle for a while. O.K., she'd never traveled in his kind of circle. She'd traveled in circles that wanted to be his kind of circle. So everything about him impressed her. He held the car door for her, and he closed her inside, and the car cost more than any two cars Annette could hope to drive. Any three cars. He said he felt special having her with him.

She also felt special. Not to mention uneasy. She had no idea how, but one way or another she was going to screw this up. She felt like—was it Moses who got a glimpse of the promised land and knew he couldn't get in?

"I hope it won't be too boring," Bishop said, "but we don't have to stay long. Shake a few hands, give me time to write out a check. They'll be happy to let me go once they have my check. Then we can get some dinner."

He looked away from the highway to grin at her—that same grin that made him look like he got more pleasure out of life than

the average run of humans even guessed at—and while he grinned
the car drove itself, because when you have that kind of money
other cars wouldn't dare crash into you. Neither would freeway
embankments. Annette grinned back and tried to remember
whether the governor was a Republican or a Democrat. She basically knew—she read the paper, after all, and the way they'd talked
at Walter's party, the Democrats were to the left of Ho Chi Minh
and almost as far past their sell-by date—but it made her uneasy
that she hadn't checked. If it had come up when she was on the
air, she'd have dodged the issue. Fine, then. She could avoid it
tonight as well.

At least she wasn't blanking on his name: Bill Ruoma.

Walter parked on Summit Avenue, among the nineteenth-
century mansions the robber barons had abandoned when they
moved wherever they moved to—Deephaven, New York, Paris—
and he helped her over the snow banks, apologizing for the recent
snowfall, for the cold, for not getting her closer to the door, for the
absence of valet parking. The wind blasted through her nylons and
turned the insides of her shoes to a layer of ice against her feet.

"Hey, it's Minnesota," she said.

It was also still November, and too early for a full-scale assault
from the weather, but she tried to be careful with Minnesotans,
even about the weather. She never knew who'd turn out to be
touchy on the subject.

"I could have dropped you at the door, but you don't know
these people: it's no fun to walk in alone. Besides, I'm looking forward to walking in with you."

He put a hand on her elbow to steer her in, announcing their
connection.

A lot of the Summit Avenue buildings had been broken up
into condos at some point, but this one was whole still, with a
marble floor in the foyer and a living room rug that could trade

even with Walter's car. It was the kind of place she'd expected Walter to live in, and it made her feel shabby in her new clothes. The host, or someone at ease enough to pass for the host, shook Walter's hand, said Bill would be late, and smiled at Annette like he'd been dreaming about her every night this past week.

"Chris Markham," Walter said, "Annette Majoris of *Open Line*."

Annette was halfway along the trajectory of a blockbuster smile, and her hand was moving through the air, ready to be shaken, kissed, clasped between two worshipful palms and treasured.

"Oh, for Pete's sake, Walt."

Whoever the hell Chris Markham was, he dropped his hand back to his side as if he'd just noticed that hers was smeared with lard, and he stranded her there with her hand in the air and her face stuck in what felt more like a grimace than a smile.

"You have a problem with that?" Walter said.

"Look, I . . ."

He looked from Walter to Annette and back again as fast as was physically possible. She'd managed to get her hand back to her side but was still having trouble with her face.

"Look, I lost a brother in that war."

He glanced toward Annette again and dodged back to Walter, visibly gathering himself together so he could say the right thing.

"Walt, I'm glad you came, the governor appreciates your support, and I don't want to ruin a very nice evening, but you'll have to excuse me, I can't shake hands with this woman."

Annette pinched her lips between her teeth to keep her face under control.

"I'm sorry about your brother," Walter said.

"I don't want to hear any more about it. Not from you, and not from her."

Walter was still saying "but you've got to understand . . ." when Chris Markham turned and left. Fled, actually. And Annette wouldn't have minded doing the same thing, and quickly, before her body took control and she burst into tears, but Walter put an arm around her shoulders and guided her past an assortment of staring couples who turned to follow their progress as they walked to the stairs. Walter kept the easy pace of someone whose imagination couldn't stretch far enough to take in loss, embarrassment, humiliation, and he murmured in her ear about their coats, and finding someplace to leave them.

The stairs passed a triple panel of stained glass, then turned and took them out of sight of the couples downstairs, and he stopped her there so he could brush the dry corners of her eyes as if he wished she had given in and wept.

"Don't worry about Chris. He used to work for the governor. He doesn't know it yet, and the governor doesn't know it, but he's a thing of the past."

She tried her voice.

"I never meant anything against his brother."

It was shaky but it worked.

"I don't want this to ruin the evening. Can you promise me this won't ruin the evening?"

She doubted she could but said of course, sure, no problem. She managed a smile, but it felt wobbly.

"Chris'll hide from us the rest of the evening, you watch. He's like a dog that just went whoops on the living room rug—he knows he did wrong and he'll stay out of our way till he thinks I've forgotten it."

They were facing each other, standing close enough to have already made certain decisions about each other, about themselves, about the rest of the evening. He ran a thumb under her eye, still as if she were crying. It almost made her wish she were, but that wasn't a door she could afford to open. Or glance at. Or remember the existence of. She'd walked through it once, after her father left, and she'd cried for months—huge, face-scrunching, ugly-making sobs that she couldn't find the end of until her mother threatened to take her to a psychiatrist. And maybe leave her there, because she was going to make both of them, herself and her mother, completely crazy with her wailing.

She'd stopped crying. This would not be a good time to start again.

Walt guided her upstairs, where they found a bed piled thick with coats and added their own.

"Ready to face the world?" he said.

"I'll manage."

"Head up, look them right in the eye, remember none of them matter. Got it?"

Her smile was growing wobblier with each try. If he didn't stop reassuring her, he'd have real tears to brush away—months of them.

"Is there a back staircase?"

He brightened: a concrete request he could fulfill.

The back stairs led them to a hallway near the kitchen—anything but descending into that foyer—and from there he led her into a conservatory.

Conservatory is a word for any room with lots of windows and no clear function, and this particular one held plants, a grand piano, a couple of loveseats, and a bar that had been set up at one end. Clusters of people were sipping their drinks out of plastic cups. In a setting like this, plastic turned into a class act. Glass would have been pretentious.

Before Walter could get them drinks, one of the clusters opened up and a man called Walter's name.

The introductions went well. No one shrank away from her. No one had lost a brother, or if they had, at least they didn't blame her for it. The man who'd called Walter over said he was delighted to meet Annette, and he asked about the demographics of her show, the technology of call-ins, and what kind of person would she say her average caller was? Walter stood beside her and beamed as proudly as if he'd scripted every word of her answers.

The governor made his entrance fifteen minutes, maybe half an hour, later, shaking hands, touching shoulders, working his way through the room like a square dancer doing a slow, solo version of the grand right and left. He was silver haired, with a nice profile, but less impressive in person than on television. Annette didn't know what she'd expected a governor to look like, but not like one more man in a suit, for some reason.

He stopped when he came to Walter, putting an arm around his shoulders to pull him out of his cluster.

"Chris told me what happened, Walt. Christ, I'm sorry. I'm really sorry. Hell, *he's* even sorry. He's hiding in the kitchen. You can go in and growl if you like, and he'll crawl under the kitchen table and wet. He sent Marguerite out to the foyer to brief me as soon as I set foot through the door. He's ready to fall on his sword if you order it."

Walter laughed and didn't order it, but he also didn't say it wouldn't be necessary. He introduced Annette, and the governor was very glad to meet her—excessively glad to meet her. Everyone over the age of six was talking about her show.

"Listen," Walter said, "why don't I give you a call tomorrow. I've got something you'll be interested in."

"Do that."

The governor turned to Annette and was glad to have met her all over again. He thumped Walter on the shoulder.

"And listen, I really am sorry about Chris. People get emotional about these things. You know how it is. He's a good man, but people get their tragedies filed away under certain labels. It upsets them to refile everything."

He smiled at Annette, thumped Walter again, and moved on.

"How do you feel about French food?" Walter asked, leaning toward her. "I know this gorgeous little place."

He put an arm around her shoulders and moved her toward the stairs.

"Why don't you get our coats and I'll find Marguerite and leave my check with her." He smiled radiantly. "Maybe I'll say good-bye to Chris, see if I can't spook him a little."

Annette started up the stairs. She appreciated Walter's thoughtfulness in moving her out of the way, but she'd have loved to see the size of that check.

The restaurant *was* gorgeous, and Chris Markham—o.k., he didn't disappear from Annette's memory, but he did shrink down to manageable proportions. She hadn't meant to hurt anyone. Surely that counted for something. They sipped their wine and asked each other all the usual questions to signal their interest, and gradually she forgave herself.

Walter told her he was an only child. He'd gone to a boarding school in southern Minnesota—the same one his father and uncle had gone to; the same one Hubert Humphrey's son had gone to, for that matter—and that led him into a discussion first about the Humphreys and then about everything that was wrong with Minnesota politics.

He came back to the Humphreys, and he'd have gone on about them—she could hear in his voice that he enjoyed not liking them—but it wasn't what she wanted to know.

"What about your family?" she asked. "What are they like?"

His father—he shook his head here—died of a heart attack just when he was set to run for the senate. Walter had been in his teens.

"He'd have won, too. That's the thing. He wanted that more than anything in his life, and he'd have had it. He'd have made a good senator. A great senator."

He sighed. He sipped his wine.

His mother was never the same after his father died and was now drinking her way discreetly through her old age. Walter himself had no children, no ex-wives, no encumbrances. He'd been engaged once, but they'd both thought better of it.

"You've spent your whole life in Minnesota?"

She asked it casually—hey, it doesn't matter to me, I'm just making conversation here—but she was looking for an explanation: if he was so deeply rooted in Minnesota, how come he liked her?

"I'm Minnesota born and bred and certified by tax records. On my mother's side, the family goes back to before statehood."

Annette echoed his smile. No problem. If it pleased him, it pleased her, and what did it matter why he liked her as long as he did.

"And you?" he asked, leaning forward. "What about you?"

"Oh, you know. Typical American family. Parents divorced, father remarried; private school, summer camp, all the usual. My mother's career took off when I left home."

She shrugged as if she really thought he did know, but it all sounded low rent in this neighborhood of almost-senators and boarding schools where you looked down on the sons of vice presidents instead of bragging about them.

"And Minnesota?" he said. "What brought you here?"

"Career. Luck. Random collision of atoms. I had a chance to break into broadcasting and I grabbed it. I'd have gone to Mudpuddle, Idaho, if I'd had to."

He smiled, looking pleased and sexy.

"You like radio?"

"I love radio. The first time I was on the air, I felt like I'd never been alive till then."

He smiled more intently and looked even sexier. She couldn't have given him a better answer. She caught a split-second glimpse of Chris Markham inside her head and looked away. This wasn't about him, and it wasn't about his brother. She felt bad about them, but they had no bearing on what was happening here. How would they be better off if she told Walt she couldn't give him her full attention tonight and wanted to go home?

From the restaurant, they went to Walter's place, and from his place they maneuvered each other to the bedroom, as they'd both more or less known they would, and no, if she was going to be honest, the sex wasn't all that good. He huffed, she puffed, and it went on too long without ever getting her where she wanted to go, but they both swore it had blown the house down and then he put on a pair of pajamas that came straight out of some 1930s movie classic and made him look rich and prudish and whole generations older than her, although there couldn't have been more than ten years between them. Twelve at the outside. O.K., fifteen, then. No more than fifteen. And forty-two wasn't old, really, if you looked at it from the right angle.

Besides which, sex isn't everything. She liked lying next to him. She liked the way he reached for her afterwards, and the way he slid over to move her out of—she was a big girl now, she could call it what it was—the wet spot. Hell, the bed was big enough for that not to be a hardship, but how many men would have thought of it? She settled her head in just above his armpit and hummed with contentment. Even his pajamas smelled good, as if someone in the next room had just finished ironing them.

"So what do you do when you're not calling the governor?" she asked.

He laughed as if the idea of him doing something, as in holding down a job, was a charming, childish misunderstanding of the world.

"I call senators," he said. "I call CEOs."

He tightened his arm around her.

"I make things happen."

She drifted a while on the idea of what he might make happen for her.

"So what are you going to talk to the governor about?" she asked after a while.

"I think your friend Stan's organization would throw itself behind his next campaign if he'd say certain things in public about Vietnam. It'll give Stan hives to back a candidate who could actually win, but I think it can be finessed. I'm very good at finessing."

"He's running for governor again?"

He laughed. Another childish misunderstanding.

"President, although it's way too early to say that in public yet. All he's doing now is laying the groundwork."

She made an I'm-impressed noise. In fact, she was impressed.

"He's got the backers, he's got the visibility, he's got an impeccable record. What he needs is manpower and a dramatic issue to bring the campaign into focus. Something that sets people on fire. Off the record? Between you and me? He doesn't set people on fire. He hasn't admitted it yet, but his precampaign is dying. And he'd be good, damn it, if we could just get him in. That's where I can help him."

She made another noise—acceptance, contentment. Of course he could help. The man was as good as elected already. She was lying in bed with the friend of a future president, he didn't think she was pushy, and she didn't have to do a damn thing but enjoy being there.

★

Walter Bishop didn't have a chef or a cook, Annette discovered in the morning, but he did have someone who let herself into his kitchen every couple of days and went through the refrigerator, clearing out anything he hadn't eaten and leaving a new batch of food that he might or might not eat.

"I'm very good with a microwave," he told Annette, demonstrating his prowess by punching the buttons. He poured them each a cup of coffee while the microwave thrummed. He was good at this too, although he didn't bother to point it out, and he wasn't bad at brewing the coffee either. The microwave's bell rang and he set two plates on the table.

"Voila. Apple Something. Specialty of the house. Eat it. It's good. You want something else instead? We have fruit salad, poppyseed bread, lasagna, other things I don't know about yet but I'll look."

Annette hadn't touched her food but said, "No, this is good. This is great."

"I could have Sherry make something else for you next time if you'd like it better. Quiche, maybe? You eat meat-and-potatoes type breakfasts at home?"

"I'm not a big breakfast person. Coffee and a muffin sometimes when I bother to run down to SuperAmerica."

He laughed as if she'd said she bought groceries at a body shop, and she felt as grubby as if she did.

"A double latte and a quart of oil," he said. "With two sugars and check the antifreeze."

It was a dumb joke but she went ahead and laughed. Hadn't this guy ever heard of gas stations selling coffee? Did someone pick up his car and fill the tank for him every couple of days too? o.k., so SuperAmerica was a step and a half down even from Perkins, and she could just as easily have kept her mouth shut about it, but Starbucks hadn't opened a store two blocks from her place yet. So what was she supposed to do, shoot herself? She didn't know whether to feel envious or superior and ended up with what felt like the worst parts of each.

They were sitting at a tile-topped table in a breakfast room that jutted out over a hill and had windows on three sides, with bare tree branches all around them, and she was wearing one of his bathrobes—royal blue terry cloth and thick as a rug—which closed low over her breasts. Every minute or two his eyes snagged on the neckline and followed it to the bottom of the v, as if he hadn't already seen her step bare-ass out of the shower and reach for a towel. Well, maybe he liked her better half hidden. She could get into that, she supposed. It wasn't her thing particularly, but it didn't bother her.

"Tell you what, I'll have Sherry bake us some muffins. What kind do you like? When can you stay with me next?"

She'd have told him muffins weren't a big thing with her, but he was running a finger down one edge of the neckline and up the other, effectively derailing the conversation. He grinned.

"Do you mind if I do that?"

"You'd know it by now if I did."

He ran the tip of his finger under the cloth.

"I'm glad you stayed last night."

She smiled a bit more. She'd have loved to be unreservedly in love with him, but some part of her was standing aside, weighing and measuring. It was touching how uncertain he was. And he was thoughtful and wanted to please her. He had great taste and an endless amount of money, and he knew everyone worth knowing. But there was also something unnerving about him.

"Try your Apple Something," he said. "Sherry's a great cook. She ran a four-star restaurant in San Francisco before she moved back to Minnesota. Very famous. Maybe it was five stars, fourteen stars—I forget. *The* place to be seen."

He radiated an intense desire for her to taste her Apple Something, and to like it. She smiled back to say it was delicious—how could it help but be?—and she picked up her fork.

CHAPTER 10

 The day before Annette's fourth date with Walter, he called to say he'd invited the governor and his wife for dinner and he hoped she wouldn't mind. He didn't say "Bill Ruoma," but "the governor," in case she needed cue cards, and she said of course she wouldn't mind. It was fine. It was great. It wasn't what she expected from a fourth date, but what the hell. Either he had something he wanted to accomplish or this was his idea of foreplay. Either way, it would be interesting.

Bill Ruoma's wife was younger than him. Annette guessed twenty years, but it was hard to tell—she kept herself in shape, and maybe she had a team of surgeons supporting the effort. Who would know? She smiled professionally—every bit a governor's wife—and asked Annette about New York and her impressions of Minnesota. Annette sat with her back straight and her ankles crossed and gave her the authorized version, which mostly had to do with the weather, and they were both so predictable that the conversation could have almost happened without them. Still, it filled the time until Walter and Ruoma got back from their tour of the pool Walter'd had installed last summer. Annette hadn't even known he had a pool, but everybody seemed to assume the women would rather sit in the living room. As the men left, the governor's wife shook her head after them and said, "Boys and their toys."

Annette wouldn't have minded playing with a toy or two herself. Instead, she and the governor's wife did as much as they could with Minnesota and New York and then moved on to Boston, where the governor's wife had grown up.

"Although that's a deep, dark secret when the press is around—you know how people feel about Easterners here. Officially, Bill found me in a cabbage patch somewhere north of Iowa and south of Canada at the age of twenty-five."

The governor's wife had a name, but Annette couldn't remember what it was. Mary Carol, Mary Margaret, Mary Norene. Something Catholic.

When the men came back, they were riding a wave of high energy and good humor, as if being by themselves had refreshed them both, and they filled the time until supper talking about problems with the pool Annette still hadn't seen, damn it: the motor that powered the current had already been replaced twice, and then there was the whole question of moisture, which might or might not create problems in the house. This was what a governor talked about? Christ, he was about as interesting as Annette's father. Ruoma's wife had quietly shut down when the men came back and was recharging her batteries with a steady flow of white wine. If it hadn't been for Walter radiating sexiness at her, Annette would have nodded off.

When they moved into the dining room, the conversation shifted to fund-raising and advertising and the personalities and quirks of various donors. The woman in the white shirt brought in salads, the door closed behind her, and Walter said, "Bill, have you given any thought yet to the Vietnam issue?"

Ruoma had a forkful of salad halfway to his mouth, which he lowered to his plate, leaving his fingers on the handle.

"I don't know if I should mention his name, but the fact is Chris and I have gone over it so many times he's nearly suicidal."

Neither of the men glanced at Annette to check her reaction to Chris's name, but Ruoma's wife did—a glance, an overdone smile when Annette caught her at it, then a sudden interest in her wine. Annette kept her own face blank, and it was surprisingly easy. The Chris they were talking about wasn't the man who'd run to the kitchen to get away from her but a set of opinions in a human body—no one she'd met.

"Chris is a closed system," Walter said. "He's not going to take in new information on this."

Ruoma looked at his fork with regret and gave up his hold on it.

"I know his biases—I take them into account—but his political instincts are solid. He considers it a fringe issue. Says it'll kill me with the party."

"He's underestimating people. I won't say that's deliberate, but I wouldn't rule it out either. This is the most powerful issue to sweep the American consciousness since—I don't know since when. The Civil War, probably. Watergate. Forget the analogies. Even if Chris agreed with us, he's cautious. I can't fault him for that, but it keeps him from thinking big. He's a good man if you want to stay where you are, but he's not the one to move you ahead."

"I don't know, Walt. You know how I feel, but this is a pretty canny guy we're talking about. He's done well for me up to now."

Ruoma lifted his forkful of salad and bolted it without breaking eye contact.

"He has," Walter said. "I won't argue that, but this issue's only begun to take off, and the train's going to leave without you if you don't jump on. Have you been listening to Annette's show? The station's going to have to add phone lines, she has so many callers. There's never been anything like this. And I'll be blunt here, all right? You need it. Distinguish yourself from the pack. Set the public on fire. I'm telling you, you can't go wrong with this thing."

Ruoma had gotten a second bite of salad down. He apologized for Chris all over again.

"It's not about Chris," Walter said. "Forget that. It never happened. This is about issues."

Ruoma stirred his salad, lifting the edges of the leaves to see what was under them. Maybe that was how he'd found his wife in the cabbage patch. Maybe he was hoping to find a younger one. He talked about fringe issues and how it wasn't just a question of what would win an election because if he couldn't win the party activists he'd never get near an election.

"It's a matter of timing," he said.

Walter had dimmed down a few watts while he listened. It made him look older, and tired.

"Look, I'm going to lay everything on the table and then I'm going to shut up and let you make your own decisions, all right? I've had a couple of meetings with Stan Marlin. I've told you about him. The Liberty Constructive? Bright guy. Not educated, a bit rough, but extremely sharp. Great blue-collar appeal. That whole man-of-the-people thing. Chris'll tell you they're a fringe group, and I admit they attract an interesting element, but damn it, Bill, basically they believe the same things you and I do, if a bit more—shall we say, dramatically? And they've got more energy than—hell, I don't know, they've got a lot of it. I'm not suggesting you want a formal endorsement from them or anything like that, all I'm saying is if you'll commit yourself on this issue, they've got all the manpower you could dream of for a campaign. And they're nationwide."

Ruoma stabbed a slice of cucumber and said, "Hmmmph."

"Bill, it's what you've been dreaming of, all wrapped up with a bow on it."

"I'll think about it," he said, "but I'll be honest with you, Walt. An outfit like that—hell, they're not even playing inside the ballpark. Anyone but you brought this to me, I wouldn't bother to discuss it."

"Yeah, but it is me."

"I'll think about it. That's the best I can do. Even for you. But I'll tell you right now, they make my scalp itch."

A few bites of silence went past while the men let the issue settle and Annette sorted through her head for something that might fit here, but before she found it, Ruoma pulled himself together and told a story about someone named Max, who'd been stopped by a state trooper the night before for drunken driving. The further he got into the story, the more he seemed to enjoy it.

"And the delicious part, the truly delicious part, is he had some woman in the car with him and her clothes—how can I put this? What there were of them were mostly adorning the back seat."

He paused to punctuate what was coming next.

"Not his wife, as you may have gathered," he said with a nod of complicity to Annette and his own wife. "The two of them barely able to walk, never mind a straight line, and the woman . . ." He laughed, shook his head, stretched the moment out so he could enjoy it all over again. "The woman's just got to throw a punch at the state trooper. Jesus, Walt, the way I heard it, she's a damned Amazon. Throws a right hook that'd make any man proud." He laughed again, stretched the moment. "Too late for this morning's papers but plenty of time for tomorrow's."

Walter had his glow back. Whoever Max was, he wasn't a friend. The tension emptied out of the room and they were united.

By the time Walter poured the cognac, Ruoma had turned charming, asking Annette about her show, what opposition she'd gotten, how she felt about swimming. His wife smiled vacantly into her glass.

After Ruoma and his wife left, Annette and Walter had another cognac in the living room. The fire burned behind glass doors, reminding Annette hazily of a fish tank, and Walter pulled and pushed until Annette was leaning on him.

"He'll come around, you watch him. I may have to pull a string or two, but he'll come around."

Annette hummed a sort of agreement.

"The only chance he has is to storm the party from below. He's got money behind him—he's flat tax, small government, probusiness, prolife, wants to dismantle the EPA—but he doesn't have the party heavies, and he doesn't have the popular appeal yet."

Annette hummed her approval. On a personal level, actually, she had no problem with abortion, but what the hell, this was politics. You made compromises. Besides, abortion wasn't the issue right now. Walter's back was against the arm of the couch, and she was leaning against his chest. It was sexy, watching him play politics. It was sexier than sex, in fact, because the thought of actual sex with him—well, it kind of depressed her, and she had to keep herself from moving to a separate space on the couch.

"Chris is dead already," he said, as if there were nothing in the world but this, and she brought herself back to it gratefully. "I give him two months at the outside. Bill'll find a different reason for letting him go—personal finances, something like that. He's in over his head and keeps right on spending. Rumors place him at the casinos a lot. The whole thing's going to come down on him any day now. It doesn't look good, a guy with finances like that being so close to the governor."

The fire burned down. The conversation burned down. Annette leaned against Walter's chest, and it was a perfectly nice chest, a chest she should be happy to lean on. Maybe what they'd done was start out wrong. Maybe she needed to let him know that other approaches were possible.

Maybe she needed to know that herself.

"Know what I'd like to do?" she said.

He shifted the wrap of his arms around her shoulders.

"Tell me."

"Tear all our clothes off and swim in your pool."

"It's not that kind of pool. It's small. You swim against the current."

"So? I take up even less room naked than I do in a bathing suit."

"You know what I mean."

She sat up and turned to face him.

"C'mon, Walt. I want to swim naked with you."

"It's an exercise pool, it's not for fooling around in."

"You don't want to fool around?"

"Sure I want to fool around, but not there."

He'd turned humorless, unradiant. Embarrassed, she thought. He had a streak of prudishness the width of his picture windows. Whatever it was going to take to make a new start, this wasn't it.

"Fine, where would you like to fool around?"

"The bedroom."

She'd remember not to suggest whipped cream, or vichyssoise.

"So let's go to the bedroom."

But she'd spooked him, and even though he nodded, he did it as if she'd suggested waxing the kitchen floor. On their hands and knees. Naked. In front of his mother.

And she was as excited at the prospect as he was.

"Let me show you something first," he said.

Christ, yes. Anything.

He led her to a room that faced out on the same hillside as the breakfast room.

"This is my delayed adolescence room," he said, snapping the light on. "I don't show it to most people, but I thought you'd get a kick out of it."

She grinned to show that she would, or already did.

Against one wall stood a pinball machine and one of those driving games where the road's personally determined to make you crash. Enough puzzles and cheap plastic games to stock a small toy store littered the shelves and coffee table, and he picked up one of these and held it out to her. Something she could play with in her clothes. She took it from him and stayed dressed, and he smiled.

"I just love these things," he said.

It was two ships with a plastic ocean between them. The point, if these things had a point, was to move the pieces around so the ships traded places.

She wouldn't have been much more surprised if he'd shown her a room full of alphabet blocks and rattles. It wasn't that he had these things—it was that he'd set a room aside for them. Whatever it meant, it was odd. She moved a piece of ocean to the right, slid another one into the newly empty spot, and handed the puzzle back.

"I was never any good at these."

"Watch."

He carried it to the couch and clicked pieces from place to place with the same concentration he'd given the governor. The ships lurched out into the ocean, tacked, detoured, passed, made their way toward the opposite port by more or less circumnavigating the plastic frame. She lost interest and looked out at the hillside, at an electronic dartboard on the cork-covered wall beside the door, at the other toys on the table. A lot of them had to do with getting from here to there in cars, in cabs, in airplanes. A set of penguins was ready to climb a staircase and skid down a slide as soon as one of them figured out how to turn the motor on. Walter was too lost in his puzzle to notice that her attention had wandered. It occurred to her, in a sour and abstract way, to tear off her clothes and turn on the penguins, but she didn't let it become more than a passing thought.

"There," he said a few minutes later, handing her the completed puzzle, the proof of his prowess.

"I'll be damned."

He radiated. She handed him the one where he had to move taxicabs.

"Do this one."

He bent over it, clicking the pieces.

She was sitting at the breakfast table the next morning when he pulled the first of his strings. He faced away with the phone to one ear, pretending to be unconscious of her, and she pretended to read the paper while she tracked the verbal handshakes and backslaps that eased the way to his reason for calling.

"Listen, I don't know if I'm doing the right thing in calling you, but I know Bill respects you and counts on your support, and I know you want to see him in the Oval Office as much as I do."

Walt turned toward the microwave—another direction that was away from Annette—while he listened to the answer.

"Well, the thing is, we've got a problem. A serious snag, and we're going to have to do something pretty unorthodox—*Bill's* going to have to do something pretty unorthodox—if he's going to get loose from it. And he doesn't want to do it. You know what he's like. He's playing it safe."

He turned to Annette finally, and Annette looked up from the paper. He listened to the phone and raised his eyebrows at her: see what I can do?

"Well, there you go," he said. "We have to make safe damned uncomfortable for him."

CHAPTER 11

 Bill Ruoma leaned his white-shirted, gubernatorial elbows on the table, framing his eggs and hashbrowns as if he were afraid somebody would come along and steal them. Or afraid the people in the next booth would overhear him, even though it was noisy enough that Stan could barely make out his words from the other side of the table.

"Walter tells me you've done quite a job with this organization of yours," the governor said.

Stan smiled his acceptance of the compliment, even though Ruoma either couldn't bring himself to say the Constructive's name, or else he could say it but was afraid someone would pick it out from under the crash and roar of dishes and voices, silverware and ketchup bottles, and then he'd find it glowering out at him from tomorrow's paper—"Governor holds secret meeting with right-wing zealot," or something like that. Stan barricaded the thought away from his smile and launched into the tale of how much the organization had grown—the new members, the new office, the nationwide network of Constructives that they were part of and how soon he'd be able to tie them together more tightly, and from there he slid seamlessly into a quick grounding in the Constructive's basic beliefs, because who could say what the governor knew or didn't know. Then he talked about Annette, who spoke directly to the American soul, and if they could just get her a national forum, she would singlehandedly unmask the secret government that was really running the country. He talked about the need for like-minded people to work together when they found common ground, not setting aside their differences necessarily but focusing for the time being on what they shared, and he heard himself and thought about Anderson, who would never have said that. Stan was in control here, making a strategic alliance while holding onto the Constructive's independence. His voice expanded with his comfort level, because really, once you get past the title and the aides, a governor's just another guy, right? He puts his pants on one leg at a time, like anybody else.

When Stan was younger, for the sheer pleasure of transcending the possible, he sometimes sat on the edge of his bed and slid both feet into his pants legs at the same time. He still wondered why, through all the centuries of pants-wearing, no one else had thought of doing that.

When Ruoma interrupted, it was in his secret-meeting voice, the voice that made Stan feel like the Other Woman, carrying on whispered conversations in out-of-the-way diners. It surprised him how much power there was in the position. Which of the two of them, after all, had something to hide?

"Stan, we're men of the world," Ruoma nearly whispered. "I don't need to explain the political realities to you. You understand the risk I'm running here—the kind of discretion I need."

Stan waited to be told, but Ruoma was too discreet to say the words himself.

"You're saying you don't want to be linked to us publicly."

"Publicly," Ruoma echoed, letting a quick silence outline the range and variety of nonpublic possibilities before he narrowed them down.

"We can agree publicly on the issues, but as far as any sort of linkage goes—well, you understand the difficulties."

Stan smiled and understood. Bishop had already talked about this. And Stan didn't need a ring on his finger. Didn't want one, as a matter of fact. He and Ruoma would use each other as long as it was convenient for them both. The trick was to make sure the Constructive got what it needed from the affair, and that it wasn't left with any embarrassing diseases.

"You know I'm considering . . . This is a ways off still, but all the same I'm considering a run for the presidency," Ruoma said.

"I've heard the rumor."

"Well, if your people are capable of some basic discretion, I think there are ways we could benefit each other."

"I think there probably are."

The next time Annette met Stan for a bad breakfast and a thick folder of research, he pointed his toast at her and made a speech about how important this Vietnam thing was.

"This is big," he said halfway through.

Annette searched her memory for the movie where she'd heard that line, but she couldn't place it.

"It's huge. It's going to change the face of American politics."

And so on. Annette frowned—an expression that passed reasonably well for attention—and left just enough of her mind in contact with the conversation to wake her if something mattered, and for some minutes nothing did. The face of American politics kept on changing and Stan's coffee grew cold. Annette fingered her watchband and kept herself from looking at the time.

"What we need to do is jump to the next level," he said, and the shift in his tone set the alarm bells ringing. She frowned with more determination. "Push the issue into the center of the public consciousness."

She nodded warily. He had something in mind, and he didn't expect her to like it, otherwise he wouldn't give it such a buildup.

In fact, she didn't like it already. He ran a hand through his thinning hair.

"Here's the thing, though. We need a new forum. Something the media can't ignore. Now, I don't want you to misunderstand, the radio show's the center of everything—I'm not talking about downplaying that in any way—but we've got to take it out of the studio, if you see what I mean."

She nodded warily again. She didn't see, but it might have possibilities hidden in it somewhere.

"Here's what I want to do."

He pushed his plate aside in a motion that said he was ready to stop the bullshit.

"We put your name all over the publicity, put you at the podium—the whole thing's infused with your personality—and we invite vets to stand up in public, talk about what they know, what they're not sure about. Same as on the show, but they're all in the same room, live and in the flesh. Very powerful. Perfect for the television cameras. Perfect for the vets themselves—they meet each other, see each other. Meanwhile we get names, addresses—we have a way to get back in touch with these people. We schedule another public forum, we can contact them, invite them back, ask them to tell their stories to the world."

Annette nodded, frowned.

"What if no one comes to the first one?"

"You leave that to me."

Annette's frown condensed into genuine displeasure.

"No actors," she said, and there was relief in that: she'd found something concrete to object to, and it was a legitimate objection. "No one pretending to be a vet who isn't. It might work for a while, but in the long run someone'd go public with it and we'd look like jerks."

"No actors. I don't work that way."

They measured each other briefly across the table: their trust, their distrust, the extent to which they didn't know each other at all. A moment of pure loneliness shot through Annette—the kind of loneliness she'd always thought Dorothy in *The Wizard of Oz* must have felt. What was she doing in this world? Where was that dry old stick, Auntie Em?

This whole Vietnam business, her brain said. *You're doing the right thing here, aren't you?*

She was. She had to be. It was too late not to be.

"So what do you have in mind?" she asked.

He hesitated, and she was about to ask again when he said, "You've got enough people calling the show to start us off."

"Calling from home, sure, where no one's looking at them. Where they can be sitting around in two-day-old underwear for all anyone knows."

Another moment of measuring each other, broken by the waitress refilling Annette's coffee cup. The loneliness was gone, and so was the doubt, and she didn't remember having felt either of them.

"Look," Annette said when the waitress had left, "you've got something in mind, and if I'm going to be part of this, I want to know everything about it."

For the first time since she'd known him, Stan looked old, although she couldn't pin down what had changed, and in a matter of seconds whatever she'd seen was gone, replaced by a flash of anger she was sure she wasn't supposed to see. It energized her, and she smiled at him beatifically. God, the power that ran through her. They could run half the lights in Saint Paul off the power she was conducting.

Not that Saint Paul had that many lights.

"It's nothing underhanded," Stan said. "I want to locate the vets who call the show, talk to them individually, find a few who'll commit to being there."

"Stan, I don't have their numbers. I don't even have their last names. Hell, half the time I don't have their real first names."

Stan blushed to the roots of his sandbar strands of hair.

"Hey, I'm sorry about that. I told you I was sorry."

Annette grinned. She hadn't been thinking about the time he called. All she'd meant was exactly what she'd said, but it was a place where he was vulnerable.

"Tell you what I want if I'm going to do this," she said, leaning across the table as if she could warm herself on the heat of his embarrassment. "I want to know if any of what we've already found out connects to the Middle East—al-Qaeda, suicide bombers, Iran, Iraq, Afghanistan, any of that. A technology like this gets loose in the world, sooner or later it'll turn around and bite its creators in the ass."

Stan's face closed down.

"Nothing I've seen points in that direction."

Of course it didn't, but then he hadn't been looking for it, and now he didn't want to. She should have brought the idea up when they were in agreement, let him think it was his own.

"Just look, o.k.? See what you find."

"I'll see what I find. Are we agreed about the forum?"

"You have to understand, I don't have numbers for my callers. Not even Nick has their numbers."

She was repeating herself, but he didn't seem to notice. Maybe he wasn't listening either.

"No problem. I'll get them."

"What are you, a magician?"

"It doesn't involve anything illegal—it's just unusual." He tapped the folder that lay on her side of the table. "I'm good at finding things out, and I'm good at knowing what to do with the information. Let's say that's my part of the job and yours is getting the station to broadcast it live. You think they'll do it?"

"Of course they'll do it. I'm the hottest thing since running shoes. They love me."

★

"Absolutely not," Len said.

Annette looked across the tundra. He had no folder on his desk and therefore nothing inside it to accuse her with. That should have comforted her, but it didn't. Nothing ever did with Len. Maybe it was in a drawer somewhere. Maybe he was going to get up and open the file cabinet.

"We broadcast off-site during the state fair."

"Permanent setup. These things cost money. And at the fair, that's the station, not one rogue talk-show host."

"Len . . ."

"No. I don't care how many callers you're getting. I don't care who wants to advertise with you. As long as you work here you follow the same rules as everyone else. You have any problems with that, I've got a box of demo tapes Kathi can bring up from the basement. I could have you replaced by tonight."

★

There's a first time for everything. o.k., this was a second time, but the first one didn't count. The point was, she didn't like the idea of calling Stan. It shifted the balance of their relationship. It let him think she needed him, let him think she was attracted to him, let him think whatever a man like Stan thought when he thought he had the upper hand. It made her skin crawl.

"I got a no on the live broadcast," she told him. "I make Len too nervous."

Six of hearts to the seven of clubs. The computer turned up a three where the six had been. No help there. She hit the undo button.

"Give me a few days," Stan said after he'd thought about it a while. "He'll love the idea."

"Stan, don't talk to him. You'll make things worse."

"Don't worry about a thing. I can fix this."

"I'm not asking you to fix it. I'm telling you we have to live with it."

"No problem. You were right to let me know."

Stan hung up the phone and didn't think about Annette's buttons. Well, maybe a little, but not enough to count. He was sitting in the Constructive's newly rented office, a barn-like room in a strip mall, where a clothing store with a country theme had failed, leaving behind half a dozen fake barn doors outlined in pine strips on the walls, giving the place an abandoned early-American look, a forefathers look. It was no place for dreaming about buttons.

He dialed Walter Bishop. It was odd that Annette hadn't turned to him herself. She didn't lack ambition, she just didn't have the instinct for politics. She needed someone to choose the moves for her. A director. A manager. A Stan. The phone rang while he watched Penny Cole write an address on an envelope. That was Penny of Penny and Ed Cole, who had once backed Anderson and who had taken a sizable chunk out of his hind end in that last meeting before he heard Annette on the radio and the winds started blowing his way. Now Penny put in thirty hours a week as a volunteer, and he needed to find someone who could bring her up to speed on the computer. But tactfully. He didn't want her to think he was criticizing.

Bishop's machine answered and Stan hung up and dialed his cell phone, which linked him to the human being and a lot of background noise. Stan explained his plan for the forum, and Len's reluctance.

"I thought as a major advertiser you might be able to hold the man's attention for a few minutes," Stan said.

"It's not me personally who's advertising," Bishop said. "You understand that."

Stan didn't exactly—he wasn't clear what the relationship was between Bishop and Bishop Milling—but he said sure, of course, but even so . . .

"I can call a few people," Bishop said.

"That's all I could ask for."

"I'm not promising anything."

"I appreciate it, Walt. I appreciate it."

Penny finished addressing a second envelope and licked first one and then the other, although Stan had bought her a handful of spongy water-holder things so she wouldn't have to use her tongue. He hung up the phone and sighed.

Three days passed, and Annette didn't mean to count them, but she couldn't help it. They took forever. She was waiting for whatever Stan hadn't promised not to do to get itself done. Mostly she was waiting to be fired. Stan would talk to Len, Len would hit the roof, Annette would be out of a job. One, two, three.

During those days, she did one show, had two days off, swam in Walter's pool—alone and with her suit firmly in place, thanks—plugged the phone in long enough to answer some hang-up calls, played a lot of computer solitaire, bit her nails, felt depressed, recited a longer, more intense version of the you're-a-loser monologue than she had for some time, bought a suede jacket—it was on sale—and borrowed five hundred dollars from her mother. The jacket was a steal, and where was the economy in passing up a bargain and paying more for it later? Besides, shopping made her feel better. For minutes at a time.

On the fourth day, Len wanted to talk to her. He looked like hell, sitting behind the battlefield of his desk—like he hadn't slept, or like he'd slept but dreamed the haunted dreams of America's veterans.

He opened a folder and flipped through the papers inside it without, as far as Annette could see, reading any of them.

"I don't like being pressured," he said.

Here it comes, Annette's brain announced.

"You study journalism in school?" he asked.

"Communications, with a minor in theater."

He grunted as if she'd said arts and crafts, basket weaving. Hell, it was on her resume. Did he think it had changed?

"Well, when I was at the U, they called the division between advertising and editorial content the division between church and state. They were that serious about it. Now, I admit the church-state division's under fire these days, and I admit we're not a news station—I like to think we're here to serve the listener, give 'em what they want to hear, maybe wrap a little education in the entertainment when we can, but our first responsibility is to serve the listener. If we can do that, everything else will follow. Corporate will be happy. Advertisers will be happy."

He closed the folder and opened it again.

"Still, advertisers do get ideas about what their money's buying."

He closed the folder and played its corner with his thumb like the tuned string of some instrument.

"You've made some powerful friends."

He gave her a cold look that stopped her from asking who they were. She wasn't sure whether the advantage lay in having Len believe that this happened without her knowledge or that she knew who her friends were and had a date to go swimming naked with them the minute she left his office.

"I'm a businessman, not some ivory-tower crusader. When a major advertiser's interested in a particular show, I have to listen. What I don't have to do is like it. You understand what I'm saying?"

It was the one thing Annette did understand, completely and without reservation.

"We'll work out your live remote, but I'll tell you what I want in return: you treat this like any other show. You're not an advocate—

you're investigating a possibility. Whoever you're involved with in this—and I mean who*ever* they are—I don't want to know about it. I don't want to see a hint of a shadow of a memory that they've been there. You understand that? Nobody testifies but vets, and nobody talks politics."

Annette understood that too.

"I don't care if you've got George Washington's ghost giving you evidence on this thing. He didn't fight in this war, and I want him in the background. If the station's going to have its name associated with this, then that's the only name I want to see associated with it."

Annette nodded.

"How big a hall you think you'll need?"

"I'm not sure yet."

"Let Kathi know and she'll make the arrangements. We'll promote it on the air. You can use your own show to pump it up. I don't know, maybe we'll do some print advertising. It's expensive and I doubt it'll put any more bodies in the room, but it might give us some veneer of legitimacy."

He looked at the clean surface of his desk.

"God knows we could use some legitimacy on this."

He looked back at her, reluctantly.

"So. If we're going to do this, we're going to do it as if we liked it, o.k.? You have a date in mind?"

"Let me look at my calendar."

"Let Kathi know. She'll take care of it. And make it soon, before I have an attack of good sense."

He flicked the corner of the folder. As far as she could figure out, she was dismissed.

CHAPTER 12

 The night of the public forum was sharp-edged and clear, and the suede jacket was way too light, but she wore it anyway, and she froze. And then it was too hot in the building, and she had to take it off as soon as she got inside, so no one except Walt got to see it, but he took it from her and stroked it as he folded it over his arm, and what the hell, it was worth the money for that moment alone.

Nick wore a pair of greasy jeans and a look like the world had done him wrong by dragging him ten suburban miles south of the station.

Stan wore his funeral suit.

Kathi had found them a hall in a shopping mall, and it was half as big as Stan had asked for but twice as big as Annette expected to fill. It was empty still, and Stan paced the perimeter like he was the only force in the room alert enough to keep the chairs from straying out of their rows. Annette watched him through two circuits, and with each revolution, her guts wound themselves tighter until she excused herself to Walter and went down the hall to the ladies' room, where she leaned against the wall, shut her eyes, and tried to assemble an attitude of perfect indifference to tonight's turnout. What she assembled instead was a case of high intensity panic over how she'd fill an hour and a half if no one showed.

Right. So closing her eyes had been a bad idea. It was a high-way to all the places she didn't want to go. She opened them and looked at herself in the mirror, and she saw that, for the moment at least, she was good: intense, pretty enough to make men think she was good looking. Long neck, short skirt. Half the time when she looked in the mirror all she saw was a collection of misassembled pieces. Tonight, though, for whatever reason, they'd coalesced, and she accepted it as an omen. This would be a lucky night. If no one showed up, she'd extemporize on bits of information that Stan had fed her. Christ, there was enough of it by now. More than she'd be able to use in a year. In six years. It would work out. Some of Stan's antigovernment people had to be vets. Stan would stand up and play expert and Len be damned. Walter would radiate at her. All she needed was half a dozen voices and she could do the rest. No one listening from home would know how empty the place was. Head up, back straight, fuck 'em all. It would work.

By the time she got back to the hall, a couple of men had set up a table to collect names and addresses, and the delivery geek who'd brought one of Stan's packets was talking at Stan, tethering him in one place. And, miraculously, seats were being filled by more-than-middle-aged men who apparently liked empty space because they were leaving chairs open between themselves and whoever was nearest—half a dozen seats, a dozen of them, a row or two. Her vets had dragged themselves here: the lost, the dispossessed, the hang-dog half-believers unable to stay home but not ready to admit to the world that they needed to be here. And she loved them all—loved them the way she'd loved George, that first vet she'd led through the half dreams of his shattered memories. It was an overwhelming, almost painful thing, that love, and she felt unworthy to channel it.

Stan called her over and introduced her to the delivery geek, Steve, who was too young to have been in Vietnam so forget about him helping to fill time. Stan had snagged him in something that was half hug and half wrestling hold, and he told her she was striking a blow for liberty. Stan thumped him on the back and introduced her to a handful of others. Except for the delivery geek and the nephew, this was the first she'd seen of Stan's people—the elves she figured must do his research—and they looked normal enough: a bit redneck but so was the rest of the crowd. They didn't have Nazi tattoos or shaved heads or, except for Stan, funeral suits. What distinguished them from the other men in the room was that they looked at each other, and talked to each other, and didn't try to pretend they weren't there. She didn't love them the way she loved the vets, but at least they didn't make her want to run screaming from the room. She hadn't known how relieved she'd be by this.

She scanned the hall for Walt and found him in a back row. He was also surrounded by empty chairs, but he looked comfortable—arms spread along the chair backs, smiling, studying the crowd as if some law of nature set him apart.

The hall was half full when she gave her before-the-show explanation of the house rules and how the mic worked, and a TV news crew was huddled just inside the door arguing about where to set up, pointing first to one side and then to the other. It was as much as she'd dared hope for, but it didn't stop there. They kept coming—singly, silently, creeping into the empty seats, leaning against the walls, too uncommitted even to sit themselves down. Mostly they were white, and normally she wouldn't have noticed that but a handful of them were black or—who the hell knew what they were—*other*, and they made everyone else *look* white. Maybe that meant she had to do something different, but she couldn't think what. So to hell with them. They were on her territory, so they could take it on her terms. She pushed them out of her mind, threw away the intro she'd prepared and after she'd explained where she was and why for the radio audience, she opened her heart and talked about what she saw in front of her: a group of men who'd been willing to risk their lives for their country but who were so stunned, so afraid of the truth they carried inside themselves, that it was all they could do to walk through a door and sit in a room together.

"I don't know what it is that happened to you, any more than you know," she said, shifting the intensity of her voice so she addressed the men in the room directly and only through them the radio audience, "but I know what it cost you, each one of you, to come here tonight, and I want to tell you this: you're the bravest human beings I've ever seen."

Someone clapped, making a flat, lonely sound that underlined the lack of applause, and she went on, recapping what the callers on her show had told her so far, inviting the audience to tell the world what they knew, what they didn't know, what they suspected. The TV camera's lights went on and then off, leaving a sense of cold and darkness in their wake. One man pried himself away from the wall while she was talking and stood by the floor mic, waiting like a high school student until she called on him. He was past fifty—shit, they were all past fifty—wearing an ironed fatigue jacket that he must have kept stashed in a closet for the last thirty years. She asked what he knew, and instead of answering, he tapped the mic, heard the drumbeat of his finger telling him it was working, and said, "Well . . ."

Then he said nothing. Dead air flowed outward: to Eden Prairie, to Bloomington, to Brooklyn Park, long, painful seconds of silence that Annette had to wade through. She focused her eyes on the back door, which opened for another straggler. She should've anticipated how skittish these guys would be. There must be dozens of them just outside, driving the freeways, listening to the radio, killing time until fifteen minutes before the show was over so they could duck in the door right at the end.

"I wanted . . ." the man said, and he looked at the floor.

"It's O.K.," Annette told him, leaning into the mic, willing the love she felt to flow outward, to enfold this man and help him speak. "If there was ever a safe place to say what you have to say, this is it."

The man cleared his throat.

"I don't have a lot to say, I just wanted to thank you for what you've done. That's all."

And he walked away from the mic, leaving Annette with her finger, metaphorically speaking, up her nose and not a damn thing she could think of to say.

"Friends," she said for lack of a better idea, "I could stand up here and go over the same old questions about whether the war happened, but most of you have heard it already, and I didn't come here tonight to hear myself talk. I came to listen. Every one of you brought a story through that door with you, or some tiny part of a story that, put together, is the story of our time and the expla-nation of our nation's pain. It's the start of everything that's gone wrong with our country, my friends, and the only way we'll ever put things right is if we assemble that story, part by painful part."

She felt the mood in the room shift, as if the men were each, separately, reaching for her. She made herself radiate into the microphone like a female version of Walter Bishop.

"I'm not asking you to say that the Vietnam War did happen, or that it didn't happen. I came here to ask you for the truth as you know it, whatever that might be."

They shifted in their isolated seats. Another minute and she'd have them begging for the mic.

"You know better than I do that the government made a pact with you when you enlisted. It promised you the opportunity to do something noble, something right and good, and you went for-ward in good faith."

A man had approached the mic and was waiting to speak now.

"What I want to know is, what happened to that pact?"

She'd meant this rhetorically, for the audience as a whole—she had another question as a lead-in for the man at the mic—but she brought her eyes toward him too early and he answered this one.

"I didn't want to do anything noble," he said. "I got drafted."

The crowd laughed. Nervousness and relief, she thought.

"Mostly, back then, I wanted to drink beer."

A reflexive laugh from the audience.

"So what do you think? Were you in a war or not?"

"I was in . . ."

He ran a hand through his hair.

"I was . . ."

"It's o.k.," Annette said. "Whatever you remember is o.k."

"I don't know if I believe this. You understand what I'm saying? I used to dream about this, but I didn't want people to think I was nuts so I never told them about it. But what I think? What I remember is I was in a tunnel. Not like with cement or that kind of thing, but a tunnel with, like, dirt sides, rock, dripping mud. Some places it's so narrow I can't stand up straight—I've got to crawl."

He turned away from Annette to look at one side of the room. Someone yelled, "Keep talking."

"The reason I say I don't know if this is true is I've got these other memories, see, and they tell me a whole 'nother story, but this tunnel thing—I mean it really bothers me. I have dreams about it. Like flashbacks. Every time I hear someone talk about the Ho Chi Minh Trail, I get the shivers, 'cause I'll tell you, that's just what it feels like in those tunnels—like what the tunnels along the Ho Chi Minh Trail are supposed to be."

Annette drew him on, or tried to, feeling for something more to the memory, but either there was nothing there or the man had risked as much as he was willing to. Either way, he'd shut down, but by the time she gave up on him, she'd found the land of milk and honey: a river of speakers flowed toward the mic. They remembered all the usual things: darkness and light, mud and rock, fear and confusion, and for a while that was enough. But the trouble was, they'd done mud and rock, and if she couldn't do better than this, she'd be last year's sensation before she'd had time enough to be this year's. The only new information was the tunnels, and that was just a variant on mud and rock. Somehow she couldn't hit the right note here, couldn't get close to them when she was being warm, couldn't get tough with them when she should have. Ninety minutes dragged past with all the speed and joy of an ice age, and she ended the show a good five years older than she'd started it. The camera crew was long gone by then, and only Stan and Walter waited at the foot of the steps to congratulate her.

"That sucked big time," she said.

"No, look at them." Stan gestured toward the rapidly emptying room, toward the table his people had set up at the back. "We broke a barrier tonight. They're talking to each other. And we can get back in touch with them."

Annette looked, but if anyone was talking to anyone, they were doing it in a way she didn't recognize.

"This isn't another one of those understated Minnesota things, is it? I don't see anyone talking."

"No, but they did. They were. Out there." He nodded to where Nick was unplugging the floor mic. "They were using you as a way to talk to each other."

Annette shook her head, not to disagree—Stan was probably right in his way—but at Minnesotans, who wouldn't turn to the person next to them and say, "Hey, this is what happened to me and it stank," they had to send the damn message by way of some third person.

"We must have a hundred names there, people we can get back to the next time we do this."

Right. And a hundred meant they had fifty. Twenty. For the first time she wondered if Stan had really managed to contact the vets who'd called the show. If he'd even tried. If he'd ever intended to. If that wasn't just something he'd said make her to agree to the show.

"We're not doing this again. It's not my format."

"Are you kidding? You're great at this. Tell her, Walt. Was she good?"

"She's always good."

"Steve." He reached an arm out and snagged the delivery geek. "Steve, tell her, was she good or wasn't she?"

"She was good. It went fine."

Stan pounded him on the shoulder and let him go on his way.

"Had a fight with the ex before he came here tonight," he told Annette. "He's been kind of down."

Nick walked past, coiling wire over his arm, without glancing her way. Who had he had a fight with? Who had Walter had a fight with? He should have been more enthusiastic if he'd meant it.

"Stan, don't humor me," Annette said. "Don't ever try to humor me. We got nowhere tonight. We spent ninety minutes, and all we got out of it was tunnels."

"Tunnels are important."

"Tunnels are shit, Stan. We need a whole memory. We need a story people can get their heads around, and we need it soon or the whole thing'll be forgotten. Things that stay the same aren't news."

"It'll come. You got to give people time."

CHAPTER 13

Stan invited Annette and Walter to join his people at a bar to celebrate the show's success, but it was only to be polite—he expected them to leave together, and so did they. Besides, she'd spent as much time with Stan as she had patience for. She went to Walter's and let him pour them each a glass of wine, and they watched the local news massacre her story. Channel four ran a quick shot of her in front of the station's banner, and the voice-over made it sound like she was claiming the sun was made of cardboard, then maybe five seconds of one of the vets saying, "It's like I've got two separate stories in my head about what happened over there, and if one of them's true, the other one can't be, but I swear I believe them both."

Great. The perfect testimonial.

"Well, there you go," one anchor said to the other at the end of it. "Would you ever have thought we'd run a story like that?"

"It just goes to show you," the other said, and she gave the camera a smug little smile before she introduced the sports.

"It's not as bad as you think," Walter said before she had a chance to tell him how bad she thought it was. "It doesn't matter what they say about you as long as they get the word out."

She nodded glumly and let him rub her shoulders, although his hands made her shoulders hurt. If it was true that some people had the healing touch, Walter had its opposite. Everything he touched hurt.

"Everything's fine," he said. "It's all going to be great."

In the morning, they sat in the breakfast room and unfolded the papers. The Minneapolis paper ran a small article—no photos, but not as slanted as the TV spot. Saint Paul ignored her. Walter glowed and cut the article out for her. On the way home, she stopped to make a copy for her mother. To hell with her father— he could find out about it for himself if he cared. She drove home, turned the computer on, and settled in to play solitaire and be quietly depressed. An hour later she realized her phone hadn't rung all morning. She checked the connection, and it was plugged in.

She kind of missed the calls.

Stan was still in his bathrobe and reading the article for the second time when the doorbell rang. Through the peephole he made out a distorted Cal Anderson, and he shifted his angle, looking for the goon squad, but the peephole had its own angle on the world, and it wasn't interested in Stan's; it let him see what it let him see, and if he wanted anything more he was going to have to open the door.

He set his hand on the doorknob. What were they going to do? Mob him? Gun him down in his own doorway while he was still in his bathrobe and pajamas? He turned the handle, opened the door and saw that there was no *they*. Anderson stood by his handsome self, and for a second the two men stared at one another, each waiting for the other to give him a cue about how to act. It was Stan who broke down first.

"You want to come in?"

Anderson stepped into the living room, snow melting off his shoes onto the carpet, and looked around like a prospective buyer. Stan half expected him to ask if the basement leaked, to open the closets and see how big they were. Flambard materialized in the doorway, a quiet presence that comforted Stan more than he'd have expected.

"Coffee?" Stan said.

Anderson's head snapped around as if Stan had blown up a paper bag and popped it by his ear.

"Coffee," Stan repeated. "Would you like some?"

Anderson shook his head several times before the motion shook loose an answer.

"Artificial stimulants, Stan. Terrible for you. Tea, coffee, heroin, cocaine—you ever stop to think they all come from the same parts of the world, and that it's the darker races who grow them and then sell them to the white race to keep it from its natural destiny?"

This was new. Anderson never did have much use for the darker races—Stan wasn't in love with them himself, come to that—but coffee? He was moving deeply into the land of the weird here.

He moved close enough to tap Stan on the shoulder.

"You could be a soldier of god, Stan. We've had our disagreements, but they're not what matter in the long run. Keep the body pure and the mind will follow. You'll see."

Stan stood and let his shoulder be tapped. He thought he should ask Anderson to leave. He thought he shouldn't have invited him in. He thought how odd it was that Ole Mainstream Anderson had reinvented himself as one of god's wackos and he experienced one of those moments of doubt that in this case consisted of the governor's face flashing on in his mind like a warning about the unexpected directions in which politics can drive a man. But it all had an underwater feeling to it, and he couldn't force himself close enough to the surface to invite Anderson back outside or himself back to the purity and smallness of his pre-Annette, pre-Walter Bishop ambitions.

Anderson turned to the living room again, then walked to the kitchen and evaluated that. Checking Stan's security, maybe. Looking for the easiest way to break in. That was one substitute for winning a vote. Stan's pajama top felt clammy on his back.

"Something you want?" Flambard asked. A quiet question. An implied danger.

Anderson turned to him, measured and dismissed him as too small to keep, and turned back to Stan, who was offended on Flambard's behalf but couldn't think what to do about it. That business Anderson had raised about him and Flambard sharing a house got in the way, because even now, god's wacko or not, he didn't want the man to think . . .

He didn't want to think it so much that he didn't finish the thought.

"The only survival will be outside the cities," Anderson said. "When Armageddon comes, the righteous have to be dug deep into the countryside. Otherwise they'll be roadkill. You understand that, Stan?"

"I've heard the argument."

"I like you Stan. I shouldn't. You're self-willed and ignorant, you pollute your body, you draw people's attention away from the things that matter, and you're consorting with a representative of the liberal media who's either Greek or Jewish or both, but the thing is I like you. You remind me of myself when I was still wandering in the wilderness."

Stan nodded, meaning not that he agreed but that he couldn't think of anything else to do.

"That woman's using you, you know. She'll use you to build her own career and shuck you off as soon as she can. The darker races are like that."

Annette was, in fact, no darker than Stan. And Stan had researched her family—she was no more Greek or Jewish than he was. Her legal name was Annie Minor; she'd only become Annette Majoris when she got her radio show.

"I'm not worried about it," he said.

Anderson considered Stan the way he'd considered the living room, asking himself if he shouldn't panel the walls. Or in Stan's case, whether the plaid bathrobe really went with the striped pajamas. Then he crossed to the front door.

"I just thought I should warn you. I wouldn't have felt right if I didn't try."

Because he could think of no other way to get the man out of his house, Stan nodded again. Then he double-locked the door.

"Jesus," he said to Flambard. "I need another cup of coffee. You want one?"

★

The next night's show gave Annette the breakthrough she needed. She'd spent an hour slogging through memories of tunnels and darkness and mud. What was it about these guys? Not one of them could remember anything that someone else hadn't remembered first. Did they dream in unison too? If one of them got up to pee, did a whole scraggly line of vets stumble out of bed all over town, shuffling barefoot down the hall to the bathroom? Didn't one of them have the imagination to remember anything on his own? She was reaching a point where she'd have welcomed calls about the hunting season or the length of the school year. Christ, anything but going back to those tunnels.

Then Sam called. Great voice, good talker, not the kind of guy whose words took root in his mouth like impacted wisdom teeth. He couldn't get them out fast enough. The answer to a girl's dreams.

"I've been listening to your show here, and I don't know if what I remember fits in the same category, because it's a lot clearer than what your callers have been telling you, but if you want to hear it I'm glad to spit it out."

"Spit it out, then, Sam. Let's hear it."

"Here it is, and you can make what you want of it. I *was* in Vietnam. I mean that both ways: the government says I was there, and I say I was there, but the thing is, that's where it happened. They took us off that plane, broke us up so we didn't stay together. You ever wonder why they did that? They didn't do that in World War II."

"Good point, there. Score one."

"I spent a couple of weeks on a base, just as if there really was a war going on, then they loaded us on a chopper, dropped us in the jungle with a map, and off we marched. Hard to believe, isn't it, but we slogged our way through the fuckin' jungle *looking* for those tunnels."

Annette hit the hot button to cover *fuckin'* with a prefab station I.D. Damn shame. It would blot out everything on either side of it.

"Extreme caution here, Sam. You just said one of the seven magic words the government doesn't want on the air. You can advocate chopping old ladies into hamburger, but you cannot use naughty words."

"Sorry. Didn't know that."

"No one does. You were saying something about looking for the tunnels."

"They told us it was an American outpost. I thought, hey, great, cold beer, hot shower, lemme at it. Christ, what did I know. Can I say *Christ?*"

"*Christ* isn't swearing. You can say *Christ.*"

"Just checking."

"Right."

He left her hanging for a second. She was getting used to dead airtime.

"It's a little choppy after this. What I know is they broke us up the minute we got there, took me into those tunnels alone—a whole fu . . . A whole maze of them. I don't know how many guys they had tucked away down there. Could've been hundreds. Could've been more than that for all I could tell. After that it's all nightmare images, the kind of things guys've been telling you, but all mixed up with knowing I shouldn't be remembering how I got there, knowing I can't let on that I do remember. Worst fear I had was they'd find out about that."

His voice was upbeat, though. No fear in it. It didn't fit, but you don't argue with a gift horse like this.

"I can't tell you a whole lot more than that. I know a lot of time passed. I remember battles, patrols, all the usual Vietnam stuff, but I don't know how much of it happened and how much is what they wanted me to remember. Hell, I even remember going on leave—had a fine ole time of it too, I'll tell you—and I don't know if that happened or not. Ain't that a—well, you know the word I was going to use. It's like waking up in the morning and not knowing if you had sex the night before or you just thought you did. Can I say *sex*?"

"All you want, Sam. You got any theories about why you can remember this much?"

He made a sound that was the noise equivalent of a shrug.

"Just a stubborn cuss, I guess. Always have been."

They cut to the ads: a new movie Bishop Milling. How're you doing, Walt? Always good to hear your voice.

It was a good night after that. Sam had broken something loose, and they called in remembering how they arrived at the tunnels, how normal American bases had stood at the entrance to the tunnels. One guy remembered a volleyball game before he was marched underground. Her last caller told her about a battle that didn't fit the Vietnam War scenario, set in a u.s.-type city after bombings that had left it looking like the South Bronx. It was as if someone had used his memories as scratch paper, writing the notes for even more horrific wars. All of it flowed toward her as freely as water, and she collected it all and flung it out into the night in a pattern that, even with the contradictions and gaps, made sense. Nick chewed his way through a bag of roasted soy nuts and shook his head, but she couldn't help that. She hadn't had a caller all night who didn't love her, and she rode their love like a wave.

CHAPTER 14

Annette's first national interview was hostile. How could it not have been? Vietnam had been the government's gift to TV news—a perfect war, dancing right across their screens—so TV was committed to the war having happened. Why should Annette have expected even-handed treatment?

She had, though. Chalk it up to naiveté, to arrogance, to whatever—she'd have agreed. She hadn't been thinking. Too many people had loved her lately; it had dulled her instincts. So when Stan warned her what to expect, she didn't exactly not listen—she just didn't take him seriously. She was the media expert. He was going into this blinkered by his ideology, expecting the media to be one unbroken force, monolithic in its hostility to anything he believed in. On top of which, the week after the producer called to set up the interview, she'd watched the show. Wallace Burke's *Sunday Night*. It was a feel-good show. Burke was out to make everyone happy.

Right. So she walked into the interview with a smile on her face, thinking, here I am: national exposure. Her only worry was her clothes. She'd heard something years ago about the kind of clothes that worked well on television, but she hadn't paid attention. Blue was either good or bad, she couldn't remember which and she hadn't had time to research it—o.k., she'd had time, but where do you find something like that?—so she wore a pearl-gray silk blouse and worried it would make her look somber. Or faded. Or sallow.

She wasn't sure what sallow was, exactly, except that it wasn't a way you wanted to look.

On the good side, of course, that kept her mind off her hair and whether her features had organized themselves into a coherent face today.

It started off fine—what was it that led her to question the Vietnam War, and what exactly did she believe had happened?—and she answered cleanly, within Len's guidelines: it wasn't a question of what she believed but of what she doubted. She had questions, not answers, and so on and so on. The whole here-I-am, there-I'm-not approach / avoidance dance. What mattered wasn't what she thought but what the veterans who called her show thought, what they remembered, the pain they carried around with them from one day to the next. The hard part wasn't answering the questions, it was keeping her eyes off the tiny picture of herself riding low on the TV cameras. Every time she glanced sideways to see how she looked, she caught an image of herself looking shifty eyed.

Wallace Burke was sixty or more, with a surgically sharp neck and jaw line, and after the first couple of questions, he launched into a speech about having been in Vietnam as a reporter and seeing a war that—he didn't mind admitting it—shocked him to the roots and made him re-evaluate everything he'd taken for granted up to then. He'd lived through a period of the country's history that, he thought it would be fair to say, each and every citizen at that time found painful, that divided families for years, and he found it hard to believe that someone would come along and claim none of that happened. It was, in fact, outrageous. Offensive. Insulting to the people who'd fought the war as well as the people who'd opposed it. Sacrifices had been made on both sides, and yadda, yadda, yadda. On top of which, to introduce a question like this at a time when what America needed was to unite against a clear threat . . .

He didn't like her. When she thought about it later, she couldn't have said why that mattered to her any more than it mattered if a caller didn't like her, but what the hell, it did. Well, o.k., maybe she could have said: he was a guy with a TV show, not some forty-year-old all-night waitress calling in when business was slow. Was that being a snob? Fine, she was a snob. Who wasn't? The forty-year-old waitress was a snob too. All Americans were snobs. It was a national virtue. It was what gave the country ambition. She felt like she'd been promised an ice cream cone only to have it yanked out of her grip in front of a national audience, and all she wanted to do was burst into tears.

"I'm not claiming none of it happened," she said. "There's no question in my mind that the country was divided, and I don't question the honesty of people who say they were there. We're talking about a mind-control experiment on a scale that boggles the imagination." And so forth. Tunnels, flashing lights, Area 51, Bemis, the Martinez letter. Martha Mitchell, for god's sake. Martha'd been on the outer fringes of the inner circles. She *knew*. Annette didn't say that she didn't question Burke's honesty, but she wasn't sure anyone would notice the omission.

At this point he opened a folder—god, she hated folders—and started handing pictures across to her: horrific things, eight-by-ten glossies of people being shot, of wailing children, of bodies. It was show-and-tell time, because with each one he had a story he wanted her to either disprove or admit to, and with each one all she could say was that photos could be staged—had he been to a movie lately?—or the stories behind them changed.

And the journalists themselves? he wanted to know. Were they in on the plot? Did she think journalists would lie?

"Not all of them, no, but you remember that *New York Times* reporter who filed stories from places he'd never been—just sat home in his p.j.s, making the things up? Journalists aren't saints. But most reporters? Listen, if soldiers' minds can be tampered with, are you going to tell me the press is immune? These are human beings we're talking about. I'm sure most of them reported what they took to be the truth."

She tilted her head to the side to give her words an edge and repeated, "*Most* of them."

They were both of them cranky by now, gnawing at the edges of each other's tempers, and when he ran out of photos, he started in with statistics: tons of antipersonnel bombs produced by the U.S. between nineteen-she-wasn't-listening and a year or three later, and where had those bombs gone if they hadn't been used and so forth. How should she know where they'd gone? For all she knew they'd been tested on our own soldiers—the deaths and injuries from that period were real enough. Then it was the Pentagon Papers. Christ, she *knew* the Pentagon Papers, she absolutely knew, but they kept slipping away from her. She dropped her voice into its most confidential register and willed herself to like this man for the next sixty seconds.

"Wallace, I'm not a historian. I don't claim to know everything about what happened, or what didn't happen. All I am is a channel for the doubts and questions of the American public, and when I see inconsistencies in the official story, it's my job to point them out. Nothing more. I have no axe to grind here and no argument to make. All I'm doing is raising a question."

Thank you, Len Bitterman.

But he ground on: the Tet Offensive, fighting in major cities—in the U.S. embassy, for Pete's sake. Did she think something on that scale could be faked?

"Not faked, no, but I believe it could be misinterpreted. Remember, what we were dealing with in South Vietnam was an unstable government, which could be dumped at will by other factions, or manipulated by either North Vietnam or the U.S., or both. What we're looking at during Tet may not have been the Communist attack as played on our TV screens but a disguised expression of the underlying factional power struggle.

"Now, I can't prove I'm right about this, but let me ask you a question. Who benefited from the Tet Offensive?"

She held up a hand to stop him from answering and rolled on before he could.

"If you take it at face value, you've got to believe two things that contradict each other: one, the Communists came out of it stronger than they went in, and two, the Communists lost fifty thousand of their best people and came out of it weaker. Now, I see a problem there. So who benefited? The one clear winner was the guy who took Hue back from the so-called Vietcong. He came out twice as important as he had been."

"Are you trying to tell me he set up house-to-house fighting in Hue, let's say six thousand deaths on both sides—that's conservative—just so he could look good?"

"Wallace, I'm not telling you anything. I'm asking questions. I'm looking at things that don't make sense and asking why."

She couldn't make herself like him any longer and couldn't remember why she'd wanted to. They were both of them wrung out, glaring at each other, and ready to bite the nearest cameraman.

★

Annette didn't watch the interview when it aired, although she should have, she knew she should have, because how else was she going to analyze her performance? But it would have been as painful as going back and reading the papers she'd written in high school. The person on the tape wasn't anyone she wanted to spend time with. She had to move on. She had to look forward. Stan told her she'd been good, though—she was a real pro. She'd held her own and made Burke look like the jerk he was. Walter said it was good that Burke was so openly biased. It helped him discredit himself. Her mother said she'd look better with smaller earrings. Even her father called: congratulations, and he had no idea he had such a famous daughter and ra ta ta ta da, and of course he had no idea because when had he last asked.

It was Len who told her they'd interviewed Stan too.

"I don't like it," he told her across the final frontier of his desk. "I don't like the station being associated with that man."

"We don't own the issue. I can't control who they talk to. Besides, he's useful."

"He's a kook. He thinks space aliens have captured the White House. You don't worry about that?"

"He's a little extreme, maybe, but I wouldn't say exactly space aliens."

"You go on with this thing, I want you to put some distance between yourself and him."

"I didn't even know they talked to him. It wasn't my show, Len."

"I don't care whose show it was. Look, no matter how either you or I feel about it, you're still out there representing this station, and I'm not about to turn it over to that bunch. You got that?"

"I've got it."

"Distance, o.k.?"

"Distance."

Len nodded. Annette nodded. He had no folder to close. She stood up, and he didn't tell her to sit back down.

"I mean it," he said when she was at the door.

"Got it, Len. Distance."

She had the door open.

"Annette."

His voice surprised her. It was the sound of one human being talking to another, almost like a friend. She froze with one hand on the door.

"Be careful with this guy. He's smarter than you, and he's using you, and when he doesn't need you anymore, he'll dump you."

"Thanks a bunch, Len. You really know how to flatter a girl."

He looked at her from across the unfenced land where, one at a time, he had grazed his flock of folders.

"I've been reading up on his organization. Do you have any idea what they stand for? Everything that man believes is poison, and if it rubs off, don't say no one warned you."

So. Did it scare Annette, the way Burke had pounded at her with the Pentagon Papers, the pictures, the bitterness of what he claimed were his memories?

Sure it did. Of course it did. How could it not?

Did it make her question what she was doing?

No.

Yes.

Not at all. She'd made a commitment. Too many people—too many sane, responsible people—were telling her she was onto something for her to question it now. And the government case didn't fit together. She drove home from her meeting with Len reminding herself of all that. She was asking questions. She was only asking questions. She was bringing peace to all the troubled veterans, and that was important. Gradually her stomach unknotted, and by the time she got home, she was settled enough to review Stan's folders and immerse herself in all the details she already knew.

How could she have this many details if it wasn't true? How could she be doing anything but helping people? Know ye the truth and the truth shall set you free. Or however that went.

CHAPTER 15

After the interview aired, the mail started, and the out-of-state calls. The callers were given the time of her show and told to call back; the mail overflowed her bottom-rank mail slot, which was below the daytime talent, below the managers and producers, below the office staff, below the temp workers. For the first couple of days, someone sliced it open for her and piled it in plastic post-office cartons, but whoever it was got tired after that and left it unopened, and Annette carried it all home to pore over. The empty post-office cartons piled up in the corner of her living room, although she kept meaning to take them back to the station.

Not many celebrities actually read their fan mail, but Annette did, and she loved every piece of it, even the letters that told her she was slime. She could measure her impact as easily by the abuse as by the love. They made up for her hang-up caller having abandoned her, and the next time she met Stan, she brought a random handful and dropped them on the table before he had time to give his folder of information its final shake.

"Look at this, Stan. It's coming in from all over the place, from cities no one's ever heard of. I'm getting buried in the stuff."

He picked up the top piece and read it out loud, half a page of handwritten testimonial to her importance in the writer's brother's life, containing no information at all, new or otherwise.

"You save the envelopes?"

She looked at him like he'd sprouted feathers.

"You didn't, did you?"

"I wouldn't have room to open the front door if I saved the damn envelopes. I'm getting buried in this stuff. Look at this one, 'Ever since I got home, everybody's wanted to use the Vietnam vets, either for a punching bag or to parade us around like heroes. Finally somebody cares about what happened to us.' It breaks my heart, Stan."

Stan put his head in his hands, not as if his heart was broken but as if he was having a quick discussion with his temper. When he raised it, though, his voice was under control, making him sound like someone tapping all his reserves of patience to deal with a difficult child.

"We need these people—names, addresses, everything."

He picked up a full-house worth of letters from the tabletop.

"I'll tell you what we're going to do with this stuff: we're going to make mailing lists, calling lists. We're going to organize a public hearing for vets in every major city where we have more than seventy-five names, and we're going to call every single one of these people beforehand. If we have to, we'll pick them up at home and carry them to the event piggyback. We're going to change the face of American politics with these. You open the letters, staple the envelopes to the backs, and pass them on to me when you're done with them. Sort the hostiles from the friendlies. You can pitch the hostiles."

"Hey, I'm not your secretary. I've got a show to prepare."

This time Stan gave her the sprouted-feathers look. Then the waitress stopped at their table and they both turned the look on her.

"You folks ready to order?"

"Eggs," Annette said. "Over very easy. Whites set, yolks liquid. Toast done just enough to melt the butter, butter spread all the way to the edges. Coffee, very hot, with two percent."

Stan ordered the same without seeming to care what it was. He watched the waitress's hind end until she disappeared into the kitchen. Then he brought himself back to the table, to the fan of mail.

"Tell you what. We'll find someone to open it for you, sort it out, take the addresses. You want to go through it after that, fine. You don't feel like it, that's fine too."

"I'll think about it."

"What's to think about? I'm offering you your own secretary, for Pete's sake. Free. No cost. Gratis."

He was offering her more than that—he was offering her a springboard to a national forum that the Wallace Burkes of the world didn't control, and she wasn't sure why she wasn't jumping up and down on it, but she wasn't. Fuck him, if any jumping was going to get done, she'd do it later, at her own damn convenience.

"That's not my format, the live appearance thing. I'll think about that too."

Stan had the face of a man trying not to make a face. She could practically hear him not-saying, *"Women!"*

"You find anything linking this to the Middle East yet?" she asked.

"Nothing yet, but I haven't gone all-out on that. It's too early."

"Stan, it's the central issue of our time. Terrorists, assault on America, Iran, Iraq—don't tell me you haven't noticed. You read the papers at all?"

He pretended he hadn't heard that.

"Throw that in, you'll weaken your impact. People can't hold two separate wars in their heads at the same time. Doesn't work."

"It does if they're linked."

"You notice what happened to Afghanistan once the war started in Iraq? Dropped right out of the news. Besides, I haven't been able to find anything. I can't give you what's not there."

By way of accepting that, Annette made a face, but in some distant corner of her mind, she found the thought comforting: he couldn't produce this stuff to order. That was good. A knot in her stomach that she hadn't known was there released itself into glorious comfort.

The waitress reappeared, carrying their coffee.

"I thought you looked familiar," she said to Annette. "You're that Vietnam person, aren't you?"

She set the cups down.

"God, that sounded dumb. You know what I mean, though. On the TV?"

Annette extended her hand.

"Annette Majoris."

"You really think they could do that? Fake a whole war?"

"I think it's possible."

"Amazing, you know. It's just hard to believe."

"It is."

On the other side of the table, Stan was winding up to make a speech, probably about how easy it was to believe about a government that made its citizens put sash locks on their windows and indoor toilets in their suburban ramblers, even if it was against their religion, but the waitress was turned toward Annette and missed the signals, so she cut him off.

"I gotta get back before my boss thinks I'm bothering you or something, but I just had to, you know, tell you I'd seen you."

She left Stan with the speech still bubbling upward in his windpipe and Annette grinning at him, all insults forgiven. A minute later, she caught sight of the waitress and a couple of men from the kitchen, all clustered in the doorway and staring at her. She smiled, then let her eyes drift to one side as if she had other things on her mind.

The arrangement Annette and Stan worked out went like this: Annette brought her mail home, stacked it untouched in the dining

room, and twice a week some woman Stan knew—Penny Something—came over to collect it and bring the last batch back, all
sorted, stacked, and stapled. It was creepy. Like sending your mail
out to be cleaned and pressed; like handing it over to be censored.
And the woman herself gave Annette the creeps. She was maybe
sixty, the wife of someone or other—Stan had mentioned his
name as if it would mean something to her—and she kept trying
to be friendly, only there was something off-kilter about it, as if
she'd memorized all the forms of friendliness but had never really
liked anyone, or else she'd liked plenty of people but Annette
wasn't one of them. She left Annette with the feeling that she'd
been stuck with a cleaning lady someone else had hired, a cleaning
lady she couldn't fire, a cleaning lady who not only didn't like her
but who also went through her underwear drawer when she was
alone in the apartment.

The mail would have dried up if first the bloggers and then
the wire services and magazines hadn't picked up the story, but
they did, doing telephone interviews; sending photographers,
reporters; writing about her without ever making contact. Some
asked five minutes' worth of questions and were gone. One followed her through the better part of a day, waited with her while
she got her oil changed, sat next to Nick through the show.
Annette half expected the woman to ride home and crawl in on
the other side of the bed with her that night. She actually gave
half a minute's thought to how she'd hide ole Perry Como's CDs.
God, that would just about kill her, seeing that in print. Pictures
of Annette ran in Minneapolis, Kansas City, Seattle, although
New York still wouldn't touch her. Pictures of her vets ran in a
Sunday magazine insert that went into papers all across the country, under the headline "Denying the Obvious." They hated her,
but the mail kept coming, and callers waited on hold for twenty
minutes, for thirty minutes, paying long-distance rates for a

chance to talk to her. When she stopped at SuperAmerica to buy coffee and a muffin, suddenly they knew her by name. The shift manager wanted to know if he had a good enough voice to go into radio himself. He'd been thinking of going to one of those schools that teach radio announcing—he even had some brochures—but maybe he'd be throwing his money away, and what was the point of that? He had a Midwestern voice—nothing wrong with it except that he sounded like everyone for hundreds of miles in any direction.

"They'll teach you how to work with it," she said. "Make it stand out more."

She had no idea if that was true, or even possible. She'd never had any real training. She rode in on nothing more than attitude and a great voice. Plus a connection of her mother's who'd gotten her the interview, maybe put in a word or two off-stage somewhere. But what the hell, it was a good idea, and if the schools didn't offer that, she'd planted an idea in the guy's head and he could work toward it himself.

He pushed her money back across the counter and told her the coffee and muffin were on him today.

It was as good as being on the air.

CHAPTER 16

 "I understand all that about mind control," Thor from Denver said. Nick typed in the cities and towns they were calling from now, and Annette used them on the air like last names. It was impressive, although who could tell if people told the truth about where they were calling from any more than they did about their names. Thor, for Chrissake. Who was going to name their kid Thor?

"What I don't understand," Thor said, "is why the Vietnamese would go along with it. I mean, what would they get out of the deal?"

"Let me explain this in words of one syllable, Thor. You start with Ho Chi Minh. I mean, here's a guy speaks eight languages fluently, knows how to order a cappuccino in eleven more, o.k.? Smuggles himself into China once disguised as a blind man, has dealings with the u.s. as early as 1940, when he's just some guy running around the jungle with pajamas and a gun. I mean, this guy's so smart he could've set the whole thing up and convinced our government they thought of it themselves. We'll probably never know. What looks possible, though, based on the information I have, is that there was a lot of genuine conflict among the Vietnamese factions, and that there was some initial genuine u.s. involvement in that, but at some point an agreement may have been reached that looked like it would be good for everyone. Our politicians got to look good because they were taking a tough stance with the Communists. The North Vietnamese got to look good because they were fighting the foreigners. The South Vietnamese got to look good because they had Uncle Sam on their side. The only people who lost were the American soldiers and taxpayers, right? The same people who usually lose: the little guy. The American middle class. What I do know is that through the International Control Commission, the South Vietnamese conducted secret negotiations with the North Vietnamese—these are supposed to be their enemies, remember. I mean, let's face it, no one wants to see their country torn to bits by a war if there's a way around it. I wouldn't be surprised if money changed hands in there somewhere, although I couldn't even begin to guess at this point who paid who, but I'd guess we're looking at a network of betrayal that reaches to the highest levels of our government. Even today, if the truth came out, we'd have politicians falling like dominoes. Are you with me, Thor?"

"I don't know. It could happen, I guess. It makes a crazy kind of sense."

"You're damn right it makes sense. Life is crazy."

She punched the next button.

"Nora from Richfield. Talk to me, Nora."

★

Another call from Len. Another meeting across the frozen steppes of his desk. Napoleon in Russia, retreating through snow up to the horses' thighs—or whatever horses have instead of thighs. The battle of Borodino. Or was Borodino a character in *War and Peace?*

Len opened a file folder and smiled. Annette smiled back and braced herself for the opening shot.

"We're going to move your show to afternoons and syndicate you," he said.

Pow, right to the heart.

"Say that again."

His smile began to look genuine.

"We can clear twenty-five stations by the end of next month. They won't be major markets, but they're stations."

She'd lost her own smile somewhere. Shot off its horse, probably and getting frostbite in the snow. She couldn't put any words together, so she sat expressionless and let him talk cities and time zones and Arbitron ratings. Somewhere along the line she realized she was grinning, and this was as much a surprise to her as anything else. Gradually the words coming out of Len's mouth sorted themselves into meaning and the meaning into thoughts and facts she had a running chance of remembering. She turned her grin down notch by notch and waited for him to come around to the question of money, and when he didn't come to it, she brought it up herself.

"We'll have to wait two or three books, see how it flies. This is a risk for us."

"A *risk*? Len, you couldn't lose on this if you tried."

He let out a sigh.

"Look, you're young, you're new at this, you don't know the business. There's a lot more involved here than you understand. We open you up to a wider audience, we open you up to public scrutiny. We open the station up to attack. You've had pretty much clear sailing up to now."

"How much will the station make on this?"

"Less than it should, frankly. You're controversial. A lot of stations won't touch you."

"Give 'em six months, they'll be begging for me."

It was the wrong thing to say. She knew it as soon as it left her mouth, even before Len agreed with her.

"In six months if they are, we'll talk money."

"Fine, then, I won't agree to syndication."

Len reached for a second folder.

"Let's review the language of your contract."

He had the page flagged: she'd granted the station the right to do everything but sell her into indentured servitude. Christ, who'd thought it would matter what she signed? It was her first contract; she hadn't planned on staying long enough to have to read it.

She called the station two hours later and said she had the flu, she wouldn't be in. She had the flu again two days later. On Monday, she left Len a message saying she was losing interest in the Vietnam issue and had been thinking it was time to move on to something fresh.

Islamic hordes, maybe. The fishing season. How women really felt about fashion.

By Wednesday he'd agreed to a $5,000 bonus as soon as the show cleared thirty-five stations, but instead of making her feel good, it made her feel like he'd choreographed every move she'd made and would have coughed up twice the money, and sooner, if she'd danced in some direction he hadn't been prepared for. She was irredeemably dumb. An idiot. A jerk. She couldn't say the right thing to Len if someone wrote her a script. And so when an agent called the next week and told her he'd heard all about her and she was hot, she was wonderful, she was great, she was his client before the phone call was over.

The syndicated show didn't feel much different from the local one: a few more calls from out of town, but the national audience had found her on its own, before syndication caught up with it. Who needed Len? The real difference was the afternoon slot: drive time, commuters calling from their cars, mothers who ran home day cares talking over the clash of pots and the wails of children, office workers calling after the boss left for a meeting at the bar or the gym, factory workers calling from their easy chairs after they'd extracted their feet from their steel-toed boots. Were there still factories in the U.S.? Weren't they all in Mexico or Indonesia or somewhere? O.K., no factory workers. Warehouse workers. Truck drivers. She knew there were still trucks. She'd seen them.

Now when she came to work there were bodies at the desks, voices talking into phones, names to remember, faces to say hello to. A producer—Amy, who turned out to spell her name Aimee— to answer phones for her. An engineer wasn't good enough any-more, and for everything that had gone wrong between her and Nick, she missed his quiet, chewing bulk behind the window, a sort of solid background she showed up nicely against. Aimee looked like she was fresh out of college. Or high school. This was her first job as a producer, and she typed with all ten fingers and was sharp and upbeat and friendly. In the control room she was all aren't-I-cute and visual noise. The Aimee Show.

After a week and a half of that, Annette ended her show with a headache and the only cure she could think of was sitting on the steps with an almost-cold beer and looking through the dark at moths and trees. In the absence of moths and trees, a blank wall might work.

Neither one was available.

Len was standing in the door of his office and called her over. Aimee stood up from her desk as if anything that concerned Annette concerned her as well, and Annette's mind scrabbled for a way to tell Len that she didn't need a producer. She and Nick had done fine together, and wasn't there an engineer on the day shift who could answer phones and chew carrots for her?

"How're you two doing together?"

Annette's mouth opened and said, "Good enough."

Aimee said, "Great," lapping her words over Annette's and giving Len a cheerleader's thousand-watt smile. Two, four, six, eight, everything I see is great. Rock, tree, bottomless chasm, I have such enthusiasm.

"Good," Len said. "That's good. Tell you what I want here." His eyes were trying to drill past Annette's surface and a hand sought out Aimee's shoulder in a gesture of protection, making it clear who he was talking to and who he was talking about. "I want you to use her for research."

"I do my own research."

"Use her. Anyone trips you up, this whole thing's going to come apart."

Annette nodded, trying to locate the part of her soul in which she actually meant yes, but it had gone south somewhere, looking for moths, trees, summer air, almost-cold beers. She smiled, but it felt off-center and unconvincing. Time did its best to pass, but it failed, and the three of them stood there like a tableau, Len's eyes telling Annette, *Don't fuck with me,* his hand telling Aimee that he was more powerful than Annette so she didn't have to worry about a thing.

Eventually time did move on, as it will if you wait long enough, even when you're with the Lens of the world, and the tableau broke apart, leaving Annette free to drive home listening to ole Perry and wondering what she could give Aimee to gnaw on.

By the time she got home, the clear answer was *nothing.* She didn't trust her enough. Except maybe with Borodino—she'd trust her to check into Borodino—but she couldn't see either Aimee or Len thinking that was funny. She'd have to come up with something. Len wasn't going to leave this alone.

She hated being in the studio when Len was around.

CHAPTER 17

Their regular waitress greeted Annette by name now, and smiled past Stan as if it didn't matter whether she knew his name or not.

"Usual?" she asked Annette.

"Yolks raw, whites set, two percent, and will you do something for me? Ask the cook to spread the butter all the way to the edges of the toast. Tell him to spread it so it laps over the crust and coats the underside."

"Got it."

The waitress took Stan's order and left, and Stan picked up the argument she'd interrupted.

"Cincinnati," he said. "We'll promote the hell out of it: Annette Majoris goes where the vets are. Court the local media, broadcast it nationally, it'll break their hearts."

"Yeah, but Cincin*nati*," she said.

By way of supporting evidence, Stan flapped a set of mailing labels on the table between them: look, see, count.

"We've got more names in Cincinnati than in any city in the country. They love you. Plus we've got a Constructive chapter that can find us a hall, provide security. And Bitterman can be convinced on this. I'm sure of it."

"But Cincin*nati*—."

Instead of arguing, Stan shrugged—hey, it's not my fault Cincinnati loves you. He set a manila folder on top of the mailing labels.

"I've been unraveling an interesting thread," he said, tapping the folder he hadn't really handed over yet.

Annette turned the folder toward her and flipped pages as Stan talked, not so much to read what was on them as to annoy Stan. Cincinnati, for Chrissake. It was past the end of the earth. But from the way she was thinking about it, she could tell Stan had won.

Aimee was fishing for something in her purse when Annette pushed through the studio door at the end of her show and she didn't look up to do the social basics, which left Annette free to contemplate her bent back, her flowing hair, and wonder if she could trust her to check some of Stan's research. The CIA and the LSD experiments maybe; the reporter—Karnow; Glenda Martinez; Nguyen Cao Ky. The nephew who gave her the Martha Mitchell column. It wasn't that she didn't believe what she was saying, she reminded herself, and it wasn't that she didn't trust Stan, but this thing was escalating—Len was right about that much—and it was making her nervous. Cincinnati, the media, the Wallace Burkes of the world. What she wanted, just to make herself feel better, was independent verification that these people existed, and that they'd actually done what they were supposed to have done. Christ, what if Stan was wrong? What if he'd set up every one of her breakthrough callers, maybe even the hang-up calls she no longer got at home? What if none of it was real?

She could have done the cross-checking herself, except of course that she couldn't. She'd tried a couple of times but it messed with her on-air attitude. You can't believe and disbelieve at the same time. You have to set one or the other aside. It felt like stretching her luck even to ask Aimee.

Aimee straightened up, holding a bottle of cold pills she'd salvaged from the bottom of her bag, and she smiled brilliantly and meaninglessly at Annette.

"I've got the worst cold," she said. "I couldn't live ten minutes without these."

Annette was still thinking about Stan, about research, about whether a private individual could orchestrate a scam on the scale she was contemplating. She nodded vaguely in Aimee's direction.

"Had it all week. Len told me to try these. They're fantastic."

Annette nodded some more. Len. Of course. You could hear it in the way she said his name: Aimee was sleeping with Len. She couldn't keep herself from talking about him, even if it was only to tell Annette about cold pills. For a smart woman, she really was dumb. So forget the research and trust Stan. Walter did. Hell, even the governor did—the future fucking president. You couldn't have that many people, and that caliber of people, involved if the whole thing was made out of smoke. Her callers couldn't all be crazy, and they couldn't all be fakes. It wasn't statistically possible. Relax. Breathe. All she was doing was raising questions.

It would all be fine.

From the moment she got off the plane, Cincinnati depressed her. For starters, it was raining, and Walter hadn't been able to come with her. Meetings, he said: fund-raising for the governor, mending fences with the religious wing of the party, and all of it had to happen on these two particular days. Plus Cincinnati was one more damn city that wasn't New York. And she was traveling with Stan. Her chaperone. Her duenna. The genie who granted her wishes but never quite the way she wished them. Wasn't that the way it worked with genies? Hadn't some book she read in fourth grade warned her about that? If he ever got her to New York, it would be to Buffalo, or to Schenectady, not to the city, and then he wouldn't understand what she was upset about. Wasn't Schenectady in New York, after all? On top of which, traveling with Stan meant sitting next to him on the plane, walking with him through the airport, letting everyone who passed by think she was his daughter, or his . . .

Nope. No one was allowed to think that. End of topic.

They'd rented her a hall that was windowless, modern, and dismal, and by the time they walked in, Stan's people had laid out their brochures and booklets and sign-up sheets, and a TV crew was setting up. Annette retreated to the bathroom. She looked in the mirror, poked at her hair. Head up, back straight, fuck 'em all; she was as ready as she'd ever be. She strode in and gave channel something-or-other news a few minutes of I'm-no-expert-but-how-can-I-ignore-what-my-listeners-are-telling-me. She held steady, looked the interviewer in the eye, and she was the people's tribune, the voice of the voiceless and forgotten, America's great and mistreated middle class. All a person had to do was listen to these tales and they'd break your heart. By that time people were drifting in, and in spite of herself, she felt a jolt of excitement. It was a different crowd than she'd had in Minnesota. They walked through the door like they weren't ashamed to be seen listening to her.

By the time she started, she was looking at a full house—O.K., a nearly full house—dotted here and there with bits of army uniforms on the vets who'd saved them and still fit into them. Or who'd stopped at the army surplus store on their way to the show. How would she know? The crowd was mixed again—a few more blacks than in Minneapolis, actually—but that was all right, she was getting used to it, and she launched her opening explanations: the floor mic, the seven deadly words, vets only at the mic, please—anyone else was welcome to call her during a regular show. They filed to the mic and waited, forming a line straight down the center aisle.

Her on-the-air opening started from zero, making it easy for anyone who was new to the show: mind control, the government, the nation's forgotten, by which she meant not just veterans but the great American middle class, the overtaxed, the overgoverned, the underrepresented, the people who were sitting in front of her today, many of them veterans but many who had been born, as she had, too late to remember the war themselves but who understood that the veterans' pain was their own.

And so on, with great intensity. Whatever doubts she'd had fell away. You couldn't stand in front of a crowd like this and have doubts. She was a channel for their pain with no will of her own.

The first man who spoke had a gray ponytail and an army-green jacket, and he testified that the blocks the army had implanted in his memory were breaking down. If he hadn't heard what other people had been through, he'd think he was going crazy. The lights people had talked about . . . He broke down and wept. The lights . . . He pulled an arm across his nose and snarked. The lights were a kind of hypnotic thing. One of his memories . . .

His voice broke. Annette was getting used to this. She almost whispered. It would be o.k. They had all the time in the world. The air was electric.

"It used to be just an awful memory, you know, but now it's all broken up with that light, the way the fan blade kind of chops it up, and I know I don't want to do what they're telling me, but they've got that light moving around, and I can't seem to help it."

She gave him half a second, then asked what it was that they wanted him to do. She expected tears, but he held together nicely.

"I don't want to tell you the details—it's too ugly, and I'm not sure I could get through it anyway—so let's put it this way: I hurt someone. I mean, you do that in war but this was . . ."

He sucked a breath in, got rid of it.

"Sometimes it seemed to me he was v.c.—you know, Vietcong—but sometimes I thought he was like me. I just couldn't tell, you know?"

Annette knew. The whole audience knew, and it murmured its knowledge like healing water lapping gently at his ankles: yes, the man could have been just like him. Annette invited him to write her at the station if he thought he could put the memory on paper any more easily than he could say it. It would help him free himself of it. And it was important. It would help her piece together a picture of what had really happened.

The fourth speaker introduced herself as a former army nurse, then tore into Annette. It wasn't just the American deaths that had to be accounted for but the Vietnamese deaths, the deforestation, the wreckage of planes that had been shot down, Agent Orange, the Tet Offensive . . .

The woman was tall, with an army jacket, graying red hair, and a neck that jutted her head forward like a buzzard's, and she let her voice get tight, which made her sound hysterical and bitchy. A fistful of people in a back corner clapped and cheered for her, but they sounded small and lost in the crowd. Annette gave the woman a minute to make herself unpopular, then signaled the engineer to cut the floor mic.

"I'm going to cut in here," she said, keeping her voice low and easy as the woman continued to push her taut voice as far into the room as she could get it. "I let you speak because I want to hear all sides, but we came here tonight to listen to people's personal experience of what happened, not to hear political speeches. If you want to call my show, I'll be glad to talk this out with you."

The woman was still yelling—she was a vet, and censorship and fear of the truth and one thing and another—and a pair of men with security armbands showed up on either side of her but she got a stranglehold on the mic, and it took them a while to pry her loose. Meanwhile her friends were out of their seats and yelling along with her "Let her talk" and "What are you afraid of?" and a few of the others—Annette's people, the real audience—were yelling, "Sit down" and "Shut up," while Annette narrated it like a football game for the radio audience: a small group of protesters, disruptive, refusing to give up the microphone, afraid of hearing what the veterans have to say, and we've heard some things this afternoon that would disturb anyone, but these people came here with their minds closed, and damn she was good. She stepped back from herself, listening to her voice, knowing how easy it would be to clutch and freeze but here she was, doing a tap dance to the crowd's uneven rhythm and not missing a step.

A few minutes into the uproar, she thought to ask the audience to stay calm and let the security people handle it, but the truth was they were already staying calm. If it had ever been true that Vietnam vets were bone-deep spooked and ready to explode into violence, it had been a long time ago. They were middle-aged now—they were older than middle-aged—and glad enough to sit and yell while the security crew handled the problem. Still, she reminded them that everyone had a right to an opinion, which cast her as sweet reason incarnate.

It was a good five minutes before the engineer could turn the floor mic back on, and by then they'd all passed through the fire together. Whatever people knew, they were ready to share, and it was in this spirit that she unearthed the first clear memory of what had actually gone on. A small, sandy-haired guy took the mic, and tears poured out of his eyes freely before he'd said anything worth crying over. Annette had pretty well written him off as a nut case and was about to get rid of him when he sketched out a scenario that jerked her to a halt. What he remembered was, in a word, everything.

"The thing you got to understand is the battles were real," he said, whole rivers flowing down his face but his voice holding steady. "They were as real as me standing here. They'd divide us up like you'd divide up teams for a baseball game, and it was our guys on both sides."

Entire watersheds drained through his eyes.

"It was our guys. I'm telling you. It was our guys."

Annette pulled at him gently, reaching for how he knew this, but she couldn't get at it. What she got instead was detail: rice paddies, jungle, a patrol, a buddy's brains blown all over a rock.

"And it was our own guys who did that. Our own guys. We'd've done it to them. Hell, we did do it to them. I don't blame them. It's not their fault. It wasn't our fault either."

Oceans flowed out of his eyes.

"They set us on each other like dogs. And they told us it was the enemy. That was the thing. We all thought we were fighting the enemy."

They broke loose after that, pouring themselves into the space he'd shown them, remembering how they'd caught glimpses of faces they knew among the enemy, just glimpses, disappearing so fast they could almost believe they'd imagined it. At the time, they told themselves they had.

Stan met Annette as she came off the stage, talking double-speed about war crimes, the UN, defense of the Constitution. He was red faced and furious. She'd never seen him so happy. Then he moved aside so the men from the audience could bunch around and tell her how even now they couldn't sleep. One by one they thanked her and shook her hand and told her they couldn't sleep.

By the time they were gone, the Ohio Constructive had packed up its booklets and brochures and Stan had come back to tell her what a success she'd been. He was the first in line and the last, the alpha and the omega, death and taxes. The last of the audience drifted out into the late afternoon, and someone from the Cincinnati Constructive bustled over to say a word in Stan's ear. Stan turned from him to Annette.

"You've hit the big time. You've got your very own protestors outside."

"No shit?"

"A couple-three dozen of them out there, all screaming their lungs out."

"Well, you know what they say: you're nobody until somebody hates you."

Stan agreed, but if he caught the joke he was hiding it well. Already he was turning to the man who'd whispered in his ear—a stocky guy in, maybe, his forties, muscles melting into fat, making him look like he was made of candle wax.

Tallow, her brain told her. Whatever tallow was, candles used to be made of it.

"How many men do we have?" Stan asked the tallowman.

"About a dozen." He turned to count. "Eleven. Plus Rog Busch's wife is still here."

"Tell you what we do. It's Annette they'll be looking for, and I don't want a confrontation when the numbers are this uneven. Is there a back door?"

"Sets off an alarm system."

"Right."

He looked around the room as if he expected some other door to make itself known to him. Was it Moses who struck the rock and turned it into a fountain? Or was that Jesus? Or Mickey Mouse as the sorcerer's apprentice? Whoever it was, it wasn't Stan, because he was still looking around and hadn't found any rocks.

"I'll be all right," Annette said. "I saw them when they were in the back yelling. They're no threat."

Stan turned to the tallowman, ignoring her.

"We'll go out as a group, keep the girls in the center. Any trouble at all, a few of the men stay behind, focus the attention on themselves, everyone else gets the girls to the car."

Annette turned away and watched the rest of the group gather itself in a huddle. She wasn't going to have an impact on what Stan and the tallowman decided anyway. She wasn't a particularly physical person—she hadn't been in a fight since Lori Katz hit her over the head with a wooden block in the third grade—and she couldn't quite take this seriously. Stan and the tallowman were comparing parking places now—who'd parked closer and where they could rendezvous if they put the girls in someone-or-other's minivan, which was parked it-didn't-matter-where-but they went on and on about it, arguing about whether close was better or ran the risk of et cetera.

They were enjoying themselves, and she gave herself over to whatever decisions they made.

It was sweet, actually, all these men trying to protect her.

They finally assembled by the door, although it took long enough that the situation's charm was beginning to wear thin, and they waited while one of the men turned the lights out and made his way back to them by the light from the heavy glass doors.

Rog Busch's wife (who the hell was Rog Busch anyway?) and an older man each picked up a box of brochures, booklets, whatever they had left, abandoning an equal number of empty boxes, and the group pushed through the doors into the raw damp outside. The younger men locked themselves in a tight orbit around Annette and the two box carriers, and the entire solar system propelled itself through a universe of jeering demonstrators, who were all wearing bits of old uniforms. Whatever else Annette had done, she'd freed those uniforms from the backs of America's closets. Within seconds the demonstrators' jeers coalesced into a chant of *liar, liar, liar,* like schoolyard name-calling, and it kept on until they were almost past, when the rhythm collapsed and a layer of men peeled away from her right flank. Annette turned to see where they'd gone, but Stan pulled her forward and to the left, and all she got was a glimpse of some half a dozen people shoving each other and the rest of the demonstrators, as far as she could tell, standing by and yelling. Then she was around the corner, still being pulled by the orbit of her planets, as if the hounds of hell, the little gray aliens, and the federal government's space program were all chasing them across the sky.

CHAPTER 18

 Rendezvousing turned out to be a lot like meeting a bunch of people in a bar and giving it a military name. How did the military ever get hold of this one lone French phrase and make it sound American enough that a guy like Stan would use it? Stan, who thought he needed shots to order a pizza.

They met in the bar of Annette and Stan's hotel, and they drank a round while they waited till the men who'd peeled away from the group to play push-and-shove with the demonstrators joined them. Then they drank a round to celebrate the men's safe arrival, and they listened to the war stories the men told, which didn't amount to much, but they'd pumped themselves to the top of a fight-or-flight high and couldn't find anything to do with the energy but tell stories and laugh too loud until they'd talked themselves down.

Annette meant to leave as soon as she had a chance to thank the warriors, but someone ordered a third round, and the glow from the men on either side of her spread outward and met in the perfect center of Annette Majoris until she couldn't tell it from her own glow, so she drank her screwdriver, which the man on her left insisted on calling a vodka-orange, and she stayed.

Rog Busch's wife (maybe one of these men was Rog Busch; how would she know?) invited Annette to her house for dinner, and Annette said she had plans but thanks, and she was damn near looped enough to wish she'd accepted. If the whole group had been invited, she'd have gone. It was the idea of being alone and growing slowly sober with this wife and presumably her husband, whoever he might be, that made her say no.

By the time she headed back to her room, she was seeing a sunburst of colored needles in the air around the elevator's globe light and she was weepily, sentimentally lonely. She stretched out on the bed and called Walter.

"The thing is, Stan was great," she told him. "They were all great. You go through something like that—it's not like you expect. You end up feeling close to people you wouldn't piss on if you passed them on the street."

That wasn't the way she'd meant to explain it. She liked these people, she just had a weakness for colorful overstatement. But even so, she expected Walter to be impressed with the revelation she'd had. Instead he got stuffy and teacherish on her, talking to her in that voice men use with drunks, hysterics, and women.

"You shouldn't underestimate these people. You're judging them on the basis of their style."

"I'm not judging them at all. Christ, I just told you, they were great."

"You see?"

"See what? I'm not saying they should all get thrown off the planet—I just wouldn't have expected to want to spend time with them. And I enjoyed it. What's wrong with that?"

They were on the edge of a fight, and she received this knowledge with the thrill of a skier looking down the slope of the ski jump. Fighting was like dancing. It was like sex. It was a way for two people to know each other. Maybe it was what their relationship needed.

"There's nothing wrong with that," he said. "All I'm saying is don't underestimate them. Those are your listeners. They're your fans."

"Don't talk to me like I'm an idiot. I'm making an observation about the world. Most of my listeners aren't people I'd choose to spend my free time with. And neither would you."

And so on, back and forth. He wouldn't cross the line to an open fight so she fought with him over that, but it was all somehow less satisfying than it should have been, and she let him patch it back together before she hung up, then she slept until she was sober enough to go out for dinner. Stan had told her earlier that he had a meeting, and she'd been looking forward to eating alone someplace nice, someplace Stan would hate, but that turned out to be unsatisfying too. All right, it turned out to be one more hue in the infinite rainbow of loneliness. No one knew who she was. She was just one more woman eating alone because she was too much of a loser to get a date. And then in the hotel lobby some guy came at her from behind a pillar like a spring-loaded monster jumping off the wall in a funhouse. He was in his fifties but big, imposing—shit, threatening—and he was yelling about Vietnam and his buddies dying and not being able to sleep, and for a second she was sure he was going to hit her, but even so she couldn't seem to make herself step out of his way, or even say anything. All she could do was stand there looking at him like he was a bug on her breakfast table. After an endless couple of seconds, she stepped backward and he stepped forward like this was some graceless, slow-motion folk dance they'd rehearsed together—Morris dancing without the bells. He was on about the jungle now, and helicopters, and MIAs, and Ho Chi Minh. She stepped sideways. He stepped sideways. He spread his arms and yelled that she couldn't walk away from him, she couldn't punch a button and cut him off, she was going to have to hear him out. Then the desk clerk appeared on one side of him and a big guy in a suit came up on the other and they asked Annette if he was bothering her. The cavalry riding over the hill. She expected him to cut and run, but he kept on yelling while they told him he'd have to leave. He didn't even look at them, and barely noticed when they grabbed his arms and hauled at them. His voice got louder—he was yelling about retribution now—and he let them pull him to the front door and out. The door closed behind them, and the lobby went silent. A tiny, silver-haired woman had set down her Barnes & Noble bag to watch—forget the books, this was live action—and a pair of Japanese businessmen had turned their backs to the check-in desk, hungry to see act two. All of them turned to Annette now, although outside the glass door the protestor and the men from the hotel were doing a pantomime of Go Away and I Would Prefer Not To. Annette stalked across the lobby to the elevator, taking care not to catch her shoes on the carpet.

Her finger, when she pushed the button for her floor, was shaking, and so was the arm attached to it. It was all a measure of her success, or at least she told herself that. You rattle cages, somebody's going to snarl, and the guy was an asshole, a loser, a man with worse taste than Stan or any of her listeners.

The elevator doors opened on her floor, but instead of getting out, she flattened herself against the wall. What if he'd brought a whole battalion of nuts with him? What if the battalion of nuts had brought *him*, and sent him downstairs as a decoy? What if the rest of them had hidden in the hallway just out of sight and were waiting to do who knew what? The doors closed. For several seconds the elevator cage hung immobile, and she could have pointed her finger at the buttons again, noticed that the finger was still shaking, and made the door open. She focused on this possibility as if it was some arcane problem in geometry—there was a lot to consider here; she couldn't just jump in. Or out, actually. Then the cage dropped and the decision fell away. The doors opened on the lobby, and a bellman waited for her to step out so he could push a cartful of luggage in. She stepped out. In spite of herself, she was waiting for someone to jump out of she wasn't sure where—the other elevator; the former ashtray, which had been given new life as a depository for candy wrappers and kleenex; the blue Samsonite suitcase squatting on the floor beside the check-in desk, its owner off wandering somewhere. When no one did jump out, she made a sharp left to the house phones and rang Stan.

Who wasn't in.

Who'd be out with his Ohio counterparts plotting the downfall of the federal government. Or its radical shrinkage. Or whatever the hell it was they had in mind for it. Christ, the one time she really needed the man . . .

She hung up the phone and marched back to the elevators, feeling like a set of neon arrows was hanging in midair, pointing to her, and above them floated a sign that read Acting Very Strange. Well to hell with anyone who was watching. Head up, back straight, and fuck 'em all. The door opened and she stepped in and rode to the fourth floor—the floor above hers. Her finger had stopped shaking. When the doors opened she stepped into a hallway identical to the one on her floor—fleur-de-lis carpet, a double line of closed doors behind which (she never really thought they would be) no one was hiding. She marched toward the exit sign—head up, back straight, if anyone jumped her all she had to do was yell *fire*—and pushed open the door.

The staircase had been transplanted from some very different building—a prison, maybe, or a housing project. It was all gray paint, metal, cement. Her heels made a sharp *tock* on the uncushioned steps, tapping out the Morse code for *she's on her way, get ready to jump out at her*. All her life she'd had nightmares about this staircase. Christ, if she didn't find a protestor crouched around the turn of the stairs, she'd find some guy slumped over with a needle in his arm instead. Head up, back straight. She turned the bend, and the stairs were empty. As she'd known they would be. No one really believes that kind of thing. It's just noise, static, the vestigial remains of a time when the species had saber-toothed tigers to be scared of. She turned the final corner and pulled at the door.

Which didn't open. She gave it a series of sharp yanks, trying to make it rattle, but it was well built. No rattle, no snarl, no one opening it from the other side and asking if everything was all right.

She looked upstairs. She looked down. Her breath came in shallow, panicky puffs, and she chose down—it was easier going, and on the first floor the door would have to be unlocked. Or if it wasn't, someone in the lobby would hear her.

Actually, not that much thought went into it. Down looked better than up, that's all. Her heels tapped out an essay on panic, on drug addicts, on the social decay that led degenerates to slump in the staircases decent people might have to use. If she got herself out of here, she'd feed the hotel manager into a buzzsaw. She was paying good money for this room, after all.

O.K., the station was paying. Or the corporation that owned her station. However it worked. The point was, someone was forking out money here and, sure, it wasn't the Plaza, but it wasn't some fleabag no-star hotel either. She had a right to expect . . .

But really it wasn't about protestors or drug addicts as much as it was about staircases and locked doors. It was about saber-toothed tigers. It was panic in its purest form, and it wasn't beholden to anything as small-minded as a reason. She hurled her weight against the downstairs door and exploded into the lobby, gaping at the carpeting, at the bellman pushing his empty cart toward the front door, at the chandelier, which was cheesy but it was a sign, a dove released directly from the hand of God to say the flood was over and here was a land people could walk upon without waders.

She stood in the lobby blinking, feeling like she'd spent the past year in a cave and her eyes had to relearn light.

As soon as they had, she tried Stan again, and when he didn't answer, she bought herself a copy of *People* and settled into a loveseat facing the front door to wait for him. She didn't like the man, but the minute he walked through the door she knew she'd be safe.

★

Stan paced in front of his hotel room's curtained window, not evenly but in spurts, while Annette sat composed and steady in the hotel armchair. She was, Stan had to admit, one hell of a woman. No fits, no hysteria. It was just as well Walter Bishop had put the moves on her first or Stan would have and—he had no illusions about this—he'd have messed everything up.

"I should've seen this coming," he said. He strode to the other end of the drapes, setting the oversight behind him, and lifted the edge of the curtain to look out. What he saw told him nothing. The usual dark-light mix of a city at night. No one floating in midair to test out secret government hardware. No solution to his problem printed on the night air. He let the curtain fall.

"Here's the thing," he said. "I could have someone with you twenty-four hours a day, but it'd drive you nuts. It can be worse than having people jump out and threaten you. So that's the first problem, is figuring out when you need protection and when you don't."

Annette nodded but didn't say anything. She was a little subdued maybe, but still, Stan had to admire her. He paced to the far end of the drapes and looked out from that side. It wasn't just the mechanics of setting up a bodyguard, although that was headache enough. It was the picture of Flambard sitting in Annette's living room with his shoes off and his sock-feet propped on her coffee table, showing the thin spot across the ball of the foot where he'd worn the fuzz off every pair of socks he owned, leaving the weave like a grid across his skin.

If someone had asked which of them he was feeling protective of, Annette or Flambard, he wouldn't have been able to say.

And then there was the problem of money. Flambard was no problem that way, but the minute she needed more than Flambard and maybe a volunteer to fill in here and there, they were talking serious money. Or more serious than the Constructive could handle without becoming even more politically indebted to Bishop and his friends than they already were.

So twenty-four hours was out, even though when he imagined someone going after her, it was the tree-enclosed parking lot of the radio station that he pictured, and second to that the bare parking lot of her apartment building, which he'd reconnoitered a couple of times. He dropped the curtain and turned back into the room.

"What makes the most sense is to have someone with you before and after public appearances. Strange cities, lots of promotion—these people want to bother you, they only have one day to do it before you leave town. It concentrates them, if you take my point."

She nodded. It made him nervous, having her leave this much empty space in a conversation. Made him feel like he had to fill it for her. He stuffed his hands in his pockets to keep them from lifting the curtains again and opening a tunnel back into the dark.

"If there's any problem—any problem at all—we'll expand the coverage. Have someone with you any time you're in public, drive you to work. Whatever you need."

CHAPTER 19

 Annette's agent, when she called him from the airport, didn't have anything concrete to offer. Sure, he was sympathetic. It was terrible, and how could someone, and she must've been scared half to, and of course he'd see what he could, but the problem was the contract, it was a terrible contract, and if only she'd brought him in at an earlier stage, but once these things were signed, and what it came down to was that it made no provision for security, and that meant that until he found a way out of the contract—and he was working on that—the problem was hers, although he did know some security outfits she could talk to if she was interested in setting that up herself. But he might as well tell her up front that they weren't cheap.

What she had to do was wait, keep a list of these issues as they came up, and have faith in him. When the time came, she'd get her own back and more.

Except for the sympathy, she might as well have been talking to Len. It wasn't going to do any good, but she explained all over again about the guy in the hotel, and the staircase. Her voice ran high on the scale, threatening to spin into the infrared. The agent gave her a shorter version of why he couldn't do anything for her yet, followed by three reasons he had to get off the phone.

★

Another show back in the studio. Two shows. Many shows. Len must've found something for Aimee to do, because he stopped pestering Annette to use her. The only research she did for Annette anymore was to put together a news summary, and Annette had to ask for it—she wouldn't just leave it in her box. Aimee had a single folder open on her desk—she must have caught the habit from Len, along with who knew what else—and she handed Annette some stapled sheets without bothering to look up, as if, hey, there was important stuff going on around here and radio shows were only a by-product, so she couldn't be bothered to look up every time the talent wanted a news summary.

Maybe she was in a snit because Annette hadn't given her anything to research. And maybe she wasn't. Screw her—there was no reason Annette had to care, except of course that she did. The woman didn't have to like her, but she could at least look up when she was being unfriendly.

Annette took the summary back to the studio to breeze through it. She didn't use the summaries much—everything other than Vietnam was out of bounds until Stan found the links she'd asked about—but you could never tell when something relevant would pop up and Stan would miss it. Besides, it made her feel professional.

The unemployment rate; Saint Paul's mayor; the Middle East; terrorists and more terrorists, plus a few suspected terrorists; homeland security; China and Taiwan; Indonesia, Iraq, Iran, and Pakistan; explosions. Nothing, nothing, and nothing. The governor was calling for an investigation of Area 51. Now that was interesting.

Ten minutes till she was on the air. She called Walter's number and got his machine.

"Hey, it's Annette. How come you didn't tell me about the governor?"

She stayed on the line a few seconds as if she expected an answer, then she hung up.

She tossed back the last of the coffee.

Five minutes till she was on the air. Aimee tritzed into the control room and gave her a stunning, meaningless smile.

She was on the air.

"Ladies and gentlemen, boys and girls, fish and fowl, this is *Open Line*, I'm Annette Majoris, and it's just you and me here, no guests, no experts, nothing to stand between us. Give me a call, because I'm waiting to hear from you."

She gave out the phone number, did the seven-second delay explanation, watched the names line up on the screen. With no warning, a weight landed on her shoulders, and she was tired to death of Vietnam. She couldn't remember if this was new or if she'd felt it before—something about it was vaguely familiar—but she wanted to talk about the length of the school year, the length of the fishing season, anything, please, but Vietnam.

The price of success.

"I'm sitting here with the news from the wire services, friends, and Bill Ruoma—that's Minnesota's esteemed governor, a very smart guy, rumored to have his eye on the presidency, for those of you who live in more interesting states or who live in Minnesota but have been in a coma for the past few years—Bill Ruoma's calling for a federal investigation of Area 51. So what I want to know is, what do you think? Can the feds investigate themselves and do an honest job of it? Is there anyone out there with memories of Area 51, and if there is, would you risk testifying at a federal investigation?"

She pushed the first button.

"Martin, talk to me."

Annette and Walter lay on their backs with the sheet pulled up to their necks. Sex hadn't gotten any better, but she'd stopped expecting it to. Well, most of the time she'd stopped expecting it to. Walter seemed happy enough with it.

The clock on his side of the bed projected the time in red numbers on the far wall. He'd explained the clock to her the first night she spent with him: it read the time directly from the U.S. atomic clock in someplace or other. Government intervention. The idea of it would drive Stan crazy.

She turned on her side to face Walter, who was breathing softly. How was it that she couldn't love this man? He didn't even snore.

★

On her way home the next morning, she stopped at Barnes & Noble and flipped through the sex advice books. They told her to find out what he liked, to find out what she liked, although not necessarily in that order. She knew what he liked—anything that didn't involve imagination—and before she met him, she'd known what she liked well enough that she'd never needed advice. It wasn't that he touched the wrong places, or didn't touch the right ones. The problem was that he touched them the wrong way—either nothing happened at all or it hurt. She could take a magic marker and draw lines and circles and arrows all over her body—touch this, kiss that, spin around three times and tickle this other with a peacock feather—and it still wouldn't help. He wasn't the sort of man who liked hurting her—it just happened. Wasn't that her luck. Here she'd found the perfect man, and she couldn't stand for him to touch her.

The manuals told her to talk to him. Right. Sweetie, you know all that moaning I've been doing? Well, it didn't mean what you thought it meant. Why don't we let my agent explain. Hell, she'd signed a contract with Walter as surely as she had with the station, and it would be just as hard to renegotiate.

She left the store without buying anything.

Later in the week she asked if he'd ever watched sex movies. She'd watched them a couple of times with guys she'd just as soon forget about, and the movies didn't do much for her—

actually, they'd been kind of gross when they weren't too silly to take seriously—but anything that expanded the range of possibilities between her and Walter had to be good. It was morning and she was rummaging through the refrigerator, feeling vaguely like she'd stayed overnight with a teenager whose parents had stocked the kitchen and gone out of town. Maybe that was why she'd thought about sex movies—it all seemed so teenaged.

When she pulled her head out of the refrigerator to look at him, he was blushing.

"You want some of this quiche?" he said.

"I mean, they're not my thing, but I just thought I'd ask because, you know, if it's something you . . . you know, it's O.K. by me."

Christ, that was graceful. How could any man resist? The good news was that Walt didn't seem to have heard: he just slid quiche onto two plates. Julia Child or whatever her name was, the woman who cooked his food for him, had even sliced it. She caught a glimpse of herself married to Walter and rummaging through the refrigerator for both of them, taking over the pushing of microwave buttons. It depressed her, although she wasn't sure why.

The microwave's bell rang and Walter carried their plates to the table. When he turned, instead of wearing the distant look she expected, he was radiating at her.

"What?" she said.

He radiated harder and set out forks and napkins.

"What?"

"Nothing. You look good in my robe."

"Huh."

She was still standing, although he had not only slid into his chair but was starting to eat.

"Sit," he said. "Eat. I have something I want to talk to you about."

She wavered, half of her wanting a fight, the other half grateful to talk about anything other than sex. Then, because she couldn't think of anything other than sex to fight about, she sat.

"What?"

He radiated. He glowed. His skin held in so much pleasure he was in danger of exploding.

"Bill's planning a public meeting with a group of so-called Vietnam-era veterans. About Area 51. He wants you to introduce him."

"Huh."

He leaned toward her, one arm on either side of his plate, bare branches behind him on the other side of the windows, his most charming smile still looking fresh on his face after all this time with no encouragement from her. He was at his best when he was working on getting his way.

"He's not stealing your format," he said. "He'd love to—it's a brilliant format—but it's yours, and he understands that. Or he understands it now that I warned him off it. He'll have to find his own format. All he's doing here is giving a speech, and he can do it without you if he has to, but he'd like your endorsement. It'd mean a lot."

The cuff of his pajama sleeve made a neat line under the cuff of his robe. She focused on that and made indecisive noises and generally put him off, all as effectively as a virgin trying to brush a boy's hand off her breast without hurting his feelings.

"This isn't like you," he said, taking one of her hands in both of his and reaching his fingers under the cuff of her robe, which was his robe, actually, she'd never gotten around to bringing her own. "You're great at this sort of thing. You're perfect."

She pulled her hand away.

"It's exactly like me. I hate live appearances. I always did hate them. Plus that guy in Cincinnati. I'm suffering from posttraumatic shock. He really upset me."

He was nodding in sympathy, one nod to a sentence, yes, yes, I understand the problem, I take you seriously, becoming more radiant and serious with each nod.

"The thing is, Annette, Bill needs you, or he thinks he does, and that means it's an opening for you—an opportunity. Last week he got rid of Chris Markham because you're more important to him than Chris is. And believe me, Chris had his uses. You want to spend the rest of your life broadcasting from a flyspeck of a station in the frozen north? This guy's going to take off, and he's going to take people with him, but if he finds out he doesn't need you—well, politics is a cold business. You'll be nothing more to him than someone he has to be polite to because you're my girlfriend."

Annette pulled the robe tighter, got up and poured herself more coffee. She didn't come back to the table but leaned against the entryway to the breakfast room instead.

"You need this guy," Walter told her. She'd never seen him this serious, or this stern. "Unless you think Stan and his people can take you to the top."

"I never said they could."

It was a lame comeback, but it was all she could manage. She commanded all the suavity and grace of a pouting ten-year-old right now.

"I'll tell him you'll do it, then?"

"I'll think about it."

He looked at his watch, which he never took off unless he was immersed in water. Even the minutes projecting themselves in a procession on the bedroom wall weren't enough to make him sleep without it.

"I've got a better idea. You don't call me by 10:35 to say no, I'll tell him you'll do it."

She didn't answer and they had a staring contest, which neither of them won.

"And I plan to be inaccessible until 10:36."

"You're an asshole."

He heard the concession buried under the words and lost the serious look.

"Ah, but one with your interests at heart."

CHAPTER 20

 The governor had chosen a VFW hall as the backdrop for his speech, and Walt swore to her that it was rented, that she wasn't walking into a veterans' organization with a vested interest in believing the war was real. And maybe he'd rented the crowd too, because it went off without a hitch and afterwards they had a late supper with the governor, who'd dumped his aides with all their clipboards but kept the high energy he'd assembled for his appearance. They went to a northern Italian place—valet parking, private dining room, a maître d' saying, "Good evening, Governor."

This was politics. The rest of it was just theater.

"So what's the long-range plan?" Walter asked, breaking a breadstick in a spray of crumbs and sesame seeds.

"Officially? I haven't ruled anything out yet."

"And unofficially?"

"Off the record," he said to Annette. "So far off the record you never heard it."

"I'm Helen Keller. Without Anne Whatshername."

"I've never seen you be coy," Walter said to the governor.

"You've never seen me have dinner with the media."

"The hell I haven't, and this isn't the media anyway—it's Annette. She's on your side."

The governor—no, that was too impersonal. She was eating

dinner with the man. Bill-the-Governor turned to Annette with his answer, as if she were the one arguing with him.

"I know you are, and I appreciate it, believe me. You're a valuable ally and a charming woman, and I respect you for both qualities. If I weren't afraid of a lawsuit in this day and age, I'd get down on my knees and kiss your hand. But when someone has access to the public mind the way you do, it only makes sense to draw a clear line between what's for public consumption and what's just between us."

"Fine by me."

"No insult intended," he said to Walter.

"None taken," Annette said.

Walter beamed, reminding Annette of why she liked him. This was his real self. The private man was an awkward front he maintained because people expected it.

"We're together on this?"

"We all love each other and swear undying loyalty." Walter turned to Annette. "Isn't that right?"

"When the waiter comes back, ask for a sharp knife. We'll do a blood vow."

"I don't think that'll be necessary," Bill-the-Governor said.

"No, I like it," Walter said. "It's right out of Shakespeare."

Bill-the-Governor looked put upon.

"Walt, what was the question?"

"The plan, Bill. What's the long-range plan?"

"Statewide inquiry into Area 51—impact on vets, impact on their families. Emphasize the families, slide quietly into the war itself—the so-called war—if the response justifies it. We've got a guy at the Vets Hospital who's prepared to go public on the mental health aspect. Call for a federal investigation and hope to hell they don't do it or they'll steal my issue. Take the show on the road late next fall."

He picked up a breadstick and flicked seeds off it with a fingernail. It was like watching someone pick at a scab and Annette couldn't keep herself from watching. To stop him, she asked, "Nationally?" but all he did was smile enigmatically and flick off another seed.

"You watch this guy," Walt said. "He's going to take the country by storm."

"Question I want you to think about," he said to Annette, "is whether you'll appear with me again. Often."

She smiled. Knowing that Walt had forced his hand made it worth more instead of less.

"Anyplace you want as long as one of them is New York."

CHAPTER 21

The offer of a show in Chicago took Annette by surprise.

"I know you've got your heart set on New York," her agent said before she could remind him of this herself, "but this really is the big time. You don't know it, but it's what you've been wanting."

Annette shifted the phone to her other ear. Something about her agent's voice made her want to say no. He was talking too fast, for one thing, as if he was trying to keep her out of the conversation even now, when he was leaving a space open so she could say what he expected her to say. And even though she knew the game, she couldn't keep herself from saying it.

"But Chicago . . ." she said.

"Chicago!" he echoed. "Great town. You'll love it. Two arguments in its favor. First, it keeps you in the Midwest, keeps you in touch with your core listeners. You've got an image to maintain, and like it or not the heartland's part of it. Annette Majoris speaks for the common man."

"There're common men in New York."

"Yeah, but the rest of the country doesn't know it. The rest of the country hates New York."

"What's the second argument?"

"Chicago station's owned by the same corporation. They're not in the New York market. That doesn't mean they can't syndicate you there—they just can't move you there. Short term, let's face it, they could save a hell of a lot of money by holding you to the current contract, but they're looking beyond that. They want you to stick around, and they know they have to spend some money if that's going to happen."

She grunted and he took that as agreement and went on to talk about money and contracts and clauses. He said they'd hang her picture in the lobby. Give her a mail slot she could reach without having to stretch out flat on the floor. She'd have her own producer.

They'd already moved her mail slot, but she let that go.

"I have a producer now," she said. "I hate having a producer."

"Doesn't matter. You need one. Learn to live with it."

"Tell them someone low-key, then. The one I have now thinks she's the show."

He said sure and switched back to money, and she let herself warm to the idea a little bit at a time. She needed a change, and she did need the money. And it was a graceful way to get some distance from Stan, and from Bill-the-Governor's VFW halls. It wasn't that she didn't want to appear with Bill-the-Governor, but she wanted to do it someplace nice, someplace where people dressed up. Whatever happened to thousand-dollar-a-plate fund-raising dinners?

If she lived two states away, he wouldn't call on her so casually.

"Did you talk to them about security?" she asked.

Her agent sighed.

"That's the one place they won't budge. They're afraid it could turn into a black hole, frankly. But at least if you want to set something up yourself, you can afford to."

In the end, of course, she agreed. Because he was right, this was the big time. Great visibility, billboards. Paying her mother back. She'd dreamed of making this kind of money. She'd even imagined asking for it, but Len had her so damn intimidated she'd never have dared to. Plus, when she talked to Walter about the move, he thought it was a great opportunity. He'd fly down to see her. She'd fly up to see him. If you had enough money, geography was no problem.

But even so, she expected not to like the Chicago station manager when she met him. She expected a more upscale version of Len, ready to wave her contract in her face and tell her she could be replaced tomorrow, but from the minute Matt Cantwell shook her hand, he treated her like someone real, like someone he had to please, and she expanded into the space he thought she'd taken.

Matt Cantwell was tall and rumpled and a few afternoon naps short of sixty, with a palm-sized bald spot at the back of his head, but he'd worked up the energy of a much younger man for this first meeting, and he leaned toward her as if she'd just become the magnetic north of his life. He couldn't pull himself away. When he took her through the station and introduced her to people, he rested a hand on her shoulder, not like he was thinking about sex but like he thought some of her magic would flow through his arm and spark up his career. She was his star, his move-the-wife-and-kids-to-a-better-suburb card, delivered into his hand at an age when the kids were probably grown and it was too late to spark his career, but who wouldn't grab at it anyway when it was right there in front of him?

Cantwell drew her to a halt beside an empty desk and asked the woman at the neighboring desk where Daniel was.

She shook her head, looking panicky and apologetic.

"I told him to be here," Cantwell said. "Here. At this desk. At this moment."

"I'm sure he just had to run down the hall or something."

She gestured in a direction that had to be the men's room.

"Well, tell him I'm looking for him. And that this is not a good beginning."

He gave the woman a look that implied she'd misread her job description, then he turned, beamed at Annette, and steered her down a different hall to show her the studios.

Daniel caught up with them a few minutes later. He was fortyish, with the look of a man who hadn't made it and had accepted that he never would. The bonds that must have once linked each molecule to the next were breaking down, leaving him slack and out of focus.

"Your producer," Cantwell said. "Daniel Gar. The man who's dedicated to making sure everything goes well for you here."

Daniel offered Annette a pale, please-like-me handshake and was glad to meet her, and when Cantwell steered her onward he fell in behind like a part of her entourage. Cantwell's hand had fallen away from her shoulder at some point, but it was back now, and Annette glowed under it. She radiated. They walked toward Cantwell's office and every person they passed looked up to soak in a reflection of her radiance.

Actually being on the air was no different than it had been in Minnesota. She'd picked up more stations, but she couldn't talk to any more people per hour than she'd already been talking to. To feel that it was somehow different, she kept a mental log of accents and imagined her listeners on a map reaching from New York to San Francisco, from the Florida Keys to Seattle.

To make the change seem more real, she hired a clipping service, and she was surprised at the stuff they sent her. In every major paper, it seemed like someone was either attacking her as everything that was wrong with America or quoting her as the final authority on exactly that subject—columnists, letter writers, op-ed pagers, it didn't matter whether they wanted her deified or drawn and quartered, it all added up to the same thing: love her or hate her, she was changing the way the country thought. Even the Department of Defense had taken time out from its busy schedule to denounce her.

Which told her that she should have held out for more money. Or insisted on New York. There had to be some way she could have moved to New York. To hell with her image. Who knew her image better than she did? Why should she take the word of people who hadn't created it? She hadn't understood how big she was—that was the problem.

And she was big. Her face appeared on billboards all over town, reminding her of how she'd let herself be stampeded. And that she should have demanded the right of approval on the picture they used, because they'd made her look like a bobble-head doll. Then a newly formed veterans organization wrote, inviting her to address its first national convention in October, and sure she accepted, and sure she was pleased, but that grated on her too. How could she have been such an idiot? When would she learn to think of herself as someone who mattered?

She rented an apartment with a doorman and a view of Lake Michigan, and she bought a Tabriz rug with silk highlights for the living room. It was $20,000 on sale and Persian, not one of your Chinese knockoffs, and when she stepped back to admire it, it glowed like the kind of money she should have been making.

Was she happy? Yes. Mostly. Who wouldn't be? It was most of what she'd been wanting and her whole body drew energy from the pavement, from the buildings, from the crush of people on the sidewalks. Walter flew down to see her. He helped her pick out a coffee table and couch, and he bought her enough plastic windup toys to reenact the battle of Borodino. They turned them loose on the uncarpeted margins of the living room, alongside the Tabriz, trying to get them all going at the same time, and they were good together until he decided to rub her shoulders.

The next day he flew home and she played computer solitaire. She talked on the phone to Stan, who now FedExed his packets to her. He said he'd found someone from the Illinois chapter who could pick up her mail the way Penny had. When she realized she was enjoying the conversation, she took that as a sign that she needed to meet people. But not at the station. She was a star there, and stars didn't need to meet people. They didn't invite people to sit on the steps and drink beer after the show.

The On the Air sign lit up.

"Boys and girls," Annette said, "ladies and gentlemen, bacon and eggs, you're listening to *Open Line*, I'm Annette Majoris, and it's just you and me here today, no guests, no experts, no one standing between us, so get on those phones and call me, because I'm sitting here by myself and I'm lonely."

She gave out the number. Three people were on the line already and behind the glass Daniel smiled unhappily at her. *Like me*, the smile begged. *I haven't done anything wrong yet*, and she did like him—she really did. She gave him the thumbs-up sign—everything's wonderful; we're gonna knock 'em dead—and his smile lost the pitiful edge and looked genuinely happy, and that charged her voice, lending it an extra volt or two. This was what she needed: not a producer but a man behind the glass to smile at her, to tell her she was the center of the universe.

After Annette wrapped up the show, she told Daniel she wanted to talk to him—could she buy him a beer?

How could he say no? Why would he want to? He knew a place nearby, but it wasn't the sort of place, exactly . . . He looked embarrassed.

"Long as everybody keeps their clothes on, it'll be fine."

She followed his car, and he was right, it wasn't the sort of place, exactly, but she kind of liked it for that. It was a refuge for men with their names sewn on their shirts, a place they kept quiet, solo vigils with the TV set and the animal heads mounted on the walls.

"It's not the kind of place I'd usually . . ." he said. "Especially with . . . But it's nearby."

"It's fine. It's great."

They took a booth near the door.

"What I mean, actually, is I spend more time than . . ."

He gestured toward the lost end of the sentence: more time here than he should, probably.

She had no idea what to say to that.

"Tell you what's on my mind," she said instead. "I want you to do some research for me."

Daniel took a palm-sized notebook out of his pocket and flipped it open on the table to show he was ready for anything.

"First I want bios on some people. Thumbnail. Just the high points. I don't need their childhood traumas, their hobbies, their pets, O.K.? All I want is what they did relative to Vietnam, any-where their paths crossed each other's, that kind of thing."

"Got it."

"O.K. Nguyen Cao Ky, Daniel Ellsberg, Lucien Conein, Tran Do, Chester Ronning, Stanley Karnow, Nguyen Khanh." She spelled them out for him. "Start with those and we'll see where it goes."

"Got it."

"Then I want some genealogy."

She gave him the nephew's name, and the uncle's, told him the Martha Mitchell story, asked him to check anything he could there, and he wrote and nodded, nodded and wrote.

"They have a waitress or something here?"

Daniel flushed.

"Actually, you sort of have to go to the bar. I'll . . ."

He rose halfway and stopped, and when Annette got all the way up, he dropped back into his seat, looking relieved to have that awkwardness behind him.

"Beer?" she said.

"Beer's good."

She came back with two glasses of draft and slid one in front of Daniel. Truth was, she didn't know much about beer. Or any other kind of alcohol. She hardly drank unless someone else was drinking. If you ordered draft, though, you didn't have to know much.

"What you want to do on this," she said, "is use the internet. Or the library. I want independent sources, o.k.? At least two on each."

"Two on each."

"You read the material I gave you?"

"Absolutely."

"Good. Don't use it. It's great, it's brilliant, it's all that stuff, but I don't want you to use it for this."

"Got it."

They looked at each other over the beers, and she tried to gauge whether she'd said too much. Whether she didn't need to normalize this somehow. It had been a mistake, the way she'd handled it. She could see that now. She should've tossed him a list and told him what she wanted as if it meant nothing. Then they could've gone out for a beer and complained about their coworkers, the management, the callers. She studied him, but all she saw was Daniel—rumpled, nervous, ready to drink beer with her if she wanted or to roll over and let her scratch his belly if the mood struck her.

"It's good material," she said. "I want to be clear about that. And I've done some independent verification on this already, but I've never had the luxury of someone who could go into it with this kind of depth . . ."

"Right.

They each took a swallow of beer. It had turned into one of those formal dances—the minuet or something—where the point was to keep a certain distance between them. It hadn't been like that with Nick.

"When you've done those, just start reading—period newspapers, standard histories, original sources, anything. Everything. What you're looking for is discrepancies, things that don't make sense. You see what I mean?"

Daniel set down his beer and said sure, of course.

"It's like looking at the space between the objects instead of the objects themselves. You understand?"

"Sure."

"Once you've got a solid sense of this thing, we'll talk about whether there isn't some connection to al-Qaeda here, the ayatollahs, all that stuff. You see anything that hints at that, you let me know."

★

After Annette left, Daniel sat with what was left of his beer. He was a slow drinker, not a heavy one, but he liked the atmosphere in bars, in liquor stores, in all the places men went to inhale a bit of someone else's misery and exhale a bit of their own. He wasn't planning on getting drunk. Any minute now he'd open his notebook and figure out how to give Annette what she wanted. But he might need a second beer before he could manage it. Hell, he might need a third.

Instead of finishing his first, he stared into his glass and wondered if he couldn't quit the job instead. The answer came back exactly as he'd known it would: no. Getting hired had been a real break, and that meant he was stuck with it. At his last job he'd gone to work one day, put his head on his desk, and simply wept because what they did was so overwhelmingly pointless. Not just the station and the program he worked on, but his life. He slept, he ate, he worked, sometimes he sat in a bar, then he went back to sleep, woke up, and did it all again. Who wouldn't weep? Why didn't everybody?

When he showed no sign of stopping, his boss patted him on the back and walked him to the door.

He was out of work voluntarily for weeks and involuntarily for months, and he was still living in a cousin's basement. It would take at least two more paychecks before he could even think about a place of his own again.

But it wasn't just the paycheck. He needed a place to go every day, even if he hated it. He wasn't the kind of person who could lay around the house and do what he damn well liked all day because what *did* he like, after all, and what made it any less meaningless than work?

He stared at the foam clinging to the sides of his glass and wondered how he could go on showing up at the station, smiling and promising Annette anything she wanted. Every day he went in, he felt as if he was picking up a tiny bit of weight—a candy bar, say, or a package of nuts—and he never got to set it back down. He had no clear idea why that was, but sooner or later it would get too heavy for him, and how would he get himself to work then?

CHAPTER 22

 Matt Cantwell had left his desk chair empty so he could sit beside Annette in the swivel armchairs where his underlings normally sat to face him. He was signaling that they were friends. They were equals. First he told her about the party the station was throwing to welcome her to Chicago. They'd invite everyone: politicians, media people, art types if she liked that sort of crowd, anyone else she wanted—all she had to do was let him know. It would be first class all the way. And while she was still thinking about who to invite and he had her feeling good, he shifted the conversation.

"I've been talking to corporate," he said, "coordinating our strategy on this, and we've come up with something that . . . Well, I'm excited about this."

Annette nodded. It made her cautious when people told her how excited they were about something. It meant they counted on her hating it and were doing the old magician routine, waving one hand through the air while the other hand reached for the rat.

Cantwell was too good a Midwesterner to wave his hands around. He kept them in plain sight on the arms of his chair, where she could see he wasn't reaching for a rat, a rabbit, her contract. Nothing up this sleeve, nothing up that sleeve.

"The strategy's the one you developed yourself, although corporate needed half a dozen consultants and five focus groups so they could reinvent it and think it was theirs all along. Public forums. Small cities. Topeka, Buffalo, Corpus Cristi, Tampa. It's a brilliant strategy. What it says to people is that just because you're big doesn't mean you've abandoned them. You go where they are, or where people just like them are. You're Studs Terkel. You know Studs Terkel?"

Annette shrugged.

"Invite him to the party."

"Sure. Great idea."

He shifted in his chair and for a second Annette thought he was going to reach for a piece of paper and write that down but he didn't.

"I admit, he's kind of a star for the highbrow, but the thing about Terkel is he never loses touch with the people. America loves its stars, but what it's really nuts about are the ones who don't move to New York, or L.A., don't have six layers of security around them, still go out and buy their own groceries."

She argued: playing small cities made her look second-rate, like she couldn't pull an audience in the top-ranking venues, but as big a star as she'd been before she parked herself in Cantwell's swivel chair, somehow she couldn't bring herself to remind him of her stardom. Couldn't quite believe it herself. She had all she could manage just keeping Annie Minor from creeping back inside her skin. She told Cantwell she was glad to do Topeka or wherever, but she wanted New York too, *had* to do New York, and he went hazy all of a sudden. Next year, he said. Maybe the year after. Once her image was carved in stone. Once they were sure the move to Chicago hadn't made people think she was inaccessible. Besides, she had nothing to prove. Had she seen her ratings in New York?

She had. She'd even seen a piece in the *Times,* finally, which cast her as a lunatic sprung from America's heartland. As if being the country's newspaper of record meant it could strip her of her rights as a native New Yorker.

She was at the office door when he said, "I hear you're keeping Daniel busy."

She left a pause that was a little longer than it should have been. "Sure am."

"I've been thinking I might've made a mistake with him—that maybe he's not a good fit here."

And there it was: a guilt-free opportunity to make Daniel disappear, and with him that awkwardness at the bar. She'd turned and was looking at Cantwell, but what she saw instead was Aimee popping up at Daniel's desk the minute he was gone.

"No, he's exactly what I need. Don't ever replace him."

She talked to Walt on the phone that night, practically begging for his support, but he went and agreed with Cantwell about small cities.

"America loves its small-town roots," he said, "even if it'd rather die than actually live in a small town. One of the things it loves you for is not abandoning its unlovable places. If it were up to me, I'd book you in the really small towns: Leonard, North Dakota; Muleshoe, Texas. The kind of places no one's heard of. And when you opened the show, I'd have you describe the town for the listeners. Bring them into the real heart of the nation."

"It makes me look bush league, Walt. Small time."

"You're big enough to go someplace small. You don't have to prove anything to anyone."

She sighed and looked out at Lake Michigan, at a block of clouds gathered to the north.

"How come everyone's so set on this?"

"Because it's brilliant. Because it's a great strategy."

She sighed again. She crossed to the computer and called up a solitaire program while he recapped all the reasons it was brilliant.

So fine, it was brilliant. O.K. She gave in, although it didn't make him happy because he'd already been happy, but still it satisfied him: everything had clicked into its proper place. They talked for a few minutes about other things.

"Be sure you catch the news tomorrow," he said when they were about to hang up. "NBC's running a story on Bill. He's looking great."

★

She watched the news, which said it was much too early in the process, of course, long before anyone was in the habit of paying any attention to the presidential race, but Governor Ruoma was surprising the pundits by taking a fringe issue and going mainstream with it, making a virtue of his outsider status, and it was an open secret what he had his eye on. Annette had never thought of Ruoma as an outsider, but everyone wanted politicians to be outsiders these days, just as long as they had access to all the things the insiders did. The news went on to say that of course at some point he'd have to articulate a position on national security issues, but so far he'd done well enough by keeping attention focused elsewhere. It quoted a political scientist from someplace or other who said, like everybody else, that it was too early to and so forth, because a lot of things could still happen, and public opinion could change very fast, but the guy could, potentially, win the election. "At which point we'll find out how much of what he says he actually means, and how much of what he means he can actually do."

And so on.

In the next day's paper, a columnist twittered about the implications of a crackpot fringe seizing the middle ground and pushing true moderates to the fringes. A couple of references to Vietnam, and one to Annette, who was the unacknowledged pole star around which the sky pivoted. An admission that Governor Ruoma stood a fair chance of winning the nomination. Much wringing of hands over the sorry state of the American political dialogue.

It was interesting. She'd never really thought what it would be like if Bill-the-Governor were Bill-the-President. Maybe she could play her cards so she'd end up as his press secretary. Or an ambassador. She could chair a commission to investigate Area 51 and the so-called war. She sucked on the possibilities like an assortment of hard candies. Did she like mint better than lemon, and what flavor was the red one anyway? In the end, what she liked best was the idea of walking into the White House as a representative of the media, the electrically charged voice of the nation's soul, the person who had first thought to question what everyone else took for granted. The person whose goodwill everyone needed because she just might set them on their ears all over again.

She folded the paper and called her agent. She'd let everyone except herself direct her career up to now, and it was time to take charge. She wanted a TV show, damn it. No, she wasn't unhappy with Chicago. And no, she didn't want to leave radio. She loved radio. She wanted both. Didn't Stern do both? Wasn't she every bit as good as Stern? Wouldn't the audience for one build the audience for the other? Wouldn't everyone benefit? Wouldn't, although she didn't say this, it suit her better when she walked into a White House reception?

All of which, apparently, made her agent nervous, and nervousness made him murmur and hum into the crevices of what she was saying as if his humming was water and he was waiting for it to wear down the stone of her plans.

"It's possible," he murmured. "It could be done, but it's all a matter of timing. The problem with building a career overnight is how easily it can crash and burn. We want to be in this for the long haul here."

"The timing's perfect. We wait too long, the momentum won't be there."

He hummed. He said that, um, actually Stern and TV were an up-and-down kind of thing and very, um, yes, and Limbaugh, um, had, but it was all very past tense; however, of course, that didn't mean it was impossible. He agreed without promising. He'd think how best to go about it. He'd put out some feelers. He'd get back to her.

She gave him a week, then she called him. He was working on a strategy. He was exploring possibilities. She had to give him time.

She gave him another week, and one more after that, but he still couldn't tell her anything concrete. In the meantime, the plans for a show in Corpus were coming together and no way were they going to let her duck out of it.

Annette uncapped her bottle of Evian, sipped from it, and set it in front of the dead mic. Traffic had been lighter than usual, and a half hour lay between her and the start of the show.

She found Daniel sorting papers. His desk was a mound of paper scraps, file folders, composting coffee cups, and stained paper napkins, with something on the bottom that might once have been a T-shirt, although it was hard to tell.

"How's the research going?" she asked.

Daniel jumped as if she'd startled him, although he'd seen her coming and had even said hello. Absolutely and definitively, he wasn't Nick. He was great on the other side of the glass, but that was his limit.

"Good," he said. "Great. I could give you some stuff now." He rampaged through the layers, talking more toward them than her. "I was waiting till I had, you know, all of it, but there's no . . . I mean, I've been printing it out as I go."

He hauled a folder out from under the phone and extended it toward her.

For a second she thought about saying, "Cantwell doesn't like you; I saved your job," but the words never got said, and she said, "Thanks," instead. Knowing the truth would make him feel bad, and she liked him. Life's strange that way.

She brought the folder back to the studio and skimmed it. Thumbnail bios. Exactly what she'd asked for. No childhood traumas, no pets, no hobbies. Anyplace one subject's path crossed another's, Daniel had highlighted it in neon pink. Nguyen Cao Ky, Stanley Karnow, all of them. He hadn't gotten the level of detail that Stan had, of course, but the people were real, and they'd been in the right places. And he'd traced the nephew to the uncle to a farm in Wisconsin. No question they were related. Even the dog show article was real, although there was no way to verify what it had replaced.

Had she ever expected any different? Of course not. Only when she was feeling down, and even then only briefly. In passing, o.k.? And if she felt extraordinarily good all of a sudden— hey, was that illegal?

CHAPTER 23

 The party Cantwell threw was everything Annette could have dreamed of: lobster salad, some guy in a chef's hat offering the guests slices of roast beef and ham, an espresso machine the size of a copper-plated Mini Cooper hissing at the end of one serving table. Plus a string quartet sawing away in a corner and an entire wait staff pushing canapés and glasses of wine. No chicken salad, she'd told Cantwell—it looks cheap—and he'd come through: she'd checked out every serving table, and there wasn't a bird to be found, either as salad or sliced.

Walt steered her from one cluster of people to the next, working his way through the people he'd added to the guest list: an Illinois congresswoman; contributors to Bill-the-Governor's campaign; Bill-the-Governor himself, appearing wifeless tonight and nibbling smoked salmon hors d'oeuvres prepresidentially with a u.s. senator and a matching pair of congressmen. It was shocking, they told Annette, talking about Area 51. Hard to believe. Deserving of an inquiry. Walt squeezed her shoulders and beamed.

"Six months ago, could you ever have imagined this?" he asked as they moved away.

She couldn't have, of course. They moved on to a handful of carefully selected Constructive members, and with them, inevitably, was Stan, who'd driven down from Minneapolis and had bought himself a new suit for the occasion. Six months ago, she wouldn't have predicted this either: he looked passable. Extremely passable. Annette shook hands. She smiled. She predicted that when Bill-the-Governor was president all the nation's files would be opened and the secrets of government would tumble forth, and if the unsleeping vets didn't shake themselves free of their insomnia, at least they'd know for certain what they were doing awake at three a.m. People gathered at the edge of whatever group she joined as if she were the only fire that would ever warm them, and all evening long no one told her they couldn't sleep. Periodically she caught sight of Daniel leaning solo against a wall or handing a stack of dirty plates to a waiter who would have found them without his help if he'd only left them where they were. Poor perfect Daniel, grateful for anything that would help him stay busy. He nodded at her but didn't come over, so she brought Walt to him and introduced them, and Walt was perfect too. Gracious. Not at all condescending.

She and Walt left while the party was still going—you never want to look like you have no place better to go—and it took half an hour to say their good-byes and reach the door. They kept getting waylaid by good wishes, by hands that had to be shaken, by people who wanted meetings with Walt.

When they got to her apartment, they collapsed on the couch with the lights out, and she snuggled into Walt's chest, too wired to suggest bed and too tired to offer coffee or some of the wine he'd brought.

"Happy?" he asked.

"Mm-hmm."

He was sitting against the arm of the couch so she could lean against him, and he wrapped his arms around her, one brushing her breast, the other at shoulder height.

"You were wonderful," he said. "I love being seen with you."

She made a noise to let him know she appreciated the compliment. Which was the truth: she did. It made her realize, though, that neither of them had ever said anything about loving each other. She was fairly sure he did love her, even if he didn't have an easy time saying the words. The second she threw that door open, he'd come charging through. If she could just bring herself around.

"You know," he said, "before you I never liked sleeping at a woman's house. I'd always find some reason to get up and go home."

She leaned against him and hummed.

"It's different with you."

"It is with you too."

He pulled her into him so that sitting together was about sex, not just nuzzling.

"You too tired tonight?" he asked.

Oh, you romantic.

"No," she said. "It'd be good."

CHAPTER 24

Every so often, Stan's mind picked a quiet time to send him a note saying something along the lines of, *Are you sure you made the right choice, throwing your support to all these political types? How sure are you that they're not trying to buy your soul?*

The morning after Annette's party was a quiet time, and his mind delivered the message at the exact moment a waiter delivered his breakfast, so that Stan had to think about it at the same time he was staring at the waiter's white shirt, the oversized platter in his hand, the way the wide-open spaces between the eggs and the bacon were disguised by a lettuce leaf, three grapes, and a twisted slice of orange, and he answered the second question decisively: if they were trying to buy his soul, they were using the wrong currency. He was paying $9.45 out of his own pocket for this mostly empty platter plus a cup of coffee and the use of a white tablecloth. He'd paid $140 to sleep in a room with stale air and a window that wasn't built to be opened. If he was ever tempted to sell his soul, it wouldn't be for life's supposed luxuries. The next time he stayed in Chicago, he'd find a Constructive member to stay with. It would be cheaper and more comfortable, and he'd deepen a valuable friendship.

The waiter set the platter in front of Stan and asked if he needed anything else. What he needed was a deep breath of honest air, but he said no, he was fine. He took a bite of egg. He'd eaten better in greasy spoons when he delivered packages for Quicksilver, before he started his own company. Better and cheaper. In a friendlier atmosphere.

The first question his brain had asked—the one about the politicians—was harder to answer. It made him uneasy sometimes, the company he was keeping. He wouldn't know if he'd made the right choice until it was too late for the information to do him any good, at which point he'd be either a hero or a cautionary tale told to the next generation of patriots to explain why political channels corrupted even the best intentions. In the meantime, all he could do was set his doubts aside and do what was necessary.

He set his doubts aside and finished breakfast. Half an hour later, he was standing outside his hotel in a cold wind, waiting for the chairman of the Indiana Constructive to pick him up and thinking how useless he felt riding around like a package in someone else's car. But the house was hard to find, he'd been told, and it didn't have much space in the driveway, and some of the neighbors got huffy when cars parked on the street. It was that kind of neighborhood.

A Jeep stopped to pick him up, he settled into the familiar shape of the seat, and he realized how much the hotel and last night's party had thrown him off balance.

He patted the dashboard in front of him.

"What year is this?" he asked. "It's a beauty."

★

Stan spent the day with representatives of the Illinois, Indiana, Wisconsin, and Iowa Constructives, painting pictures of the brilliant future they would create if only the state organizations could agree to form a network.

For months, Stan had been sending Annette's fans his pamphlets on the so-called war and on Area 51, along with information on the Constructives, and since every state organization had a separate brochure, all of them had kept Stan supplied, and most had kicked in money to cover the cost of mailing. And every one of them had picked up members from it. That didn't make the Twin Cities a national office, but it had gotten people used to the idea of cooperation. And it had put Stan in touch with at least one person in every state organization.

"What we're looking at is a national issue," Stan told them. "We don't coordinate our efforts to deal with it, we'll be like mice attacking the cat one at a time."

The Indiana chairman nodded a steady rhythm to Stan's words and he looked—well, *proprietary* was the word that came to mind, as if driving Stan out here had given him an investment in what Stan said. There was a lesson to be learned from that—the one he'd taught himself earlier in the morning, when he was looking at his breakfast: don't be afraid to impose on people; it ties them to you.

"What I'm proposing," Stan said, "is a national convention, and a national office to coordinate our efforts. Coordinate. Not dictate. This is a voluntary organization, and we're an independent bunch. I'm not fool enough to think I could change that, even if I wanted to. But we can't afford to stay insulated anymore, not in times like these."

Indiana nodded and Stan nodded back. They were old friends, bonded to each other by one Jeep and fifteen miles of tollway.

CHAPTER 25

By the time Annette left for Corpus, her agent still couldn't tell her anything solid about the TV show, although it wasn't for lack of pushing on her part. He had the right people interested, finally. He could almost promise something would happen, but when she pressed for details it all turned to smoke.

In spite of which, she still had to do the show in Corpus. She stepped out of the airport into a crowd of supporters, and she shook hands and gave a quick interview while Stan hovered, uneasy in his background role. After a few minutes he stepped in to cut the interview short. They had a schedule, they had appointments, they were too important to stand in front of TV cameras all day long, although whatever Stan's rush was it wasn't Annette's. Still, it wouldn't have looked good to argue about it in public. She could chew him out later. So with the cameras still rolling, they made an aggressively noncelebrity exit in a minivan driven by some guy who must have been a Constructive member because Stan seemed to know him already. She'd begged Cantwell for a limo—she'd even offered to pay for it herself—but you'd have thought she'd suggested assassinating the entire Supreme Court the way he reacted. She had an image to keep up. She couldn't run around in limos. She was one of the people. Annette Average. She couldn't set herself apart. The station would be glad to arrange for luxuries—what did she want? all she had to do was name it—but only if they could be hidden. So here she was, riding in a minivan with a grimy Snow White doll from some fast-food restaurant rolling around next to her on the seat while Stan and the driver cranked each other up about the tyranny of posted speed limits. With all the money the station was pouring into this trip, they'd created an exact replica of what Stan himself would have set up.

On top of which, the air conditioning wasn't reaching her, Daniel was sitting in the seat behind hers honking his nose into— she hoped—a kleenex, and Stan had brought along the red-faced delivery geek, who he called, with an absolutely straight face, her bodyguard. She'd checked into the cost of professional security, but even with the new contract, money seemed to be going out faster than it was coming in. There was rent. There were clothes, restaurants, furniture, credit card bills, stuff. Plane tickets to Minneapolis to see Walt. She didn't know where it went, it just went. Took one look at her and ran screaming in the other direction, and she still hadn't paid her mother back, although it was on the list. It was high on the list. Which drove her to Stan for security. What the hell—he was supposed to be good at this stuff. And he understood the situation in a way no professional would. Besides, Cantwell had made a big point of saying that if she hired security it had to be unobtrusive. Corporate's fourteen focus groups and its herd of consultants were very concerned about that, and he'd implied that corporate would be watching.

The thing was, there'd been threats. Those had been the first words out of Stan's mouth when he parked himself next to her at the Chicago airport. Nothing they couldn't handle, nothing she should worry about, but he'd told the local people to alert the police all the same so they could provide presence, as he called it, at the forum.

The minivan's owner interrupted the moment of outrage he was sharing with Stan long enough to tip his words over his shoulder and tell Annette he listened to her show every chance he got, leaving an opening for her to move into the conversation, but she wasn't in the mood. She said thanks, she was flattered, and she let Stan move back in while she watched the land roll past—flat land, flat buildings, as if someone had let the air out of everything. If they got any flatter, the roofs would be splat on the ground.

It was the amateur hour. She had a national audience and a traveling show, she had dinner with a future president, and her agent was allegedly negotiating for a TV show, and it was still the fucking amateur hour.

They slid into their hotel anonymously. She'd insisted on that so there'd be no pickets, no pop-up protestors, but when it came down to walking in and registering, she could as easily have been some sales rep pushing textbooks, or shoelaces, or wooden legs. She could've been anybody. She followed the bellhop to her room, tipped him, unlocked her suitcase, and hung up the blouse she'd brought for the show—off-white, simple, the top button low enough to keep a crowd tightly focused. She stuck her nose in the flowers the station had sent and ate one of the chocolates that Cantwell must've thought would substitute for a limo. They were nice and all that, and she tried to appreciate them, but what she really felt was *so what?* They didn't mean anything. They didn't thrill her.

She hung up the clothes she'd wear for the show and called her mother at work.

"Why do you have to go to Texas?" her mother said. "Kennedy was shot in Texas. They walk down the middle of the street carrying guns and don't think a thing about it."

"I'm already there, Mom. I haven't seen any guns. Mostly it's just big hats. And boots. I've seen lots of boots."

"Don't make jokes about this. I'm worried. They're crazy down there."

They could carry guns in Minnesota now too, but there was no point in saying so. Annette pushed her shoes off and stretched out on the bed. She had a suite facing the water, a king-sized bed. The best Corpus had to offer, or so Cantwell swore.

"I'm not making jokes. I'm serious. It's under control."

She pulled the spare pillow out from under the bedspread and piled it on top of the one on her side. The right thing to say next was, "I've got a bodyguard," but she couldn't say it. Even thinking the words brought up too clear a picture of the sorry excuse Stan had found. It was too depressing to talk about.

"Call me as soon as the show's over, Annie. I'll be frantic. Have you talked to the police?"

"Sure, Mom."

"Well, are they giving you protection?"

"They will, Mom."

"They *will*? What about now? Where are they now?"

And so forth. She was a public figure, an American citizen. She had rights. She should call the police back and demand them. It was the squeaky wheel that got the attention and they'd do as little for her as they thought they could get away with. On top of which . . .

Annette shifted the top pillow. Two pillows were too thick and one was too thin. She shifted the phone to the other ear and promised she'd call the police, promised she'd call her mother back after the show, promised anything else her mother wanted although that was as much as she actually remembered. That was another thing she hadn't expected: that by the time she became an important national figure she'd still be on the phone getting instructions from her mother like some ten-year-old. She never thought of people at this level as having mothers, much less getting instructions from them.

Walter had promised her a police escort for the show in South Bend. Bill-the-Governor was on good terms with someone or other there. When she got home, she'd tell that to her mother.

She flipped through TV stations with the mute on while her mother talked, then without the mute once they'd hung up. She read the room-service menu and the descriptions of the hotel's restaurant, pool, and weight room, its bar and coffee shop, and then she flipped through the TV again. When she'd made the full circuit, she read a page of fluff on the wonders of Corpus Cristi, and she still had two hours before she was due at the auditorium. The longer she hung around, the more her mother's worrying was turning into her own, damn it.

Eventually, because she didn't see any way around it, she called the geek, who told her Stan had gone to meet with the local people. Which explained his hurry at the airport.

The geek rode down the elevator with her and slouched, head down, across the lobby beside her. If he was on the lookout for problems, he expected them to rise out of the carpet. *Talk Show Host Attacked by Hotel Carpet; "I was expecting this," said vigilant bodyguard.*

"Tell me your name again?"

"Steve. Flambard."

Said vigilant bodyguard Steve. Flambard.

He pushed open the door and held it for her.

"Where're we going?"

She looked in both directions, and they looked equally hot. From what she'd seen, downtown was more of an idea than a place there—a memory of the days when America was America and downtown was where you went to shop. She wasn't sure downtown would have sold anything she wanted, but it made her lonely to think she'd missed out on it.

There wasn't time enough to look for a mall.

They walked along the water—a lagoon sheltered from the gulf by a spit of retiree-infested sand—and Flambard kept his eyes fixed on the sidewalk in case someone meant to attack from that direction. The water made her realize how much she missed the Hudson River, the Staten Island Ferry, even the Circle Line boats that packed tourists in hip by money belt and showed them the sights from a safe distance.

"You ever been a bodyguard before?" she asked.

Flambard shook his head.

"Drove a delivery truck till the wife left me. Done a lot of training, though. Unarmed combat. Target shooting. Explosives. Nighttime surveillance."

He walked with his hands deep in his pockets, surveilling the cement.

"You got a gun now?"

"You mean here?"

"No, in your grandmother's attic. Of course I mean here."

"Can't take a gun past the metal detectors."

"So you check it through in the suitcase."

"Huh. Hadn't thought of that. They let you do that?"

How the hell would she know?

"So if anyone comes after me, you're supposed to do what, bite them? Insult their mother? Recite 'The Song of Hiawatha?'"

He lifted his eyes off the ground and actually looked at her.

"No one's trying to *kill* you."

"You don't know that and neither do I."

She'd stopped walking, and Flambard shambled to a stop half a step ahead.

"I thought . . . From what Stan said . . ."

"Forget Stan. Nobody's stalking Stan."

"Stan knows this kind of thing."

He didn't say it as if he was arguing. He was placating, and he looked as if he'd have cheerfully thrown himself in the lagoon rather than have her mad at him if only they'd had the foresight to walk on the lagoon side of the street. The guy was a real

Minnesotan: terrified of someone talking to him head-on. He had no trouble with the idea of knocking heads together if the job required it—hell, he probably knew how to blow up a federal building—but he came unglued if she raised her voice. She breathed in, breathed out, reminded herself that patience was a virtue, even if it wasn't one of hers, and tried to find a new approach with him.

"Look, I'm worried," she said. "We go along acting like nothing's going to happen because we'd all go crazy if we didn't, but there have been threats, and there was that guy in Cincinnati, and they worry me."

Flambard nodded some more, agreeing with everything and waiting for her to stop being emotional so he could go back to doing exactly what he'd done before.

No wonder his wife left him.

"Oh, hell, let's just keep walking," she said.

Stan appeared at the hotel in time to escort them to the auditorium, to Flambard's visible relief, and he brought along a new local guy with a big hat and a fancy we-got-a-back-seat-in-here, ain't-we-something pickup truck. Grand style. The stretch limousine of the pickup world. He'd even covered the back with a snap-to-the-sides vinyl thing that made her wonder what people actually hauled in these things. The local was in his forties—well fed, smirky faced, wearing the boots that went with the hat. She wouldn't have thought before today that Texans really wore those hats. He glanced at her legs as she came out the hotel door and ignored the rest of her.

Stan seemed to think she needed conversation, so he told her there were demonstrators and they'd have to go in through the loading dock at the auditorium.

A smooth man in social situations, old Stan.

They hustled her in through the back with the three men surrounding her so tightly she damn near tripped on them. The metal door slammed behind them and they eased away, giving her space to straighten her skirt and brush a hair out of her face. She detached herself and escaped down a cinder-block hallway until she found a women's room where she looked in the mirror, reviewed the introduction she had in mind, slowed her breathing, set her jaw. Head up, back straight.

It would all work out fine.

Fuck 'em all.

She stalked onto the stage in front of a packed hall, the entire audience pounding its hands together at the sight of her. There was nothing on earth like that rush. She crossed the stage on a cushion of applause and tore into the preshow explanations—the floor mic, the seven deadly words, vets only at the live shows, please—with every bit as much commitment as Lincoln put into the Gettysburg Address.

It went well. A nurse testified about the ravings of her patients—at the time she'd dismissed them; the men were in pain, in shock, sedated, traumatized, dismissable in one way or another, but in retrospect, after what had come out, she had to think back and it all sounded different now. The audience nodded and uh-huhed like the backup singers in a doo-wop group while Annette sang the soprano line—the biggest betrayal any government had ever et cetera—soaring solo above them all.

She was still smiling when the denunciations started. First it was a huge slab of a guy who started in about what he personally remembered, not to mention Da Nang and Tet and especially My Lai, which of course he *did* mention, because why would the government deliberately fake a P.R. disaster like that . . .

It wasn't meant as a question, but she cut in to explain about mind control, the point being to see if soldiers would violate their own beliefs, because that was the test of how well the control worked. Although it may have been a mistake that the men involved actually remembered it.

"That's what you've got to remember, that the guys running this thing weren't gods. They were feeling their way through. They made mistakes. If they hadn't, we'd never know that it happened at all."

He said yes-but. She was dismissing the experience and sacrifice of a whole generation, and who did she think . . . It was the standard rant, and he got some cheers, some applause, loud but not solid—the pitter-pat of a pissed-off minority. She gave him a minute to stake out the territory, then she cut in with regret: she wished she thought he was right; she understood the power of his memories and how hard they must be to disbelieve. It went against every human instinct. Meanwhile she signaled the engineer to cut the sound to the floor mic—she'd told Daniel to be ready for this, and to make sure the engineer was too—and the vet let her take the conversation away and move to the next person in line. Maybe it helped that they had a couple of big guys hovering beside the mic smiling and adjusting it up and down to each speaker's height. Maybe it helped that he knew who the person behind him was, because this next one opened by saying he was a vet, then went into a speech about what it would take to create a delusion on this scale.

"We're talking not just the military and the press here but the entire population of the Indochinese peninsula, whole industries in this country, making everything from ammunition to beer, plus the Congress, the antiwar protestors . . ."

His friends were going nuts, her vets were yelling at them, and the TV cameras had their lights on, panning the room, hoping to catch the first stages of a brawl, and it was going to be Cincinnati all over again. She cut in to agree that it did boggle the mind, but how could any honest person ask her to ignore the evidence of, and of course he kept yelling when his mic went dead, and his buddies yelled with him while she said she was going to have to ask him to respect, and the security guys got hold of him but not tight enough, because he managed to haul off and slug one of them. The TV crews were damn near trampling each other to get a good angle, and all the while she was asking everyone to stay calm and let the security crew handle it, nothing would be solved by attacking each other physically, but oh, damn, it was a hell of a sight, all these overaged soldiers hurling themselves at each other one last time before Social Security and arthritis took them off the battlefield forever.

She narrated it for the radio audience: a fight had broken out on the floor. A handful of protestors, disruptive, refusing to respect the . . . One of the security men had taken a blow, and there was no telling at this point just how serious the damage was. The man who'd attacked him was being led outside. Wrestled, actually. Meanwhile a couple of protestors tried to storm the stage and were blocked in the aisle by . . . It was hard to tell but it looked like a combination of audience members and security men.

She caught a glimpse of Daniel in the back, tucked into the sound booth with the engineer and looking as baffled as if the entire audience had turned to snow and Cantwell had forgotten to issue him a shovel.

It went on longer than Cincinnati had, and she began to repeat herself. That was the problem. Here she was, narrating one of the great prizefights of history, and she knew shit about boxing. People hit each other. How many ways could she say that?

CHAPTER 26

 After the demonstrators were dragged out, what was left of the show went smoothly. They did tunnels and lights and the horror of knowing they'd violated their most deeply held moral et cetera in the service of no-one-knew-what. The cameras had gone home but it went smoothly, and she'd learned to be grateful for that. The time passed. When it was over, they applauded. They crushed in around her at the steps down from the stage—Cantwell loved that, the way she climbed down to the audience after the show—and they wanted to shake her hand and tell her that they loved her, that she'd brought meaning to their lives, that they still couldn't sleep. Stan and Steve Flambard hovered behind her, one at each shoulder, her guardian angels, her Scylla and Charybdis, and Daniel was nowhere to be seen. She didn't need him for anything in particular, but she'd have liked to see him.

They left by the loading dock door, the same way they'd come in. The driver—Mr. Hat, Mr. Look-at-Her-Legs—said the demonstrators outside had gotten rowdy enough that a bunch of them had been hauled off and arrested, mostly for blocking the doors, but one for attacking a cop.

He turned in his seat to grin at Annette.

"Sweetheart, they just hate you."

She grinned back: fuck you.

"Mike, you better move us out of here before we have trouble with them ourselves," Stan said. In the few hours they'd been in

Texas, his accent had shifted sympathetically southward so that now it came from no identifiable part of the continent. "And head away from the hotel, why don't you, so they won't know where Annette's staying. We had some trouble with that in Cincinnati."

Mike grinned at Stan the same way he had at Annette, as if he thought they were both soft, and he started the truck.

They'd have gotten away clean if Mike hadn't taken Stan literally and made the first available left—away from the hotel, sure, but directly past the demonstration—just as a handful of demonstrators decided the show was over and started across the street to their cars. Or that's how Annette reassembled it afterwards. What she knew at the time was that the pickup stopped at the corner, giving her a glimpse of cop cars, demonstrators, and picket signs, and she felt a rush of Christmastime greed— all this for me? Then someone was pounding the hood of the truck, and Mike had the door open, yelling that this was a new fuckin' truck, and Stan was yelling at him to stay put and get the truck the hell out of there, but Mike was out the door by that time, hurling himself into what was suddenly a crowd and slamming the door behind him. Stan leaned over to punch the button down on the door.

"Stay with her," he ordered Flambard, reaching to open his own door and haul Mike back, but Flambard was out the door already and looking happier than Annette had ever seen him.

The whole demonstration was streaming toward them by now, surrounding the truck, and Flambard and Mike had disappeared into a sea of bodies, shoving and swinging. Stan was yelling, "Goddamn it, Steve," after Flambard, sounding one part pissed off and three parts scared for the man, and over the top of it all rode the metallic sound of a cop's bullhorn warning everyone of a coming apocalypse if they didn't break it up and go home.

Someone started rocking the truck—up, down, left, right, nothing too bad yet, but any minute it would cross their minds to tip the thing.

"Get them out of here," Annette shrilled. Her voice was high and hysterical, and she knew that what she was saying didn't make sense, but she couldn't stop herself. "Get them out of here."

The demonstrators' yelling was muffled by the truck windows and the pounding, but Mike was right: they did hate her.

Stan said, "Shit," and he squeezed his bulk into the driver's seat and put the truck in gear, lurching it a few inches forward, pushing far enough into the wall of bodies to scare people but not far enough to flatten anyone—plowing them forward, making them scramble to the sides. Annette's voice shrilled on, making even less sense than it had when she'd wanted him to move the demonstrators. He lurched forward again, lay on the horn, lurched forward. He was getting into it now, finding his rhythm. Lurch-honk. The pitch of the shouting shifted; they were mad at him now, and it was gut-level, you-scared-me anger. If he and Annette had stepped out of the truck together, they'd have shoved her out of the way to get their claws into him.

"Keep an eye out for Steve and Mike," he ordered Annette. "We'll pick them up on the fly if we can spot them."

"Are you kidding me? We open those doors, every lunatic in Texas is going to pour in here."

Lurch-honk.

"Just watch for them."

The hood broke free—there was open street in front of them, and at the edges of the crowd the cops were in a fight of their own, pulling people away from the pack. She caught a glimpse of Flambard, or thought she did, pulling a bigger man into a choke-hold, before some straggling section of the audience poured out of the auditorium and joined the uproar and she lost him.

Everywhere, small knots of civilians flailed at each other. How they could tell who to hit was a mystery—both sides wore the usual uniform fragments and looked alike to her—but they seemed to be finding each other. Maybe they did it by smell. Maybe once the fight started they didn't care who they hit. She leaned forward, hands digging into the upholstery of the front seat as if hanging on would keep her safe. It did, at least, keep her from saying anything more. The truck was rolling steadily now, and the demonstrators were dropping away on the sides, a few of them running, keeping pace as long as they could, then they dropped away too, and Stan stopped the truck long enough to slide the seat back.

He drove—straight ahead, right, left, any direction but toward the hotel.

"I'm going to take the back way in, drop you off, then see if I can't get Steve and Mike out of there."

Annette hiked her skirt, climbed into the front seat, pulled her skirt down, and buckled the seat belt. It gave her a sense of normalcy to have the seat belt around her.

Stan headed away from the water, intent and serious now that he'd proved himself by breaking the truck loose. He was John Wayne. He was Batman. He was the entire Special Forces. As soon as he'd seen Annette to safety, he'd parachute in behind enemy lines and rescue his men.

Annette straightened her skirt again, grasped the seat belt with both hands and watched the empty sidewalks roll by. The world was sane again, in a Texas sort of way. A Mexican-looking woman walked a toddler across a street. A scruffy white guy in yet another cowboy hat unlocked a car door. Everyone else was either at home cultivating their yuccas or in front of the auditorium throwing punches at each other. And no wonder. Downtown was a wasteland.

"You know where you're going?" she asked a couple of blocks later. Her voice was stabilizing—a little shaky, maybe, but without the hysterical edge.

"Should be up here a few more blocks and on the right."

They drove a few more blocks, and a few more after that, and got tangled up with a canal, and with the piers supporting a freeway bridge.

"Problem is, with Mike driving I wasn't paying enough attention. It's a mistake, counting on someone else to take care of things."

Annette watched the streets go by, watched the time go by, watched Stan deflate from superhero to hero to just another man who wouldn't stop to ask directions.

"I'd feel better if you'd see me to the room," she said at one point.

"Can't leave the truck anyplace they'd spot it. You'll be safer if I drop you and take it somewhere else."

Which made sense, damn it.

He dropped her at the hotel some fifteen or twenty minutes after they'd broken free, and she scuttled across the lobby to the elevator and tried to wedge a chair under the doorknob of her room. She'd seen that done in the movies, but the chair back was too low and she had to settle for shoving it against the door, where it would do no particular good if somebody broke in, just scrape across the carpet as the door swung open and give her something to trip over as she tried to escape.

Everyone was gone by the time Stan got back to the auditorium—vets, protestors, police, all of them swept away as cleanly as if Area 51's little gray aliens had beamed them up for experiments.

He circled the block a couple of times with the vague sense that everyone would reappear the next time he drove past. When they didn't, he broadened his search area, but the fight might as well never have happened for all the evidence he could find.

That left him with a truck that wasn't his. He drove it back to the auditorium, parked it, and walked to the hotel.

He found Flambard in their room, examining his face in the bathroom mirror.

"Doesn't look too bad," Stan said.

"Took it mostly in the ribs. They'll be sore in the morning."

He dabbed at a cut in the corner of his mouth. Stan leaned against the doorway, feeling a sense of relief that surprised him. Anger would have made more sense, but it was locked away someplace, and he didn't have the pin number.

"I drove back to see if I couldn't get you out of there," he said after a while. "I didn't like leaving you, but Annette gets—well, hysterical's what she gets. We've got to keep her away from that kind of thing."

Stan nodded his agreement with himself. It wasn't that he'd forgotten how calm she'd been sitting in his hotel room in Cincinnati. He remembered it clearly, but today canceled it out. It showed him a deeper truth about her, and a more satisfying one, and he offered it to Flambard by way of apology.

"Wouldn't've happened if Mike hadn't been such a damn fool," Flambard grumbled, although he looked delighted, as if he'd been needing someone to hit for a long time.

Stan sighed.

"I've got to let him know where his truck is."

CHAPTER 27

Annette's agent called when she was in the bathtub, and she lay back and listened to him tell her machine that he'd set up a meeting for her in L.A. and that all the omens were good. She was surprised that she didn't leap out of the tub and drip water all the way to the phone but it scared her—deep down, what-am-I-going-to-do terrified her—to think about that meeting.

She waited until the next day to call him back, and she had him change the date of the meeting.

In L.A., she was met at the airport by an absurdly good-looking guy holding a sign with her name. He said Mr. Bowdwin had wanted to meet her himself but something had come up—a minor crisis, nothing serious, but he wanted it settled and out of the way so he could give her his full attention this afternoon, and he hoped she'd understand.

He took her garment bag as he talked. He was tall and in his early twenties, with an athletic body under the suit. A would-be actor waiting to get the same break a thousand other would-bes were waiting for. He steered her toward the doors and talked about the weather, the city, the traffic he'd seen on his way out, working on the assumption that they were buddies, or that they could be, and she let her mind slip out of reach. At some point he said, "But hey, you don't want to hear about me," and she smiled a hazy agreement.

The airport doors opened in front of them, and they stepped into L.A.'s fabled, smog-filtered sunlight. He opened the limo door for her. He closed it. She smoothed her skirt, sat back, and told herself to get used to this. It was just another form of transportation. Sure it was what she'd been wanting, but it was also the opening move in the game, and she couldn't let it impress her.

She grinned into the long, empty space in front of her. She loved every wasteful inch of it.

Her hotel was built around a courtyard: a pool, flower beds, palm trees that looked as improbable as if someone had come along and stuck peacock feathers in the ground and everyone had agreed to pretend that they grew there naturally. Just L.A.'s little joke on the rest of the country. The lawn had grass as rich as a hand-knotted rug, and sprays of water rising out of the ground, leaving an edge of damp where they brushed the path.

She unpacked, admired the flowers on the coffee table, and deciphered the signature on the card, Saxon Bowdwin. Her agent had warned her about the name. "Saxon as in Anglo," he'd said, "and he's not open to jokes about it," but as long as the man thought to send a limo he could call himself Visigoth and it'd be fine with her.

In the refrigerator she found a bottle of wine, and she examined the label. She should learn about wine. Really she should. She couldn't tell if this was a good wine or an ordinary wine or a fantastic wine. It had a nice-looking label, for whatever that was worth—gold lettering, black background—and she decided it was another good omen.

Her meeting was in a restaurant—light, airy, very California, very indoor-outdoor. Bowdwin and some other man were there already, and Bowdwin didn't look like her idea of Hollywood. For one thing, he was wearing a tie. And he was short, with the sunless face of a man who spent his days basking in the blue glow of a computer screen. But her agent had said the man was brilliant. He knew everyone. He was *the* person to know. He introduced himself as Saxon—we're all first-name here—and before she'd had a chance to slide into the booth, he was already telling her he loved her show, and she was better looking than Larry King; she was smarter than Barbara Walters.

"Is the hotel all right?" he asked.

"Fine. Nice. Very comfortable."

"And the flowers. They did get them to you?"

"They're beautiful. I can smell them from the next room."

"Perfect. Wonderful."

He'd gotten to his feet when she walked in, and they were still standing. He turned to the man left sitting in the booth.

"Raymond," he said by way of introduction, as if this explained everything, and Annette shook hands with him. An assistant, then. A Daniel. They were all standing now, Raymond trapped by the booth and awkward.

"I'll tell you why I asked about the flowers," he said. "We sent flowers once to . . . Well, I shouldn't use names here, but someone I very much wanted things to go well with, and she never got them. I didn't find out until later, when I heard she'd told—well, another person, a close friend—that she felt we'd taken her for granted. The whole thing fell apart over that one mistake. So I ask now."

"They got there."

Annette and Bowdwin slid into the booth. Raymond sat back down, and they all radiated goodwill at each other. Bowdwin went on to talk some more about the flowers, and the hotel, and the restaurant, and we're talking about a seriously boring conversation here, but Annette hung in with it, smiling and making noises in all the right places and waiting for the business talk to start, but it still hadn't happened when the waiter presented himself and recited the specials. Bowdwin stopped him after hearing only two.

"Can I order for us all?" he asked Annette. "They have this . . . You'll love it."

"Sure. Of course."

"You're not vegetarian, macrobiotic, anything like that? You don't do food allergies, low fat, low carb, South Beach, North Beach, any of that?"

"No. God, no."

"Of course, no. Of course."

He turned to the waiter, canceling out what was apparently an embarrassing question.

"What we want here is the free-range chicken, but we don't want the red sauce. You remember that vodka sauce you had last week? That's what we want."

He turned to Annette.

"It's magnificent. I can't have you come all this way and not try it."

He turned back to the waiter.

"That comes with a salad?"

The waiter shook his head.

"We've got to have salad. House dressing, I think. On the side. What about an appetizer?"

Annette nodded. To have said no would have been to mark herself as a barbarian.

"The crostini, I think, but no goat cheese, just a sprinkling of asiago and have the chef broil it till the cheese barely melts."

The waiter wrote, showed a nicely capped set of teeth, and disappeared, and in another minute Annette was going to be hearing about the hotel and the flowers again, or the restaurant and the chicken, because as far as she could see the first person who admitted they were here to talk business lost.

"So what do you think?" she said. "Do these restaurants really buy free-range chickens or do you think they buy the factory type and charge free-range prices for them?"

Bowdwin looked like she'd just murdered the Easter bunny.

"They couldn't. Word would get out. People would find out about it."

"Who'd know? You're looking at a slab of meat. It's dead. You can't ask how it spent its formative weeks."

Bowdwin's expression shifted as she talked until by the end he was pointing at her.

"There," he said. "That's it exactly. That's what we want you to do."

She smiled and waited. This was the first time she'd been with people whose decisions would control her career and still felt like herself. Wasn't her attitude what they wanted her for? How could she lose, then? She was poised to ride whatever wave this was that had lifted Bowdwin, but it dropped before she got her chance.

"Maybe not. Too small. Too parochial. Why don't you tell me instead—what do you have in mind? Run me through your for-mat—say your first half-dozen shows."

"Live audience," she said, leaning forward, relieved to be rid of the make-nice stuff. "Guests, a mix of experts and personal testi-mony. Opposition. I'd just as soon we weren't dealing with physi-cal fights and having to drag people out during the show, but let's be honest here, I'm at my best when someone annoys me. It goes too smoothly, I get bored."

"Perfect," Bowdwin murmured, and, "Of course," and, "The audience'll love it."

"I'm not committed to this," Annette said, "but I've been thinking we could use news footage, a kind of re-creation of the so-called war—a *You Were There* kind of thing, except we don't know if anyone actually *was* there. Take it apart, frame by frame. Find the places it doesn't hold together."

Bowdwin nodded, but with less enthusiasm.

"Just a possibility," she said. "Topics. I'd like to move beyond Vietnam. I'm getting boxed in by that. It's important, it's crucial, but I'm capable of something bigger here. Area 51, of course, and what's happened to Project Sunrise since the war. I've never had a research staff, so we haven't been able to follow up on that, but you don't invent a technology that powerful and then mothball it. It's being used somewhere, and I want to know where."

Bull's-eye.

"What I'd like to look at, did the CIA pass it on to the mujahedin they trained in Pakistan? It could explain the suicide bombers."

Bowdwin nodded, looking properly somber.

"What else?" she said. "Pentagon's black budget. CIA's. FBI's. Where's the money going? What agencies don't we even know about? We've got an entire secret government here, and the American people have barely heard about it."

"O.K."

He was ticking off the topics on his fingers to see if she could come up with half a dozen.

"Vets hospitals. Are any of their programs using mind-control technology? How are they coping with mind-control victims?"

He lopped off another finger, although she'd thought that was two.

"Elementary schools. We may crash and burn on this one, and if we do, I want to be sure it happens before we go on the air with it, but there are people out there who claim phonics drills are the baby sister of mind control. Is it true? I'm not convinced, but now that I think about it—and all I'm doing is talking out loud here, O.K.?—maybe that's our format: put them on the air, let them make their case, investigate it, see if it holds water. If it doesn't, we say so ourselves. Sort out the real from the fantastical. Don't let the guests know where we stand till they're on the air or a lot of them'll back out."

"That's it," Bowdwin said. "It's new. It's unpredictable. It's brilliant."

He turned to Raymond.

"I love this woman. She's a genius."

By the time the limo dropped Annette back at the hotel, it was late afternoon and she was elated and edgy. Plus they'd had a couple of cognacs after lunch, and they'd been as good as anything she'd ever tasted at Walt's. So she was elated and edgy and a little blurred, and she wasn't ready to stop feeling that way, so she brought the wine bottle she'd found in her room outside, asked the bartender at the poolside bar to open it for her, and ordered an empty glass, then she settled herself in a chaise longue and poured the wine. She held the first sip in her mouth, searching for the subtleties of Bowdwin's commitment to her show in its taste and its undercurrents.

As far as she could tell, he loved her, but she wished she could have had Walter's opinion. Because there it was again: she'd always considered alcohol something a man should know about—a bit of arcane knowledge that was part of men's charm. She couldn't decide whether she wanted to invade that territory. On the one hand, it would be useful. On the other, what if she liked men less once she learned their secrets?

On a nearby chaise, a man looked up from a sheaf of papers and smiled—the kind of noncommittal flirting that was easy to back away from if she didn't signal back. He wasn't as good looking as the limo driver, but he wasn't bad, and he wasn't a limo driver. Beak-nosed, around thirty. One of those intense men she didn't associate with California.

"I need an opinion," she said.

He lowered the papers to his lap and waited.

"The wine." She held up her glass to show it to him. "I want to know what someone else thinks of it."

He shuffled his papers into a stack and transplanted himself to the chaise next to hers.

"Wait," she said. "Don't go anywhere."

She brought a second glass from the bar and filled it. He held it up, moved the glass in a circle so the wine whirlpooled inside, and contemplated the way the light flowed through. It was a lovely gesture. She had no idea whether it told him anything about the wine, but it was enough to convince her that she didn't want to know. Suppose she found out the gesture really was an expert's. She'd start judging with him, and judging his judgment, and she'd never be able to admire the gesture again for its own sake. Suppose on the other hand that the gesture meant nothing—that he was doing it for no good reason, or just to impress her. He'd be pitiful. Either way, she'd lose the ability to fall in love. Or fall in attraction.

He lowered the glass, sipped, held the wine in his mouth the way she had, and closed his eyes to draw his attention inward. Annette let her eyes shift away—to the blue and green tiles ringing the pool just above water level, to the play of light on the water, and from there to the Mexican-looking maid pushing a cart of sheets and cleaning supplies along the open-air corridor.

"Lovely," the man said eventually. "The descriptive words for wine are silly. You know: crisp, fruity, all that kind of thing. All wines are fruity, for god's sake. They're made from fruit. And crisp—this is a liquid. Liquids aren't crisp—they're liquid. But it's a nice wine."

He put his glass down.

"Expensive?"

"I'd think so." He picked up the bottle. "It's not a brand I'm familiar with, but I'd think so. Tell me why you want to know."

"I'm trying to understand the intentions of the buyer."

"I'd say it's safe to marry him."

She smiled. She thought about Walter and decided he had no bearing on the situation. What she had with him was a committed relationship, of course, but this wasn't about relationship. This was about bodies.

Walter owed her that.

"It's not a question of marriage."

"Then sign the contract. Just check with your lawyer first."

He set the glass down and extended his hand.

"Paul Dexter."

"Annette Majoris."

"Of course. From the . . . I knew I should know you."

That killed the conversation for a few seconds, and they both looked into their wineglasses for the next line. She should have said Annie Minor and had her fling incognito.

"So can I ask what you're doing here? Aren't you based in New York or somewhere?"

"Somewhere, unfortunately. Chicago."

"Chicago," he echoed as if he were sucking meaning out of the word. "And what brings you to the promised land?"

"Let's just say I'm exploring possibilities."

"Intriguing."

"It's holding my interest."

He waited, practically batting his eyes to get her to say more. If straight men could be said to bat their eyes, because this man was definitely straight. She knew that from the way the air between them vibrated.

"What about you?" she said.

He left an open space.

"I might as well confess: I'm launching a new magazine. National circulation. Very hip, very visual, but depth too.

Entertainment, style, politics, personalities. Celebrity profiles. Top-quality writing. We're still in preproduction on the first issue, but we've had a great response—advertisers, focus groups . . ." He shook his head to cut off a speech he'd delivered so many times it practically spoke itself. "You don't want to hear that."

She opened her mouth to say the polite thing—of course she did—because that was part of the dance, you listened to each other as intently as if words were the only thing you had in mind, but before she got anything said he went on.

"Why I'm *here*," he gestured to the pool, the hotel's stucco walls, the climbing roses, the city beyond, "is meetings. Everything worth doing in the world, it all comes down to meetings."

She refilled their glasses.

By the time they were halfway through the second glass, he'd pulled his chaise closer to the low table and they were both leaning heavily on the arms, pulling toward each other and lobbing bits of conversation back and forth to keep from moving toward each other too quickly. She learned about ad sales and the vagaries of freelance writers. He learned about Minneapolis and Chicago and what a relief it was to be out of the Midwest and away from the grating dreariness of live appearances, and all the while she ran her mind down a list of everything she'd unpacked, looking for something she could invite him back to her room to see, or share, or taste, but she came up empty. The wine was her best card, but she'd already played it. Could she invite him to admire her flowers? Did she have any etchings? She filled their glasses and asked if he'd join her for dinner later—she'd love to have company. The shadows got longer. She talked about Stan and his people, and Bill-the-Governor's VFW halls, which were great as a political strategy but whatever happened to black-tie receptions? She didn't talk about Walter, because she didn't want to spook the guy, but she did say it was a pleasure being someplace where people weren't embarrassed to live well, and that was the only time she felt she was being unfair to Walt. Through it all, Paul smiled as if he thought she had no one but him on her mind. He was a good listener, a sexy listener, the kind of man who makes you think nothing's more interesting in the world than what you have to say. They were sitting in shadow now. The maids had wheeled their pushcarts off to some supply room and disappeared. A gardener bent over one of the irrigation nozzles and did something with a screwdriver, then he went away too. A silver-haired couple paraded majestically past the pool, the ends of a silk scarf wafting behind the woman like an expensive perfume.

"I think I saw a coffeemaker in my suite," Annette said. "And I'd love a cup of coffee before supper. Can I tempt you?"

He picked up his papers and was tempted, and she actually got as far as brewing the coffee, and even pouring it, before they abandoned the pretense for something more interesting in the bedroom, and it had been a long time since Annette's body had done what she used to count on it being able to do. It restored her faith in herself that it still could. Damn, she felt good. She ran a hand down Paul's chest, which was feathery with dark, curling hair, and she kissed his nipples.

"I'm glad I met you," she said.

"You know what I'd like to do, maybe for the second or third issue of the magazine, is do a profile on you. Not on Vietnam, not on your show or your vets, just on you. Who you are, how you came to be that way."

"Sure. We'll talk about it."

"You'd make a great cover."

She grinned.

"I mean, I think we can agree to respect certain limits. We don't have to tell the world everything we know about each other."

"We'd better not, sweetie, because if you start that, I've got a bigger audience than you do."

She was still glowing when she got off the plane. It wasn't until she set her garment bag on the floor of her own apartment and walked to the window to admire Lake Michigan that she let the glow drop away and began the transition that would allow her to call Walt.

CHAPTER 28

Weeks went by without any solid news about the TV show. There were possibilities, Annette's agent said, and then there were setbacks. There were delays. She had to be patient. She had to let him handle things. She had to listen to more metaphors about the natural rhythm of one thing or another. Time passed, and then more time passed. Walter flew to Chicago. Annette flew to the Twin Cities. In the world around her, something seemed to have shifted, making her visible in a way she never had been before. She could hardly leave the house without someone recognizing her. The woman who worked at the dry cleaners hated her and let her face go cold when Annette pushed through the door, then she disappeared into the back for the pure pleasure of making Annette wait. But the love was at least as hard to deal with as the hate. At delis, in parking ramps, in drugstores, people stared, people whispered her name to each other, people wanted to tell her about their lives, about their brothers, sons, husbands, neighbors, cousins, and all the awful things that had happened to them, not to mention the awful things that had happened to their sleep patterns. Couldn't anyone in the country get a decent night's sleep?

It should have been flattering but instead it was like one of those dreams where you're minding your own business and suddenly realize you're buying a box of tampons on TV. Live. In your underwear. And you're holding the box so that *super absorbent* faces the camera.

"Call me when I'm on the air," she told the people who talked to her, turning away and trying to look fascinated by a display of stuffed cabbage, of aspirin, of nylons. "I'd love to hear from you when I'm on the air."

And then Daniel wanted to talk to her after the show again—the same bar, the same awkwardness over who was going to buy, the same fumbling for something to say. When he finally got around to was on his mind, it was some guy who'd given him an earful about the the war being real and did Daniel have any idea what he was doing to people, working for Annette? He was killing people. *Killing* them. Vets who'd come through the whole war in one piece—men that people like him owed their freedom to—they were dying because of him and Annette, and Daniel wanted to tell her every word of the conversation because even if this guy hadn't given him a single piece of information about who was dying, and how, and why, he'd left Daniel deeply and competently spooked.

"It's all just talk," she said, her voice as gentle as if she was on the air and he was coming to her through the wires. "It doesn't mean a thing. It's just some guy with a bug up his ass pretending he knows more than he does."

"Don't you ever think, though, about whether what we're doing is right?"

He whispered it, as if he was afraid she'd hear him.

"I do, often, and it is."

He nodded miserably.

"Daniel, you've heard the callers. We're saving lives here."

Another nod.

She said the same thing three different ways without getting anything more than that nod, and tried a different angle.

"It's not your problem anyway. It's my show, my decision, my issue. You're just doing your job."

No change in the nod.

An age later, when she got up to go, she patted his hand and left him to his half-finished beer. All the way home she thought about the way he slumped in the booth. He was rumpled and didn't quite fit together, but he'd always been like that. Hadn't he always been like that? He had, but even so she thought about it again the next day when she saw him at work, and almost every day after that. He never brought the topic up again though, and she never found the right time to bring it up herself. Still, it changed the way she felt about him. He'd opened himself up to her. How could she not—after a fashion—love him?

She spent more and more time in her apartment playing computer games, watching the lake and the traffic. She called her agent, who said Bowdwin was making progress, things were coming together, and he himself was talking to the corporation that owned the radio station. They were being stubborn, but it was all a game. They wanted something from her, that was all. She had to be patient. These things had a rhythm of their own. He'd take care of everything.

She was worn out with being patient, though, and the apartment was closing in on her, so once a day she took herself to the only refuge she'd found, a New Age bookstore and café where the staff and customers would have rather ripped raw red meat off the bone with their teeth than admit they listened to her show. She sat there in perfect anonymity, and if the food was alfalfa sproutish and the staff was too ethereal to wipe down the tables between customers, she didn't call attention to herself by complaining.

In December Annette's agent called her at the station to say he'd have everything in writing by New Year's. She could bank on it.

"Talk to them about security, o.k.?"

"I'll bring it up, but you know what the problem is."

"Push it. Right to the edge. This is important to me."

He said fine, and right to the edge, and she hung up with that odd mix of elation and suspension that follows promises.

She set the elation aside as too risky.

Because the thing in L.A. with Paul had changed nothing in her life, she pretty much forgot that anything had happened there other than the meeting with the Visigoth, and so it surprised her when Cantwell wanted to talk about an interview she'd given to some magazine. He hadn't figured out a way to be mad at her, but he did sputter out that some people in corporate were upset.

She skimmed down the page he handed her and said she was upset too, and where did people get off, writing this sort of stuff?

She was serious about it. She hadn't given any interviews, and she had no idea where this mess had come from. She'd let her clipping service go, otherwise she'd at least have had some warning.

A second later she remembered the guy by the pool. Mr. Magazineman. Mr. Journalist who didn't even have a journal yet. Paul Whatshisname. She shook her head to keep the realization off her face, but the elevator that once held her expression in place was in the midst of crashing to the basement, and it was hard to believe that the drop didn't show.

"I can't control what they write."

"Just tell me you were misquoted; that's all I need."

"Misquoted? Believe me, I never even gave an interview."

He nodded without looking any happier.

"And then there's this business with Daniel . . ."

She gave Cantwell as blank a look as any she could have wished for, and he found a section on the jump page and handed the magazine back. Daniel said he'd done research for her but that he hadn't found anything yet that would make him doubt the war's reality. It kept him up nights, wondering if they were doing the right thing. It absolutely tore him up.

She stared at the page. To her right lay outrage: Daniel was her producer, the man dedicated to making everything flow smoothly for her. When Cantwell wanted to can him, she'd protected him. She'd drunk beer with him, smiled at him with a full heart. What more could she have done? To her left, though, lay relief: he hadn't noticed the weapon she'd handed him when she asked him to double-check Stan's work. Left or right? It was no contest. She closed her fist around outrage.

"Jesus F.," she said.

"I hardly need to tell you that we'll be looking for another producer."

"Christ, though. I liked the guy."

Cantwell nodded a somber acknowledgment of her loyalty.

When she got home, she skimmed through the article looking for names she recognized—especially her own—and what she found wasn't all bad: she was attractive, with long legs and a voice that made every man capable of turning on a radio think she was talking to him alone. She had singlehandedly brought everything people thought they could rely on into question. But she was lonely in the Midwest, a woman who appreciated the good things in life, trapped in a round of VFW halls and cinder-block convention centers because they'd become part of her image. Very sad tale of a celebrity at odds with her image and surrounded by political zealots to whom she'd mortgaged her soul.

Had she actually said anything about cinder block? The whole conversation was hazy. Hell, who'd been listening? At the time, she hadn't thought conversation was the point.

Paul had also interviewed Nick back in Minneapolis—had she mentioned Nick to him? was it her fault Paul had found him?—

and Nick hadn't said anything about drinking on the back steps, but he had dredged up the time a caller had been defending smoking bans and Annette had told her regulation was completely out of hand and claimed a Keep Our Children Safe from Salmonella Bill was working its way through the state legislature. It was going criminalize parents who kept pet guinea pigs, hamsters, mice, white rats, and lizards of any sort, and what kind of country were we becoming if little Ryan and Ashleigh couldn't keep iguanas in their bedrooms if their parents saw fit?

She'd forgotten about that one. The caller had yapped at her like an outraged Yorkie, and Nick had thought it was pretty funny at the time, but now all of a sudden it was a sign of irresponsibility. It had been past midnight, for god's sake. It had been a joke.

She set the magazine aside and stared out at the lake, but the magazine pulled her back and she read the article again, starting at the beginning this time and forcing herself through to the last expendable paragraphs. Paul had even dredged up someone who claimed to be the ex-girlfriend of the first vet to confirm her theory about the war. The woman couldn't remember what name her ex had used on the air, although Annette could—it was Michael—but she said she'd watched him make the call, and he'd winked at her when he dialed and said, "Listen to this."

So she'd listened, and he claimed to have fought in a war that had ended before he'd even gotten himself born. She listened to the catch in his voice and was halfway ready to weep herself. Even when she knew he was lying, the man could break her heart.

He hung up the phone and laughed so hard he got the hiccups.

She broke up with him that night.

The ex-boyfriend had declined to comment.

So, did reading that make Annette wonder? Well, it rattled her, of course. She had an extended bad moment over it. But when she came down to it, all Paul had was the ex-girlfriend's word. He couldn't prove the ex-boyfriend was even the caller, never mind that the call had been made the way the ex-girlfriend claimed. But even if every word the ex-girlfriend spoke was the capital-T Truth, sometimes it takes a lie to shake loose the larger truth. Because what was she supposed to do with all her other callers? Dismiss them? She had too much other evidence to be wrong about the war.

She looked out at Lake Michigan. Hell, she'd read worse than this without getting so badly rattled. It was because she'd slept with the guy—that was why it was getting to her. It was because she'd told him about cinder-block convention centers and VFW halls.

Then Walter called. Stan was livid, and Bill-the-Governor wasn't what he'd call happy, and he'd talked to them both and settled them down a bit, but what the hell had she been thinking?

"Christ, Walter, I said a few words to this guy. The rest of it he made up."

"That's what I'm going to tell them both, and that's what you need to keep saying. And I'm going to stand by you on this, but I want you to know, I'm not the only one who noticed how close this is to the way you feel about things. You haven't exactly kept your feelings a secret."

"Look, I'll fly up there. I'll talk with them."

"It'll be better if you let me handle it."

"Walt, I need to fix this myself."

He didn't like it but at least he didn't ask why, and that was good because how was she to explain that her relationship with him was one of the things that needed fixing? Because this mess had made her realize that she really could lose him, and that she didn't want to. It had made her ask herself what she wanted and she'd answered, L.A. and Walter both. Excitement and safety. TV and radio. New money and old. There was no reason it shouldn't be possible, but she couldn't take him for granted.

★

It didn't go badly when she met with the governor. It was all just business. These things happen, he said. The media, he said. "And what you said—what they said you said—well, when you come to think about it, it's more of a problem for you than it is for me."

She dropped her eyes to the carpet on his office floor, not exactly acknowledging that it was a problem but still not arguing about it either. A part of her actually agreed—a problem was floating around out there somewhere—but then she brought her eyes to the hard surface of the governor's desk and to the harder surface of his face, and they left no room for problems or vulnerabilities. Her moment of ritual abasement was over. Or it wasn't exactly over, because he kept on talking, but she'd passed its low point.

"You'll forgive me if I give you a piece of advice," he said. "I'm at least twice your age, and you're used to being on the other side of the microphone, so . . . Well, the point is, you never want to let your guard down when you're dealing with the media. First thing, you learn to tell them from the start when something's off the record, just the way I'm telling you now: this is off the record, because even though I'm not talking to you as a representative of the media right now, I never forget that you are one and could start working without telling me about the switch. Next, you watch what you say even when you're off the record, because you don't want to tempt people into sin, right? And when you're speaking on the record, you figure out what you want to say and then that's all you say. Over and over. Not another single thought. You want to talk about the weather, you find someone else to talk to or next thing you know you just made a policy statement on global warming."

She agreed. She thanked him. She listened humbly while he went on for another ten minutes, and she kept a smile on her face and ate shit, and they were friends when she left, although she felt like an asshole—the producer, in fact, of all the shit she'd just eaten. She couldn't imagine that she'd ever look at him without feeling that way all over again.

With Stan it was harder. Well, yeah, there had been that business about zealots and mortgaging her soul, and he and his boys had sounded pretty dreary, but she wouldn't have thought Stan was the sort of man to be offended by dreary. Or by being called a zealot.

So O.K., everybody had their little vanities, and he was going to clean the smudges off his by using her as a polishing rag. No problem. If she'd managed to sit through Len's lectures all that time, she could make herself sit through Stan's.

So they sat across from each other at the same Perkins where they'd always met, and neither of them ordered anything more than coffee, and she should probably have known right then that this wasn't a good sign.

First he ran through a speech about Constructive members and what they expected of him, and then about the phone calls he'd been fielding, all of them asking what kind of person he'd tied the Constructive to if she could turn around and say things like that.

"Stan, I told you. Walt told you. Misquote. I didn't say that. Any of it."

He made a gesture with his hands, sweeping that out of his way and almost taking his water glass along with it. He didn't care who'd said what. It had been printed. Alongside her name. That was what mattered: people's perceptions.

Just listen, she reminded herself. *Just shut up and listen*, and for an endless five or ten minutes she did listen. She heard about the problems she'd caused just when he was pulling together a national network of Constructives, and he didn't necessarily like it either but they were linked, the two of them, him and her, and they might as well get used to that. It was a marriage of sorts. He had to know he could trust her. So goddamn it, she had to think before she went whining in public about her personal likes and dislikes.

The way he was reacting was out of proportion to what the article had actually said, and it didn't make sense to her until he started talking about himself.

"Look," he said, "I don't fly to Hong Kong to buy my clothes, or to Singapore, or wherever it is that Walt goes to buy his. O.K.? That's how it is. That's who I am. I don't eat at restaurants where it's too dark to read the menu. O.K.? You don't like that, fine, don't eat with me, don't be seen with me. It's not that kind of marriage. But don't go out in public and run me down because of it. Especially when you're using my research and asking my people to guard your hind end."

He'd worked himself up to deliver a real scolding and he'd have gone on but she'd run out of silence, somehow.

"For Chrissake, Stan, I told you . . ."

"Without me you'd still be talking to three listeners in the middle of the night."

"Yeah, and so would you."

They glared at each other. Her answer hadn't made sense but they both knew what she meant, and it was a joy to be this cleanly furious with him.

"You need me," she said, "and if I needed you before, I don't now."

"Fine," he said. "Wonderful. We just got a divorce."

He dropped some money on the table for the coffees, and he walked out.

★

She drove to Walter's, pushing the rental car over the speed limit until a furious kind of peace flowed upward from the tires, through the steering wheel, and into her arms. To make the turn into Walter's driveway without ending up in the trees, though, she had to slow down, which meant she was raging again by the time she slammed her garment bag down in the entryway.

"He just dropped the damn money on the table," she told Walt, but he didn't seem to understand what an insult this had been, and she was too riled to make sense of it herself.

"I tried, Walter. I walked in there ready to eat shit, really I did, but he just pushed me too hard. I mean, it's not like he had anything he wanted me to do, or undo, or patch back together for him. He just wanted to pound me over the head so he'd feel better. So he could tell people he had."

Walter uh-huhed her as if all he heard was the emotion, not a word of the content.

"You know what he talked about was us being married. Me and him. The two of us. It was creepy. It was like all this time what he really wanted from me was sex or something."

Walt moved her into the living room without breaking the flow of her diatribe, and he uh-huhed her some more. When she slowed down, he poured them each a glass of wine, and she accepted hers and burst into . . . Well, not tears exactly but they would have been if she'd been able to cry. A kind of choking was what it was, the body's lower forty-eight working to push out tears and her throat refusing to let them pass.

He took the glass back, set it down, and sat on the edge of the coffee table in front of her, waiting for a sign that he could touch her.

"You don't know what it's like," she choked out between squalls of not-tears. "People don't talk to you that way. Why do they think they can talk to me that way?"

She knew the answer, of course—he was a man and he was rich—but he shook his head as if this hadn't occurred to him, or as if it would be impolite to mention it.

"It's one thing from a governor, although he didn't . . ." she said. She almost-cried some more.

"But a guy like Stan . . . Talking to me like he thought there was something . . ."

"He's just letting off steam," Walt said. "Lets him feel better about himself."

"Yeah, but what about me?"

He moved to the couch and nuzzled her neck.

"Now we have to make you feel better."

She shook her head to keep her hand from pushing him away.

"I'm not ready to feel better yet."

He laughed and said that was fine, he could wait, and he handed her wine back. She had no choice but to accept it.

Annette lay on her side next to Walter, the fingers of one hand tracing the shoulder seam of his pajama top, wondering whether she'd marry him if he asked, whether he'd move to Chicago to be with her if she did, whether he'd follow her to New York or L.A., whether she'd spend the rest of her life not liking sex.

He rolled on his side to face her.

"You feel better?" he said.

She had, a tiny bit, until he reminded her that she'd been feeling worse, but she said "Mm-hmm."

She smiled and ran a hand along the curl of his ear, and he hummed with pleasure. How could someone be so good at feeling pleasure and so bad at passing it along?

They'd never talked about marriage, any more than they'd talked about love, but the possibility was marching between their bodies like a cat. Sooner or later they were going to have to either scratch its ears or squirt water in its face to get it off the bed.

She settled herself against him, back to front, and his arm swung over her.

"I love your hair," he said. "I love your voice. I love the back of your neck."

She thought about Michael, that first vet—that first alleged vet—who'd called her. She thought about the catch in his voice, the way he'd almost cried on the air. He'd been as real to her as Walt was right now. It was . . . well, it was unnerving, a little.

There had to be a way to confirm Stan's information. Something definitive. Something she hadn't tried.

Walt pushed her hair aside and kissed the back of her neck.

"I particularly love the back of your neck."

CHAPTER 29

 Annette drove to work directly from the airport, threading words together for a letter to Stan: *there is too much at stake to let our personal feelings disrupt . . .* No. *Both of us have too much at stake . . . We all have too much at stake . . .*

It was too bad Daniel was gone. She could have dictated half a letter to him—the phrase she'd been sharpening, an offer to continue trading Stan's research for access to her fan mail, then blah blah blah until the page was full, sincerely yours— and when he brought it back she could have added a squiggle resembling a signature and shoved Stan-fuckin'-Marlin out of her mind.

Cantwell would let her borrow someone to type the letter, but she didn't want half the station knowing her relationship with Stan was held together with safety pins. She didn't want them to know it existed at all.

Fine, then. She had time, she'd type it herself, and when she breezed into the open office and past what had once been Daniel's desk, most of her mind was working on the blah-blah-blah part, trying to fill that in. She glanced at Daniel's desk, expecting a twinge of regret—the transience of all things mortal, something she'd liked about Daniel, how he could betray her? that sort of twinge—but there Daniel sat, straddling his desk chair, and she registered an oddity about the scene before she had time to break the oddity into its component parts. It didn't even register as something wrong yet, just something odd.

"But that's the thing of it," Daniel was saying, underlining some point he must have made just before she swung around the corner. "You don't see what we're doing to people."

He wasn't talking to Annette—he hadn't seen her yet—he was lecturing Cantwell, and Cantwell was standing there and letting him. So that was one oddity. Or two, really. Another was the cluster of people standing beside Cantwell, all gathered up between Daniel's desk and the back wall and looking, well, odd. Annette drifted in their direction with all the self-direction of an ant washing down the drain.

"If it's about the job," Cantwell said. Uncertainty was already undermining his words but all the same he added, "I could . . . ," before he gave up the offer.

"It's not that," Daniel said. "You can't change a single thing that matters. That's not in your power. And I'm not asking you for anything. In a sick sort of way, I think you did me a favor."

He turned to Annette and smiled—not his please-like-me smile but a real one, as if he was genuinely glad to see her—and here was another bit of strangeness: this was beyond any question Daniel, but it wasn't the Daniel she was used to. He'd gotten himself up in a suit, a tie, the full body armor of the powerful man, and even if it wasn't quite the suit a powerful man would have bought, it had given him a confidence she wouldn't have thought he was capable of. All the apology had gone out of him.

Her eyes followed the suit sleeve to his hand and noticed that it was resting on a gun the way some other hand might rest on a dog's head. Good ole Shep, always there for him. He didn't gesture Annette into the cluster of people, but she clustered in as if he had. She was an ant. This was where the water had carried her.

He must have used it to gather them all up, and it had left behind the current that swept her in.

O.K., she wasn't thinking clearly. Right at that moment it seemed like the only thing she could do.

"But here's the thing," he said. "Here's what I'm trying to get you to understand. I gave up my soul for this job. I told myself, you know, I told myself it was O.K.: I could do the job, pick up the paycheck, think whatever I wanted in my spare time. I thought, you know, everybody has to make compromises. That's what making a living's all about. But the thing is . . . The thing is . . . Hell, now the job's gone, I didn't need to do any of that. I could drive a cab. I could work at Kinko's, wait tables, flip burgers if I had to, but the thing is it's not about keeping the job, it's about who I am after I helped . . . Do you have any idea how much damage we've done?"

He glanced at Annette as if she were the only possible person to direct this question to—his old friend Annette—and she opened her mouth to say something but no words came out. She liked this version of him, oddly, as much as she'd liked the rumpled, apologetic one. Or more. He was someone she might have really talked to, if she could have talked at all.

"I've been talking to people. Vets. Vietnamese refugees. We're tearing them apart."

Daniel picked up the gun, not like a man who wanted to scare anyone, but because it was there, and because he wanted to think about it more closely.

"The question is, how am I supposed to go on when I gave *me* away to keep my job?"

He looked at the gun, then at the huddled mass in front of him, then waved it vaguely toward them, not exactly threatening but not exactly not threatening either. Who could say, once a gun was in someone's hand, what would happen next? The gun waved toward Annette and seemed to consider her for a long time before it meandered on and she could breathe out.

At the back of the crowd, somebody whimpered.

"You know how they say you have to put the gun inside your mouth if you want to be sure it, you know, does the job? You know what I'm afraid of? I'm not afraid of dying—I'm pretty much looking forward to that. I'm afraid of the taste. If you could just put it to the side of your head, it'd be easy."

And he smiled again, directly at Annette, before he pointed the gun toward his mouth. She drew in, her muscles working to make her so small she wouldn't be present when he pulled the trigger, but instead of shooting, he extended his tongue until it touched the barrel. The same voice at the back of the crowd moaned, higher this time. The woman next to Annette huddled into her, as if he were pointing the gun at them again.

"Daniel . . ." a woman said, an admin assistant in her fifties who Annette knew well enough to nod at when she saw her by the coffee machine.

"It's not that bad," Daniel said. "The taste. It's not that bad."

"Daniel. Please."

It was the same voice, and it was, in the context, eloquent. Those two words contained everything a person could possibly say.

"It's o.k.," he said. "Someone always pays a price for the kind of thing we do here."

He'd lowered the gun to his lap, and he studied it for a second.

"Actually, a lot of people are paying the price already, so it's only right that some of us do. Don't you think? We all know it's wrong."

He raised the gun and swung the barrel toward his mouth again. Annette closed her eyes, and when nothing happened she opened them, expecting to see that he'd taken another lick of the barrel and was setting it back down. She half expected him to smile and say, "Licorice," but his lips were closing around it, and she was just sending her eyelids the signal to close again when noise filled the room and the back of his head exploded. Her eyes closed, but behind the lids, she continued to see the inside of his head on the outside, flying loose. The woman next to Annette clutched at her and Annette clutched back, although she couldn't have said who she was clutched to. Someone screamed—a man's voice. In the movies, it was always a woman who screamed, and this registered as another oddity. Then he stopped, and the voice at the back moaned again. A few minutes passed. Or maybe they were seconds. Annette kept her eyes shut.

Cantwell's voice said, "o.k., people," as if he were calling a soccer team together. Nothing followed, but it brought enough normalcy to the situation for Annette to disentangle herself from her neighbor, squint her eyes open for some ragged fragment of a second, and turn away from what had been Daniel so she could open them the rest of the way. She was looking at the side wall, the water cooler, a man who sold ads and was now sitting on the floor with his head on his knees and his back wedged against the wall. She held onto that view, although it didn't quite block the images behind her eyelids.

"o.k.," Cantwell said again. "o.k., let's . . ."

The words hung there for a while.

"Would somebody . . ."

The moaning had stopped at some point and now it started again.

". . . call the police. Would somebody call the police."

Nobody moved.

"Janice, please."

The admin assistant who'd said Daniel's name, back when the name still belonged to someone, worked her way into Annette's line of sight and then out, following the wall like someone walking a high ledge, bracing her weight on an outstretched arm to step over the ad salesman on the floor, and it made a kind of sense to Annette that she'd work her way around the room this way.

Annette shielded her eyes so she could turn to where Cantwell stood. He drew a breath, visibly inflating himself.

"O.K.," he said again. "O.K., this is a tragedy—we're all devastated—but it's ten minutes to the hour, and we have a station to run. Annette, can you handle your show?"

Annette opened and closed her mouth a few times, soundlessly, like a fish.

"Right. Paul, find a tape—old show, any show, doesn't matter which show. Quick. Everyone else, let's move to the lobby, please."

They broke apart reluctantly—one person, three people, the man on the floor levering himself up and waiting to see if he fell down again. Annette followed the invisible ledge, her eyes tracking the line of the wall, careful not to look down.

In the lobby, Cantwell seemed to run out of orders. The man from the floor dropped himself into a chair. A woman said, "He used to stop at Starbucks on his way to work sometimes and bring me a coffee, you know? I never once asked him to. It was such a sweet thing." Annette's mind was stuck on narrow focus, moving from one detail to the next and unable to assemble them into a coherent picture. Speakers in the ceiling were broadcasting the show before Annette's, a testosterone jock called Marcus who Annette had never liked, but it occurred to her now that he was sitting in a soundproofed studio and had no idea what he was about to walk out and see.

The woman who'd talked about the coffee was crying. Paul raced in.

"Storeroom's locked. Keys aren't . . ."

He shook his head to show how thoroughly the keys weren't.

"Keys, people," Cantwell ordered, and Annette half expected

them to materialize in his outstretched palm. "People, who has the keys?"

No keys appeared. He looked at his watch.

"Annette, you're going live. Give us fifteen minutes, twenty minutes, I don't care what just happened—you do it. We'll cut to a tape a.s.a.p., even if we have to chop the storeroom door down. Just hold it together till then. Paul, fill in for . . ." He didn't say Daniel's name, just nodded his head toward the open office they'd all just left. "Everyone else, I want those keys."

★

Annette dropped herself in front of the microphone and focused on the tabletop, willing it not to slant, since it never had before. When her will didn't affect its tilt, she brought her eyes to the window separating her and Paul, who did the countdown on his fingers and pointed at her. The sign over the door lit up, and she was on the air.

"Ladies and gentlemen, boys and girls, peanuts and popcorn."

A hairline crack appeared in the smooth surface of the words. The table was still slanted, and she wondered, in the back of her mind, if that mattered. If she could ignore it, did that mean it wasn't a problem?

"I'm Annette Majoris, this is *Open Line*, and I'm waiting for you to call me."

She gave out the number, explained the seven-second delay, said all the things she'd said so many times she could have repeated them in her sleep, and after that she was flying free—no net, no safety harness, no script, just her and the microphone, her voice winging invisibly through the air. She punched the first button.

"Tim from Aberdeen, talk to me."

Tim talked. He told her he'd been in Vietnam—Khe Sanh, other place names that bounced off her mind like marbles—and he'd brought home a Zippo engraved in Saigon with a rhyme he couldn't repeat on the air, but he'd also brought home some memories, and he wanted to tell her about them.

Annette should have cut in there and told *him* about his memories, but she didn't. He had a slow-moving voice, and she was grateful for every extra second that gave her before she'd have to come back in and say something. He'd worked his way through all the places he'd been and moved on to the buddies who'd died in each of them, and then to an old mama-san in some ville he didn't even know the name of and a couple of kids on a water buffalo who'd gotten shot just because they were in a place where their people had lived from the beginning of time, and he didn't say what happened to the water buffalo but Annette's mind flashed her a quick picture of . . . Who was it who'd talked about shooting that chicken? She saw blood, feathers, bone, and except for the feathers it could as easily have been Daniel, or the water buffalo, then the picture was gone and Tim was saying again that he'd been there, that he knew he'd been there, that it was real, every—excuse the French—goddamn death and injury, every bit of blood and bone, and she should have cut in there, too, told him how unreliable memories are, how easily we can be fooled by them, but she couldn't. She was seeing that chicken. She was seeing Daniel. Everyone he was talking about was as real to her as the two of them, and they were all of them filling the studio.

"I don't mean to get emotional about this," Tim said, but he was emotional, and his voice broke. "But the thing is . . . The thing is . . . All these people who say it didn't happen? You have no idea what that does . . ."

His voice broke again, and he stopped talking. Just shut down without bothering to say, *Tag, you're it.*

She would have liked to tell him about Daniel—wanted that so much that nothing else seemed possible—but she knew she'd never get the words out, and that left her sitting wordless in front of the mic.

On the positive side, the tabletop had stopped slanting.

"Tim," she said. The break in her own voice matched the one in his, leaving a crack considerably larger than a hairline.

"Tim, I'm . . ."

The next word wouldn't come out. Dead airtime leaked out of the cracks and flowed into the wires.

"Hey," Tim said after an endless amount of time had flowed past. "You O.K.?"

"I'm . . ."

The sobs at the back of her throat tore loose. On the other side of the glass, Paul stood up, his body looking for a way to intervene and his mind not supplying it.

Annette fought back the next sob. When she could produce human speech again, she said, "Tim, I'm sorry. Really I am." Her voice wasn't much more than a whisper—sand against gravel—but it was at least a voice, and it left Tim speechless the way no amount of argument would have. Between the two of them, the station was spending she had no idea how many hundreds of dollars a minute to broadcast silence into offices and kitchens, into cars and barber shops. Or maybe it was thousands of dollars. She had no idea. At stations around the country, engineers were thumping their equipment on the side to see if they could bring the signal back. On the other side of the glass, Paul was holding up five fingers and mouthing *please*, and she stared at the fingers as if they were a message from another planet.

"I'm sorry," she whispered again, not so much to Tim this time, or to Paul, or even to her listeners, but to—well, to whoever. She didn't stop and ask herself who she was apologizing to, just stood up and looked around, saw the frame tethering the glass to the wall between herself and Paul, saw the fake wood of the tabletop under her mic, and she saw it all with a clarity she'd never experienced before. Each object was perfectly defined and heartbreaking and beautiful in a surprising and beauty-less way. Even the silence filling the studio was perfectly balanced and beautiful. Then she unslung her purse from the back of the chair and walked out. Behind her, the microphone picked silence out of the air, shot it through wires, and hurled it across the country. In the hallway, the speakers amplified her silence before they picked up a series of high, quick beeps. Somewhere along the line, Tim had hung up. Paul cut the connection and there was silence again.

By the time she reached the lobby, Paul had cut to an ad. The lobby was abandoned—everyone was off scrambling for the keys, or battering the storeroom door down. It didn't matter. All that mattered was getting through the outer door and as far away from the microphone as possible. She seemed to be crying again, but it was only water this time, with none of the sobbing that had kept her from talking a few minutes before, and so it had nothing to do with her, or it only had to do with her face, not with her lungs, her thoughts, her self.

By the time she got her car started, someone had thrown on an old Carpenters album and was broadcasting it into her front seat.

CHAPTER 30

Annette drove home. She thought about going to a hotel, a motel, some anonymous place where no one would know her, but the act of finding one, or choosing one and then getting herself there, was beyond her. And she couldn't count on anyplace being anonymous anymore. Wherever she went, someone would know her. So she drove home, she locked the door behind her, and she swiveled a chair around so she could stare out at the lake. Sometimes she wept—huge, ugly, face-scrunching sobs—and sometimes she didn't, and some distant part of her brain noted both acts and judged them equally odd.

The phone rang and her answering machine picked up. Cantwell wanted to know if she was all right, and wanted her to know that what had happened was unfortunate but it wasn't irremediable.

Irremediable. Was that even a word, *irremediable?*

She should call him, he said, as soon as she got his message.

Silence closed back in. She wasn't weeping, and if she could sit entirely still and do nothing but watch the lake she might not need to ever again. The sky grew darker and the lake harder to see.

The phone rang and a reporter left her phone number. The phone rang. Her agent. The phone rang. Her agent's secretary saying her agent really did need to talk to her. The phone rang. Another reporter.

If she could make herself stand up, she could unplug the thing.

The phone rang. Walter said he hadn't caught the show but he'd heard about it, and he wanted her to know it wasn't the end of the world. There were plenty of ways to explain what she'd said. She should call him. He was worried about her.

What had she said that needed explaining? That she was sorry? All she'd meant was that she'd never meant to hurt anyone. That Daniel was dead and the chicken was dead and the kids on the water buffalo were dead and for all she knew the water buffalo was dead too, and damn it, she was sorry about all of them. She didn't know if the war was real or not real, and she didn't care. Daniel had been real, and Daniel had thought the war was real, and now Daniel was dead, and if she'd never gotten into this thing that would never have happened.

The thought of having to explain any of that upset the stillness she'd been sustaining, and she wept again.

The phone rang. She got out of her chair, unplugged every phone in the place, and sat back down. It was too dark to see the water and she stared into the dark. She rained used kleenexes, one at a time, onto the floor beside her chair. Time had stopped meaning much, but at some point she took herself to bed, not because it was time to do that or because she wanted to sleep but because it struck her as a better place to feel awful. When she woke up, it was light out, and she moved back to her chair and stared at the lake. Time passed. She felt something she recognized as hunger and found a handful of cookies but after a few bites, chewing didn't seem worth the effort. Daniel came into her mind, straddling his chair, with no apology left in his body, and she turned her mind away from him by making lists of the things she needed to do. She should call Cantwell. She should call her agent. No, she should call her agent first to make sure of what to say to Cantwell. It was the pressure. It was Daniel's death.

Cantwell should never have asked her to go live after what happened. All she'd meant to say was . . .

She should call Walt before she called anyone and let him tell her what to say and who to say it to. She should ask him to fly down so he could put his arms around her while she buried her face in the smooth front of his shirt, where no memory could reach her. They could stay that way forever. She'd be lifted so far outside herself that even if she did have to leave the shelter of his shirt front, she wouldn't mind. If there had ever been a time when she hadn't wanted Walt, she'd been wrong. He was a good man. She hadn't realized how important that was.

She called no one.

Sometime in the afternoon she grew hungry again and found a can of smoked oysters. She ate them and stared at the lake.

It was getting dark again when the door opened and Walt stepped in.

"I was worried about you."

He set his garment bag down, and it pooled against his leg.

In the movie she'd watched in her imagination, this had been the scene where she'd flown to him, but it was strange how hard it was to leave the chair. Plus, there was a lake of kleenex at her feet that she'd have to wade through. And the empty oyster can, the uneaten cookies she'd dumped on the end table, not to mention that she was wearing exactly as much makeup as she'd been born with. Still, she made herself stand up, and she crossed the floor and buried her face in his white shirt, and he did wrap his arms around her. She waited to lift out of herself, to melt into him, but her mind was still ticking away inside her head, reminding her of how things should be and how they weren't.

"When you didn't answer your phone . . ." Walt said. "I was calling you most of last night, this morning . . ."

She pulled away enough to point her head in the direction of the nearest phone.

"I unplugged it. I unplugged all of them."

She swung back to Walt—was he following this?—and he nodded.

"I can't talk to them."

She couldn't seem to get her voice up to a normal volume either.

He nodded some more, and he seemed to be measuring, calculating, making lists, trying to get an estimate of her dimensions and vulnerabilities so he'd know how many packing chips he had to pour around her if she wasn't to shatter when he shipped her back to the studio. Then he drew away from her to lean his garment bag against the wall and she was free to scoop up the trash and spin the chair so it faced into the room.

"Tell you what we'll do," Walt said, "we'll find a spokesman to deal with the press. Spokes*person*. Say you need some time out of the public eye, you were deeply affected, all of that. All perfectly true, all perfectly understandable."

She reached for a fresh kleenex but kept herself from doing anything worse that getting teary.

"Have you called Cantwell?"

She shook her head.

"Pivotal. Cantwell's pivotal. Got to talk to him, let him know it's under control. I'll give him a call."

He walked to the window and looked out.

"The issue of the apology has to be addressed," he said to the glass, to the lake she'd been staring at all day. "Leave that open to interpretation, and hell, it could mean anything. The press'll massacre you."

For a few seconds he seemed to have forgotten her, then he turned back.

"Here's what we say. You were devastated. You'd just witnessed this . . ." He ticked his head to one side. "We'll have to give a clear picture of what it was like, but anyway, this horrific scene, and there you were with a caller upset about deaths he seemed to remember, and it was no time to argue politics, or even realities— you just heard his pain and you resonated with it and were sorry for it. It wasn't a retraction or even an apology, just a moment of old-fashioned human sympathy, and is the world so far gone that we can't understand that? Is that close enough?"

She sniffed and nodded that yes, it was close, although it was also several sizable states west of the target. It was some- place where the chicken, the mama-san, the kids on the water buffalo had never been, someplace where Daniel had never straddled his chair and talked about having no self to go back to. Someplace where he'd never stuck his tongue out until it met the barrel of his gun. Someplace . . . Jesus, all of that was inside her, and she wanted to tell Walt about it, but she had no reason to think talking wouldn't make it worse. What good were words going to do when your producer's just splattered his head all over the office?

She could almost taste gunmetal on her own tongue.

Still, she had nodded, so Walt got down on his hands and knees and plugged in the nearest phone. She hadn't expected that. She'd thought there'd be more time, more talk, the gradual disap- pearance of what she was feeling, a slow return of the person she'd once been. Instead, she felt like she'd been snapped out of REM sleep to find Walt waltzing her along the roof edge, barefoot and thirty-seven stories up. In a high wind.

Walt dialed the phone.

"And get me your agent's number," he said while it rang.

She nodded and backed toward the bedroom, not because she had her agent's number in there, but because she needed— intensely, wordlessly—to get away from Walt and the telephone he was holding.

"Jerry," Walt said. "Walter Bishop. Long time. Very long time. How've you been?"

Annette closed the door, putting a slab of painted wood and a drywall sandwich between herself and that easy voice trading verbal backslaps and hiya-buddies with Jerry, whoever the hell Jerry was. The first of the puzzle pieces Walt would have to click from one place to the next before he could move her from the safety of her bedroom back into that studio. Her breath was coming in short gasps and she lowered herself to the edge of the bed, giving herself over completely to her body's reality show, which involved snatching breath desperately in and in and in again. Oxygen was about to be rationed, and the participants were stockpiling.

She curled on her side in the staleness of unmade bed, of pulled sheets, of side-skewed comforter, and packed more air into her lungs. The rise and fall of Walt's voice worked its way under the door and through the wall, the drywall serving as a sounding board for his ease in the world. He said good-bye to one person, hello to the next person, and the exact words were muffled, but in spite of herself, she could fill in content to match the tone: it's been too long. We'll have to get together. Click, click, another piece happy to be shoved from here to there so she could be moved forward.

Her body snatched air. Even lying down she felt lightheaded and her hands tingled. Her mind's video camera sent her a quick shot of the studio, of the microphone, nothing more than the actorless setting but it was enough. It was too much. It was the most desolate place she'd ever been.

She sat upright and sucked air in. She couldn't go back to that endless round of callers—the attackers, the complainers, the physically and psychically wounded, the unsleeping ocean of need she'd somehow called forth. It wasn't the physical place. She couldn't go back on the air and be the person she'd been in that place. Not after what Daniel . . . Not after . . .

She curled back onto the bed, followed the tingling up her arms, and caught a glimpse of the person she used to be, bobbing like a rubber duck on the sea of callers, sure that nothing could pull her under, and she had just started mourning the death of that self, remembering how clever she'd been, how sure of herself, how attractive, and had just understood that that self was as dead as Daniel was, when Walt came through the door holding the phone in one hand and using the other to block the mouthpiece.

"It's Cantwell. You don't have to say much, but you do have to talk to him."

She pushed herself upright so she could shake her head.

"I can't. Tell him I can't."

He turned her palm upward and set the phone in it.

"Talk to him."

Annette looked at the phone. She looked at Walt, who smiled as if he knew something she didn't and walked out of the room, leaving her with what might as well have been a live hand grenade. Cantwell's voice rose from the plastic, tiny and demanding, and her body made another grab for air. She lifted the phone toward her face.

"I can't," she told the phone.

"Annette?"

"I can't."

"Listen, I should never have asked you to go on. I didn't have time to think how it would affect you . . ."

"I can't listen to them. I can't go back in there."

Her voice was pleading with him, and she listened to it as if it were somebody else's. A wisp of silence blew past, and then he was talking again, a little too fast, a little too loud.

"It doesn't have to be today. Take some time. Get away . . ."

He'd have gone on but she cut him off.

"I can't do it anymore."

Her voice this time was definite, absolute, and still somebody else's. She let the phone sink to her lap, stared at it for a while, then hung up.

Walt came through the open door, and he argued with her. This was a career decision, something that would affect the rest of her life, and she had to think about more than just how she felt today. At a minimum, she should give herself time. She could always quit later, but she had a gift, a presence, something very few people possessed. She shouldn't just throw that away, because if she walked away from this . . . Well, what were the odds that she'd have another chance? He threw arguments at her like dry bread to the overfed ducks in a city park, and she paddled close enough to see what he was offering, then watched while it soaked up water and sank. She didn't want another chance. All she wanted was an end, a way to disappear, a way not to feel what she was feeling. She sat with the phone in one hand and let his words drop into the water all around her, and she wondered if Walt would still want her now that she wasn't Annette Majoris, Radio Personality. It came to her with a sense of surprise that he would, that it might suit him to keep her like a duck he'd taken in because it had a broken wing. She could live entirely inside his house and program the microwave for them both.

She wondered what she'd do with herself between meals.

He sat down next to her and put an arm around her shoulder.

"I'm being insensitive, aren't I? I'm so focused on what I want you to do that I'm not leaving you time to figure it out for yourself."

She could have said yes, he was being insensitive, only he hadn't given her time to figure that out either, and she understood with the clarity of divine revelation that there was no way she'd be able to make herself sleep with this man again. If he was a good man, then being good wasn't good enough. Her body wanted nothing to do with him, and she leaned far enough away to dislodge his arm.

"I can't touch you?"

"I can't do this, Walt. I can't do any of it. I'm sorry—I wanted to, but I just can't do it anymore."

He looked like she'd run over his pet duck.

CHAPTER 31

 Stan hadn't caught Annette's meltdown in real time. He found out about it the next morning instead, by opening the paper as he sat over his coffee: Producer. Majoris. Apology. Not available for comment.

He reached for the phone, but Walter Bishop wasn't available for comment either, and he was relieved when he couldn't reach Annette, because what was he supposed to say to the woman? No one at her old station in Minneapolis could tell him anything, and he'd never cultivated any contacts at the Chicago station other than Annette, of course, and the producer.

All of which told him that he'd let his network go slack, but beyond that it told him nothing, so he focused on the information he did have and vowed to tighten the network's strings until they were so taut that they'd whisper when a fly brushed past. Which was a satisfying image but no practical help at all. He sat back down at the kitchen table and finished his coffee. It had gone cold, and he never had liked cold coffee, but it gave him a sense of normalcy, or at least of its possibility, to finish what he'd poured himself, and he clung to that, because he understood already that this was the end of things as they had once been and that whatever came next would be immeasurably worse.

The golden age was over.

He called Bishop again and left a message, and he called Annette again and didn't.

Bishop waited till the next day to return his call, and his voice was flattened and dull. If he still had his chipmunk cheeks, they were no longer stuffed with pleasure. He said Stan's name, he said his own name, and having established both, he waited for Stan to fill in the blank, as if he'd lost the power to direct events.

Fair enough. Stan was the one who'd left a message.

"I wanted to ask," Stan said, and then he left a blank space of his own. This was a touchy business, and he wasn't sure how personal a question he was trying to ask.

"About Annette?"

"About Annette."

A second or two dragged past, pulled by oxen who'd been taxed and regulated out of all job satisfaction.

"She's not coming back, Stan."

Stan understood *coming back* geographically and was struggling to figure out the impact of this information. The oxen lumbered past, dragging another second behind them. *Clop,* very slow *clop.*

"Her show's dead. Over. Kaput. I tried to tell her we could fix what she said, but she can't do it anymore."

Clop.

"That's too bad," Stan said, "because she was . . ."

The thought dangled and Bishop cut in before either the oxen had to struggle past again or Stan had to figure out what, exactly, she had been.

"She really had something, didn't she?"

His voice lifted for a moment. They might have been talking about the blameless dead.

"She did. She really did."

Clop.

When Bishop came back in, the lift had gone out of his voice but the mournfulness was gone as well. He was flat again but ready to get down to business.

"Here's the thing. She's left an absence, not just on the air but politically, and we've got to address that. I don't have to spell this out for you, Stan."

Stan said no, he didn't, but he waited for Bishop to spell it out anyway since people always did once they said they didn't have to.

"The thing is, if people like you stretch the boundaries of the political arena, it's people like Annette who let you be heard. I mean, she was fearless."

That slight lift again, and Stan agreed: fearless. Absolutely.

Bishop sighed, then shook himself free of his regrets, his memories, everything that stood in the way of the task at hand.

"I'll get to the point here. I've been talking to some people—the governor among them, and believe me, Stan, he thinks highly of you. I'm still missing someone who can keep Annette's audience, but I'll find that, and if we move quickly enough, we can hold on to a number of the stations that've been carrying her. We'll lose a few—there's no help for that—but if we find the right person, they'll be back."

"What do you need from me?"

"At the moment, nothing. I just want to make sure you're on board. What I'll want from you very soon is the same sort of help you gave Annette but with a broader focus."

"A broader focus is good," Stan said.

When he set the phone down he hung suspended between the future, which was either a great opportunity or complete corruption, and the past, when he had been pure but wandering uselessly in the desert.

He had no choice but to go forward, and he walked down the hall to the living room, where Flambard was just yanking his feet off the coffee table.

"Steve, you'll let me know if I'm doing the wrong thing, won't you, with Walter Bishop and them?"

Flambard looked at him blankly, then came into focus around the question.

"Sure, Stan. No problem."

Stan wasn't convinced—he'd agreed too easily for it to mean much—but it warmed him all the same. Steve would be a kind of political mood ring. As long as his socks rested on Stan's coffee table, then Walter Bishop and the governor hadn't claimed his soul.

★

Even before Walt picked up his garment bag and left, Annette's mind had already begun dividing everything she owned into categories: things that she knew held bad memories and things that might not; things she could fit into her mother's apartment and things she couldn't; things she loved and things that were just things. For days she drifted through the apartment picking things up and putting them down, sorting them into piles and then forgetting which piles were for what and starting new ones, but none of it mattered, really. It was all just stuff.

It was odd that the thought of moving into her mother's apartment didn't depress her. Or maybe it did but she was too depressed already to notice an extra shot of gloom pumping through her bloodstream. She spent hours looking at her furniture, staring at it the way she'd stared at the lake: it was fascinating, but it was meaningless. She could look at it for hours, but what the hell, she was done with it. Let the building management have it. Maybe it would balance out what she owed on the lease.

In the end, after all her lists and piles and divisions, her decisions about what to take were random. She took what caught her eye, what fit in her car, what she could bear to look at. The suede jacket and the computer went with her and the windup toys and the skirt she'd bought for that first party at Walt's stayed behind. She gave the doorman a twenty to roll up the Tabriz and tie it to the top of her car. It left on outline of grit on the floor to mark where it had lain, and she thought about sweeping it up, but what was the point? Instead she closed the door behind her and followed the doorman to the car.

She'd just crossed into Indiana when she turned on the radio and picked up a man's voice, a voice so easygoing that he seemed to have slipped into the passenger seat beside her and propped his feet on the dash, and in spite of herself, she kind of liked him. Her hand was reaching for the knob to turn him off—she wasn't ready to like anyone yet—when it hit her: she was listening to her show's old slot. This was her replacement.

Her hand kept moving and turned off the radio.

Silence. Or not silence but wordlessness and the sound of tires on the highway and of cars slicing through air.

She thought nothing. Her hand turned the radio back on. Who knew why. Perversity maybe. Sick fascination. It was better than letting her mind pick its own amusements.

For a while all she heard was the voice—its tone, its texture, the way the man behind it would be leaning forward in his chair to bring himself closer to his audience. America's best buddy, creating himself out of a series of tricks that anyone who'd been in front of a mic could spot.

America's best buddy took a quick dip into outrage before he settled back into buddydom, and she was about to turn him off again when a second voice came on, and she realized that this wasn't a caller. He was interviewing a guest. The sonofabitch had changed her format. Her foot pushed down harder on the gas pedal until driving became a soothing form of violence.

By the time her brain was ready to absorb actual words, America's best buddy was talking again, telling her that history mattered, that she couldn't just think of it as one more school subject that had bored her.

Fuck him—how would he know what bored her?

"We look to the past to tell us who we are," he said, "and for much too long now this nation has been ashamed of its history."

"Exactly," the guest said a little too precisely on cue. "And that's because we've been lied to by everybody from the abolitionists to generations of liberal historians with an axe to grind, from a quota-happy government to multicultural activists pushing for preferential treatment."

The guest's voice was professorish, but comfortably so. Pipe smoke, tweed jacket, lots of footnotes, of course, but as long as you tell a good story no one reads the footnotes.

"Now, I've spent years traipsing around the South, poring through old documents, and what I've learned, in a word, is this: that slavery in this country was by no means as widespread as we've been led to believe, or as harsh. What's the true story? That free blacks all over the South have been counted *as if* they were slaves—their memories demeaned by the very people who claim to be defending them—and the reason they were miscounted is because they decided, of their own free will, mind you, *decided* to live on the plantations, where a relatively small number of other people genuinely were slaves. Why did they stay? The evidence argues that the conditions suited them. Remember, they chose that life. They could have left at any time.

"What does that mean for you and me? It means slavery is not a defining element of our history. It means we have nothing to be ashamed of. It means that black and white citizens of this country can meet finally as true equals, the whites without apology, the blacks with no one to blame. It means everyone starts with a clean slate. No special holidays, no special treatment, no special history months."

Annette sighed. She hated to admit it, but what they were presenting had a built-in constituency. It was pretty far out on the fringe still, but if you had the gift you could take fringe and turn it into the blanket. Then you could shred what had once been blanket to make a new fringe.

An Escalade cut in too close to her front bumper and she lay on the horn. The Tabriz sliced her line of sight into two unequal sections, reminding her of everything she'd lost, of every card she'd moved to the wrong place in the wrong order, but instead of wanting to weep, she was visited by an odd sense of lightness. Whatever had happened to the blanket and the fringe, it didn't matter. Or it mattered, but only to her pride. She was free of Walt, free of the insomniac veterans with their uneasy memories, free of Stan and the war and everything connected to the war, free of *Open Line* and the person she'd been on *Open Line*. What she was left with was personality, style, a great voice—everything she'd started with, plus a damn nice rug. It would be a shame to let all that go to waste because one person had been unhappy with his choices. And that hadn't been her fault. She'd never forced Daniel into anything. He'd stayed of his own free will. She'd done her best for him.

She twisted the radio dial until both men were gone and she heard nothing more than her wheels humming against the pavement, and for the first time since Daniel stretched out his tongue to test the barrel of his gun, she wondered if she couldn't transmute what had happened into something good. She'd let everyone but herself direct her life, and now she was free of them all. She'd been brought low and she'd repented. It had taken a tragedy to show her what mattered in life, but weren't Americans hungry for something that mattered?

She couldn't find the words for what it was, exactly, that mattered, but they'd come to her. All she needed to know right now was that people could embrace someone who'd known tragedy and found her way back. Her redemption would make their own mistakes more bearable. She brushed away tears. Everything that had happened had been necessary to bring her to this point, and now she could be reborn. She could help other people be reborn, and they would love her.

It wasn't marketable yet, but it would be.

The cords tying the Tabriz to her front bumper vibrated as they cut through the air, and the road ahead rushed toward her, blank with possibility.

COLOPHON

Open Line was designed at Coffee House Press,
in the historic warehouse district of downtown Minneapolis.
Fonts include Caslon, Confection, and Copperplate Gothic.

FUNDER ACKNOWLEDGMENTS

Coffee House Press is an independent nonprofit literary publisher. Our books are made possible through the generous support of grants and gifts from many foundations, corporate giving programs, state and federal support, and through donations from individuals who believe in the transformational power of literature. Publication of this book was made possible, in part, through special project support from the Jerome Foundation. Coffee House Press receives general operating support from the Minnesota State Arts Board, through an appropriation by the Minnesota State Legislature and from the National Endowment for the Arts, and major general operating support from the McKnight Foundation, and from Target. Coffee House also receives support from: an anonymous donor; the Elmer and Eleanor Andersen Foundation; the Buuck Family Foundation; the Patrick and Aimee Butler Family Foundation; Stephen and Isabel Keating; Mary McDermid; Stu Wilson and Melissa Barker; the Lenfesty Family Foundation; Rebecca Rand; the lawfirm of Schwegman, Lundberg, and Woessner P.A.; the James R. Thorpe Foundation; the Woessner Freeman Family Foundation; the Wood-Rill Foundation; and many other generous individual donors.

This activity is made possible
in part by a grant from the
Minnesota State Arts Board,
through an appropriation by the
Minnesota State Legislature
and a grant from the National
Endowment for the Arts. MINNESOTA
STATE ARTS BOARD

TARGET.

To you and our many readers across the country,
we send our thanks for your continuing support.

Good books are brewing at coffeehousepress.org